THE
KNOWING

THE
KNOWING

DAVID GRAHAM

URBANE
Publications

urbanepublications.com

First published in Great Britain in 2017 by Urbane Publications Ltd
Suite 3, Brown Europe House, 33/34 Gleaming Wood Drive, Chatham, Kent ME5 8RZ
Copyright © David Graham, 2017

A CIP catalogue record for this book is available from the British Library.

ISBN 978-1-911331-09-4
MOBI 978-1-911331-91-9
EPUB 978-1-911331-90-2

Design and Typeset by Julie Martin
Cover by Author Design Studio

Printed and bound by CPI Group (UK) Ltd, Croydon, CR0 4YY

urbanepublications.com

For Henry

"To know, is to know you know nothing. That is the meaning of true knowledge."

— Socrates

"Protect me from knowing what I don't need to know. Protect me from even knowing that there are things to know that I don't know. Protect me from knowing that I decided not to know about the things that I decided not to know about. Amen."

— Douglas Adams, *Mostly Harmless*

"I know nothing!"

— Manuel, *Fawlty Towers*

PROLOGUE

Imagine a world where something we embraced, and came to rely upon, suddenly turns out to be our worst nightmare; something that made trillions of dollars worldwide and is the economic mainstay for the biggest companies in the world; but also something that caused teenagers to run amok and kill their families and themselves.

The 'something' turned out to be the toxic electromagnetic soup of the telecommunications industry and the technology it spawned. That was on top of trans fats and copper that had been eating away at children's brains without anyone realising it.

Countries were split on the issue: the UK went for an all-out ban; the US took the more expedient route of locking up the offending article – teenagers, in other words. The use of executive orders swept the problem conveniently under the White House carpet.

Banning the technology proved to be a bonus for some, as electromagnetic radiation had been blocking paranormal abilities. Dai Williams was a case in point. He called his talent 'hocus focus' and it allowed him to 'ping' human minds to discover what made them tick. He could also do it to pigeons, although that was never particularly productive.

MI5 were particularly interested in Dai's talent, as was a certain member of the Royal Family. But Dai had never expected to save her life. Then, through meeting a fellow lost soul in MI5's secret research establishment, he discovered that he was telepathic. It was certainly a long way from his childhood in Pontypridd, South Wales, and his grandmother's kitchen, with a large pot gleaming mysteriously in the centre of the table.

CHAPTER ONE

A decent pot-bellied, cast iron cauldron typically sold for a £100. One that was antique and tarnished by heat might easily fetch double that sum. Use by an accredited witch – specifically, a member of the Dynion Mwyn tradition – could send the figure sky-high. It was reputed that a well-used cauldron absorbed a witch's hexes into the metalwork, thereby making incantations more effective. Lesser witches had attempted to debunk that idea by insisting cauldrons should be thoroughly cleansed before every new incantation. They were the sort who wore latex gloves to handle wooden spoons and kept a sharps box in the kitchen.

To complicate matters, Welsh folklore remedies had become available in disposable, ready-to-boil cauldrons marketed under the Cymry Originals brand, complete with an ostentatious logo of giant leeks crossed like swords under two golden harps. Any self-respecting witch would have viewed that as the end of the line for their hard-earned tradition. The royal approval was yet another nail in the coffin. It was like homeopathy and Bach flower essences all over again.

The worst insult to the witches' calling had been the bitching and badmouthing from north of the border. It had become nastier and more personal since the shutdown of the internet and social media. Sending cats' eyes in the post marked an all-time low. But at least they were the sort taxidermists used.

So, all things considered, Wales wasn't currently the best of places to be practising witchery. Witches had been advised to keep a low profile, limiting their activities to the occasional bit of folk healing, with coffee mornings for mutual support.

All that was quite academic to the three Welsh girls currently peering into an empty cauldron, considering their next move. Ceri, Dilys and Bronwen liked their magick delivered with *Grimm* determination and lashings of David Giuntoli, whom they had already accorded the title of 'Honorary Welshman'. He'd know a good potion if he saw one and wouldn't have time for fripperies like wands. They were for stupid kids who knocked themselves out walking into walls at railway stations.

All three would-be witches had been outfitted courtesy of the Halloween section in a local supermarket. 'Gold Witch' had seemed an absolute steal at just £3. They'd also considered the 'Mental Patient' blood-spattered straitjacket costume, but Bronwen's mother was a social worker and thought the mentally ill deserved more respect than a few pence-worth of garish polyester. A gorily-streaked plastic meat cleaver was an optional extra and even Bronwen's mother thought it looked realistic.

It was all for show, of course. They'd no need of such embellishments, but it kept their mothers happy and ignorant of what they were really up to. Halloween – or, more accurately, *All Hallows' Eve* – was just around the corner and provided the perfect cover for their activities.

Modern witchery had honed potion ingredients down to freeze-dried essences of magic that could be bought over the internet. Currently, they had no internet thanks to the government, so they'd had to improvise – after tossing salt over their left shoulders, crossing their fingers and reciting a few Hail Marys. There was also the chance that Ceri's mother might enter the room while they added an eye or two of newt, so they had the music system turned up loud and playing Super Furry Animals.

•••

Their history teacher had suggested the idea. They'd wanted to do something culturally relevant for their GCSE project. Miss Donn had brought in a newspaper clipping with the heading: 'WITCHCRAFT THRIVING IN THE WELSH COUNTRYSIDE.' The article went on to say that there were 80 witches active in South Wales. There was no mention of familiars, broomsticks, steaming cauldrons or the best witches' outfitters. In fact, it was impossible to see in what way witchcraft was actually thriving. The reader might have concluded that 21st century witches spent all their time reminiscing about their best spells and smelliest potions. Ceri and her friends had been left wanting to know more, but contact details hadn't been included either.

So, one afternoon after school, the three of them walked up the steps of Pontypridd Central Library, hand in hand, in search of the truth about Welsh witchcraft. Bronwen was momentarily distracted by the hand-knitted poster for 'Knitting Nanna's Knitting Circle' next to the men's toilets. She'd never progressed beyond monochromatic plain and purl, so the idea of making chunky willy warmers, in all colours of the rainbow, was hugely attractive. Dilys seemed intrigued by the notice for the 'Lilac Lounge Reading Group', which showed two young women in diaphanous dresses, their arms entwined, smiling joyously and reading from the same book. Ceri made a mental note to look up what 'Sapphic' meant. She dragged Bronwen and Dilys away from their temptations and they found a trainee male librarian whom they charmed into ordering a rare treatise, with the title *A Course in Welsh Witchcraft*. Ceri was convinced their hitched hems had helped, although Dilys's alteration had overstepped the bounds of public decency by several inches.

Two weeks later, the trio collected the book from the library. They'd had to promise, on pain of death and a date or two, to give it the care and attention it deserved. The volume was leather bound, about two inches thick and had a deliciously musty smell. The front cover was embossed with peeling gold leaf. The names of the joint authors, Taliesin einion Vawr and Rhuddlwm Gawr, sounded strange and exotic. Bronwen wondered whether they spoke Klingon. Some of the pages were stuck together and Dilys suggested that it must be because of ectoplasm. She was always getting the supernatural confused, poor dab. Two Post-it notes had been left in between pages: one consisted of numbers written in green ink and the other read, simply: 'Siandi Da'aan'.

Bronwen nudged Dilys. "I told you he fancied you," she said smirking.

"No, it's Ceri he likes," Dilys countered hastily, her cheeks reddening.

"That's strange," Ceri said, oblivious to her friends' comments. "'Da'aan' is similar to our teacher's name. Sounds really ancient, though. You don't think they're related, do you?"

"Dunno," Dilys mumbled moodily. Ceri guessed she was trying to square up her thoughts about the book-sharing bibliophiles. It'd certainly be frustrating if one read faster than the other.

"Could be," Bronwen said, surreptitiously popping

the Post-it with the librarian's telephone number into a pocket.

Ceri continued thumbing through the brittle, brown-edged pages marked by the Post-it and read that Siandi Da'aan was a local witch. Unfortunately, she'd died a 150 years ago and was unavailable for interview for a GCSE project by any conventional means. She sounded a force to be reckoned with and Ceri thought her story would provide a good background to their work. There was even something of a connection with Queen Victoria that Ceri planned to chase up.

Soon after that they found Ceri's great grand-mother's cauldron. Elizabeth Williams's home had been left to Ceri's family on her death. It wasn't much more than the usual two-up two-down miner's cottage, but a previously locked door off the kitchen had led them to a treasure trove of a cupboard that included the cauldron and a potions book. It was almost as if the cauldron wanted to be discovered. It wasn't exactly that it called out to Ceri, but the door did keep on opening by itself in her vicinity, so she'd felt compelled to investigate.

Their first task was to deal with some mean-looking spiders. Dilys and Bronwen ran screaming out of the kitchen when one of the pot's occupants climbed up the side and peered at them with its eight beady eyes. Ceri thought they'd been placed there as guardians. The library book had mentioned about using a black cat to free a cauldron from protection, and Ceri managed to cajole the neighbour's moggy into dispatching the spiders by opening a large can of tuna.

The cauldron itself was about a foot in diameter and sat on feet that reminded Ceri of a bird's claws. It took all three of them to transfer it to the kitchen table.

"Gosh, that weighs a ton," Dilys said, mopping her brow.

"You're so unfit, you," Bronwen said. "Just you watch me lift it on my own." She strained her puny muscles, but the cauldron remained where it was. She looked puzzled. "Humph! You try, Ceri."

Ceri picked the cauldron up with one hand and put the handle over her shoulder like a handbag. Dilys and Bronwen stared at it disbelievingly.

"Ceri bach, are you Superwoman or something?" Bronwen asked, her eyes wide with surprise.

"No, more like Superman," Dilys said. "She's always forgetting to put her knickers on under her trousers."

Bronwen and Dilys snickered into their hands. "Ooh, ah, I lost my bra, I left my knickers in my boyfriend's car," they chanted in between giggles.

"You're tossers, both of you," Ceri grumbled. "If you're not going to take it seriously, I'll tell Miss Donn that the project was too much like hard work for you."

"Sorry, Ceri," Bronwen and Dilys said together, still stifling sniggers.

"Anyway, according to the course in witchcraft we're *meant* to be studying – " she gave them a censorious look, " – variable mass is a feature of a true witch's cauldron." Ceri deposited the cauldron with a clang back on the table. She flicked a finger at the metal. "It's got a clear sound, too, so it must have seen some good potions over the years. Bronwen, can you pass me the book?"

No matter how long Dilys and Bronwen looked at the potions book, it just read, 'Recipes'. They'd even tried holding it above their heads so the light struck the cover differently. The appearance of the book was like something their grandmothers would have put together over the years, complete with oil spots, food stains and lingering smells from the stove. The recipes inside, in spidery black handwriting, were just like their nans' homeliest food. Dilys was particularly taken by a sticky toffee version of bara brith and planned to search for Medjool dates to add to her next baking session.

Everything fell into place as soon as Ceri looked at the book with her left eye closed while standing on her right foot. The word 'Potions' and her great grandmother's name had a flickering quality. She'd heard of the term 'illuminated' applied to books, but the letters on the cover almost seemed on fire. Ceri glanced around the kitchen to see where her mother had put the fire extinguisher. She deposited the book carefully on the kitchen table and flipped open the cover, watching out for sparks. The book was remarkably neat and organised. She didn't recognise the handwriting. It certainly didn't look anything like Granny Betty's old-fashioned squiggles. Her eyes were drawn to the last entry in the list of contents: 'DANGEROUS HEXES'. Now, what might they be? She turned the pages cautiously, getting a glimpse and the occasional whiff of potions as she flicked through the book. And then she saw it: 'Divination Hex – to gain insight into a question, situation or individual by way of an occultic, standardised process or ritual'.

•••

Ceri stared into the cauldron, searching for a sign that they were right to go ahead, but the blackness was all consuming and the vessel wasn't about to give anything away.

"Come on, Ceri," the habitually impatient Dilys said. "We've delayed this too long already. He'll be out of our reach soon."

Bronwen nodded her approval and folded her polyester-clad arms across her large golden bosom. "Yeah, Ceri," she said, "you listen to Dilys, you."

Ceri shot daggers at them and sighed to herself – followed by wishing she had the guts to stand up to her friends. She was such a ... what was the expression her mother used? ... *sad arse*, that was it. What they were about to do had been a good idea at the time, but now ... well, she wasn't sure. Perhaps it was the family resemblance ... and his good looks ... and a few other reasons she wasn't about to admit. Freed from the kitchen cupboard and its guardians, the cauldron had also been chomping at the bit – or whatever cauldrons do when they want a piece of the action. Her mother had blamed the putrid smell coming from her room on her, when it was actually the cauldron throwing a stink under the bed. She'd been tempted to try a hex right there and then, but the library book had warned the reader that a hex in haste is worse than a spell at speed.

Ceri turned to check that the door was still closed and then extracted a glossy sheet of paper out of a plastic bag. She glanced at it briefly before pressing her right thumb against the face in the photo and muttering two words under her breath. She passed it to Bronwen and Dilys who repeated her actions.

"Are you sure this'll work?" Bronwen said, ever the doubting Thomas, as she handed back the photo. "After all, they didn't have inkjet printers in your gran's day."

Ceri had already considered this. The hex might carry more force if the colours leaked from the photo into the cauldron. And there were still the other items in the bag. She carefully placed the photo on the bottom of the vessel. With her smartphone confiscated, she'd had to dig out an old digital camera to take the shot from the TV screen and the end result was a bit fuzzy. Dai looked far too pleased with himself. Was that because the Queen had called him 'Sir *David*'? Of course they were proud that someone from Pontypridd had been knighted, but getting engaged to an English girl with a Welsh surname really took the mickey. And if he was using witchery ... well, that could be dangerous. More pertinently, they were jealous of what he'd been up to and wanted to know how he did it. Ceri reached into the bag again and withdrew two items. She put one of them to her nose.

"What does it smell of, then, Ceri?" Bronwen said, wrinkling her nose. "Did he use that horrible Brylcream stuff my dad gets from Bryn the barber?"

Ceri sniffed the hairbrush. She had little experience of men's hair products, but she didn't imagine Brylcream being one of the usual odours emanating from the boys' changing room at school. She couldn't detect any smell. She inspected the brush: dark hairs were clinging to the bristles and a fragment of Dai's DNA might still be there. If it wasn't his DNA ... well, that could prove unfortunate. At least there was the back-up of his much-chewed toothbrush.

Ceri added the hairbrush to the ingredients in the cauldron. Dilys and Bronwen tipped the contents of colour-coded sachets on top of the photo – freeze-dried eye of newt included. Ceri's final contribution was critical: a Christmas card Dai had sent to her mother shortly after he moved to London. He'd included a photo of the Park Estate tower block and drawn an arrow pointing to his flat on the top floor. Her mother used to say that Dai had never been blessed with brains. Ceri agreed; the addition of the picture was as good as using a laser-guided missile.

Incanting a hex was straightforward as long as nothing got missed out. There seemed little chance of the hex going astray with all the extras added to the cauldron. It was really the equivalent of the failsafe computer systems on an aircraft. The three girls started reading aloud from the page Ceri had copied out of Granny Betty's potions book. It had been taken from a section headed 'DANGEROUS HEXES' and the top of the page had a roughly drawn skull and crossbones as a warning. The hex was a divination spell with some added bells and whistles. The add-ons designed to get inside Dai's head were what warranted the equivalent of a HAZMAT label.

He is the one who went away
He is the one who was led astray
He is the one who must be made to pay
He is the one whose mind we open up

As they repeated the incantation, Ceri stirred the contents of the cauldron with a wooden spoon that looked as ancient as the pot itself. Although there was nothing liquid in the vessel, an opaque film spread over the photo until the only part visible was Dai's face. And then the strangest thing happened: smoke erupted through his eyes and billowed up, filling the vessel. The three of them peered into the murky depths and glimpsed fragments of the photo: a spike of hair here, a glimmer of gold there, his eyes watching them all the time, his mouth taunting them with a sweetly innocent smile. It was as if Dai's image was being disassembled while they stared. The cauldron had also started producing heat despite the absence of a flame. The clouds swirled around, but they were going anticlockwise, contradicting what they'd learned about the Coriolis effect in physics lessons.

Ceri watched her friends' faces. She could see the contents reflected in Dilys's and Bronwen's eyes. The girls' mouths gaped open, their silver fillings glinting in the eerie light emanating from the cauldron. Ceri stopped stirring and the vapour swiftly swallowed the spoon until all that was left was the handle. She dropped that before her fingers disappeared too. The spiralling gas seemed to bear an intelligence – as well as an appetite for wood. "Thanks, wholesome young wench. I'll have more of that, if you don't mind," she imagined it saying with a hearty, sulphurous belch. Except this was a B&Q decorated front parlour in 21st century Wales

– not some filthy coven of hairy old hags covered in pustulent boils. Those cost a little bit more and Dilys said they squeezed out authentic looking pus. With her current blight of teenage acne, she'd become quite the expert on skin eruptions.

Modern theories about witchery mentioned quantum mechanics. It was a bit over Ceri's head – they'd only just started GCSE physics at school, after all, and Mr Ellis the teacher could barely tell a quark from a quack – but the gist was that, statistically, there was a bit of everything in everybody. Witchery just made the connections stronger. An incantation nudged mind-boggling things called fundamental particles into forming cutely-named quantum twins, which could really be anywhere the witch wanted. The simplest way of using them was for the equivalent of a long-distance call. But if they were at the beginning and the end of a divination hex, it was as good as a striker kicking a football into goal. And judging by the activity in the cauldron, a score was just about to happen.

What had been a rotating wispiness like sticky candyfloss had coalesced into a shimmering golden orb about the size of a tennis ball, hovering at eye level. The colour came from specks of light within the orb, and as it spun faster, the flecks lost their individuality. It had also started to emit a breathy, moaning noise. Ceri was tone deaf, so she had no idea of the pitch, but it sounded like the organ in St Dyfrig's Church that had an out-of-tune pipe. Then she recalled that her great grandmother used to play the harmonium, so perhaps that was the explanation for the wheeze.

Ceri exchanged a quick look with Dilys and Bronwen and they redoubled their efforts at chanting the hex: "He is the one, he is the one …" They'd collapsed in giggles when they first practised the incantation in the kitchen. Dilys had added 'om … om … om …' Daft bugger, she was. But now it was deadly serious. A tingle of excitement shimmered up Ceri's spine. Sweat had started to bead on their foreheads. Somehow, the orb had gained energy and spun ever faster, firing darts of light in every direction. Bronwen's and Dilys's eyes were out on stalks. Quantum level connections were being made. It was the point when so much could go wrong. Ceri imagined the skull and crossbones cackling and rattling at her. She didn't think her mother's household insurance would cover witchery-related damage.

The flashes of photons were meant to seek out the appropriate quantum twin wherever it buzzed around. Once connections were made, every subsequent contact should have had a higher chance of success – and then the hex could start its business. Except it wasn't quite happening on this occasion. The energy seemed to have hit an invisible wall and bounced back into the orb. The orb continued to send out yet more sparks. Ceri glanced anxiously at Dilys and Bronwen, but they seemed lost to the fairies. They probably thought the orb looked like the Snitch from a game of Quidditch. Theirs clearly had no need for wings. The orb was getting whinier.

Ceri didn't register much of what happened during the next few minutes. The sparks found their targets, although not quite as intended. There must have been something particularly attractive about the 'Gold Witch' costumes. And polyester – even cheap polyester mass-produced in a Far East factory – has the capacity to stretch ... and stretch ...

•••

Joan Edwards was surprised at how excited the girls had been to see Dai on the six o'clock news, standing in the Buckingham Palace quadrangle alongside his girlfriend. Ceri had even taken a photo of the TV screen. Mrs Edwards couldn't recall any other occasion when her daughter had shown the slightest interest in her cousin. Although he wasn't exactly the black sheep of the family, no one really understood him. Leaving Pontypridd for London was one thing, but choosing to live on the 20th floor of a tower block just seemed strange. So, too, was how he'd somehow ended up at Balmoral Castle and saved the Queen's life. Perhaps he'd acquired resuscitation skills at some evening class – and been in the right place at the right time. But a knighthood? Incredible. Still, he'd turned out a tidy boyo and Grandmother would have been pleased as Punch the bookie on Grand National day.

Mrs Edwards had been going over the details of the Queen's visit to the Royal Glamorgan Hospital. It amazed her how much protocol had to be followed, even down to the brand of toilet paper in the loo. She'd never considered before that such a thing might be awarded a royal warrant. She suddenly became aware of a strange whining sound emanating from the living room. The music the girls had been playing on the hi-fi – a Welsh pop group with a name more stupid than usual – was also strange and whining, but this new sound had a droning quality that jarred.

Up until then, Mrs Edwards had done her best to avoid prying, as Grandmother had always insisted young'uns should find their own witching way – even when celebrating Halloween using the back pages of her potions book. Ceri's mother wasn't blessed with magickal abilities herself, but she'd picked up the basics over the years. She'd been waiting for Ceri to show an interest and her daughter had finally passed the first hurdle of separating the cauldron from its guardians. It had been so helpful of her history teacher to take a special interest in her studies. Still, it was a hazardous business for those without a real calling, so Mrs Edwards thought it best to check that nothing was untoward.

Mrs Edwards slowly opened the door a crack … and stood rooted to the spot, mouth agape. She'd never expected in a month of Sundays to see Ceri and her friends transforming into golden beach balls. They were making pig-like oinking noises and it definitely wasn't through the pleasure of eating from a trough. A golden orb span ominously above the cauldron, reaching out to them with ghostly, sparkling tentacles. The air in the room was charged with electricity and Mrs Edwards felt her hair lifting from her scalp. There was a pungent, chlorine-like smell that reminded her of the aftermath of a heavy thunderstorm. She also detected the unmistakeable acrid odour of fear.

"Help us, Mam," Ceri gasped, "we're choking!"

Dilys and Bronwen couldn't even manage a feeble "Help!" between them. Bronwen's lips had turned a shade of blue that Mrs Edwards had just learnt about in a first aid class. She reached instinctively for her mobile phone to dial 999 and then swore as she realised the futility of the gesture. There was no alternative: she'd have to release the effects of the incantation with a pair of scissors. She made the sign of the cross. It was a pity damage from an undelivered hex hadn't been covered on the first aid course; Grandmother used to say that dealing with an errant hex was like applying sticking plaster to a severed carotid artery Mrs Edwards prayed to the first patron saint she could think of and hoped she could dodge the streams of energy coming from the orb.

Bronwen's oink had become a pathetic wheeze. Mrs Edwards dived in with the scissors at the neck line, somehow avoiding the sparks. The dress fragmented following the first cut and the pieces of fabric were sucked into the cauldron with a sudden whoosh. That was followed by the pot expelling a cloud of paper fragments with a regurgitant burp. Bronwen clawed at her throat with both hands, as if trying to pull air into her body. "Fuck," she screeched, in between drawing deep, wrenching breaths. She didn't seem aware that she was naked and getting bigger by the second. Grimly, Mrs Edwards realised her error: the dress had been containing Bronwen's expanding body. She ran into the kitchen and grabbed a roll of cling film. Returning to the living room, she wrapped the plastic around Bronwen's torso, hoping it would hold up until she got help. The girl's eyes were wide with terror.

"Just hold on, Bronwen bach," Mrs Edwards said. "Help will be coming soon." She glanced at Ceri and Dilys. They'd wrapped their arms around their chests, which seemed to have helped their breathing. "See what Ceri and Dilys are doing," she said, pointing at Bronwen's friends. "Try to slow down your breaths so you don't get lightheaded."

Something on the carpet caught Mrs Edwards's eye:

it was the photo Ceri had taken of Dai from the TV screen. Somehow, the pieces of paper had been reassembled. It was only too clear what her daughter and friends had been up to.

And then there was the orb, still hovering and spewing energy in all directions. It would set fire to the house if she didn't do something. She didn't have time to look through the potions book. *Where's the knowledge when one needs it?* And then she remembered Grandmother's bedtime tales about the gods and goddesses of the four elements. She'd thought it unfair at the time that water always won. She ran back into the kitchen and grabbed the nearest saucepan. *Would tap water work against whatever the orb was made of?* she wondered. She tutted to herself. This was no time for indecision. Holding the full pan in both hands, trying not to spill a precious drop, she imagined herself as Addanc, the fresh water faery of Wales, up against the wickedly fiery Brigid, and heaved the contents at the orb. The water went everywhere, including over the three girls. Their look of surprise was nothing in comparison to Mrs Edwards's abject astonishment when the orb fizzled, shrank to a pinprick and then promptly vanished down the nearest throat.

•••

Lieutenant Dale Franklin, a dead ringer for Harrison Ford in his hunky *Star Wars* days, surveyed his penthouse apartment from the super king-size bed – a bed he currently shared with Sergeant Steve Abrams, partner in love *and* crime fighting. He threaded sleepy fingers through his mussed-up hair and examined the pillow for strands that had abandoned ship overnight. Steve's wavy locks cast a dark halo on the neighbouring pillow and seemed destined to remain attached come what may. As usual, follicular envy loomed large in their relationship.

"Cool haircut," Dale said, screwing-up his eyes to examine the 20-something man who'd just appeared on the flat screen at the end of the bed. He was smiling and holding up something that glinted on the screen. A girl stood next to him, but she didn't look too pleased to be there. "Nice suit, too."

"You don't mean the Hoxton fin?" Steve snorted disdainfully from his recumbent position under the 800 thread count Egyptian sheets. "Nah, dude, that's so yesterday. His girlfriend must've made him get it. She's so stuck in the past." He stared forensically at the screen. "The suit's way too shiny." He looked some more. "And she's pregnant."

"Why's it called a 'Hoxton fin', then, Mr Smartass?" Dale hated him for all that hair.

"Dunno, dude. I must've read it somewhere," Steve said, defeated. Even Steve wasn't that smart at six in the morning. He seemed to brighten at the thought of something and levered himself up. "But when we go on vacation to London, perhaps we can find out. There's probably some museum for ancient haircuts – you know, footballer's perm, Beatles' mop-top, Beckham's fauxhawk ..."

Dale rolled his eyes. This was way too much hair talk. "Yeah, yeah, I get it. And like Chief Scanlon's gonna pay for flights after our all-expenses-paid trip to LA. No way, Jose. He's still blaming us for his addiction to oxynuts."

"Well, at least his cardiologist must be happy. And Sam's business is taking off. It's a win-win for everyone."

"Try asking the chief's wife. She's having to get in Genovese pesto and beetroot chutney from the deli. And that doesn't come cheap at Sam's hiked-up prices."

Steve's tousled head disappeared back under the sheets. Dale's claws retracted. Steve's ex's oxymoronic healthy doughnuts had become a legend in their brief lifetime and an army of bakers were churning out the low-calorie, low-fat pastries with exotic, but wholesome, fillings. But Dale couldn't avoid letting loose darts of jealousy whenever Sam's name got mentioned. And it wasn't because of his taste in leather pants or the ease with which he pummelled dough into submission.

Dale glanced back at the flat screen. The Queen had quite an assembly line churning out knights and dames of the realm. He recalled his first sight of Dai Williams in the Burn Center at LAC Medical Center. It was sure hard to imagine him as a 'Sir' back then. Hell, he was just so weird looking. The pantyhose thing covering his head was something else. He'd said it was for his protection. Dale chuckled to himself. They'd certainly come a long way in a few short months. But so had the whole damn world. The only people applauding that were the anti-technology new agers – and his mom and dad had just signed up. Fucking wimps! "Wash your mouth out with ..." *Sorry, Mom, Dad. I'll try to behave. Promise.*

But at least they could still use cell phones in the US. He wondered what would happen to the tens of thousands of scrambled-brain teens who remained in detention units on executive orders. The healthcare budget had been blown apart. He sighed. *Oh Jeez.* He might be losing his hair but that was a whole lot better than life as a teenager. Their attorneys must be having a field day.

But, hey, something was stirring below. Dale closed his eyes and leaned back against the pillow. There was still a half hour before they needed to shower. *Yeah, I've sure come a long way thanks to young Steve ...*

"Er, sweets," Steve said with exquisite mistiming, deep from beneath the sheets, "is it okay if I go see that guy Joseph on the psych ward? He sorta got to me that day in the ER and I owe it to him to check on how he's doing."

"Yeah, whatever dude," Dale mumbled, his mind on far more pleasant things than some kid with a scrambled brain and a penchant for exposing himself.

•••

The Two Rivers psych facility was situated a couple of miles south of Arrowhead Stadium, the home of Kansas City Chiefs. Steve had been to a couple of rock concerts there but never a game. Somehow he'd managed to resist American football being engrained in his adolescent psyche. But baseball was okay – so long as it didn't involve duplicitous pitchers and being made the laughing stock of his year.

The Metro bus crawled its way in the muggy heat of early fall. Steve sat at the rear, just as he used to in high school. He'd usually pass the time fantasising about his latest crush – making out on the back seat included. He shifted to the least stained patch of upholstery and glanced around. 'No Cell' signs were prominent, but half the passengers had phones clamped to their ears. He thought of his friend Dr Cathy Svenstrom at the Centers for Disease Control and Prevention who'd worked with them on the Marshall case. It wasn't every day that a high school jock killed his parents and himself and left triplets as witnesses. Uncovering the cause had been a team effort, of course, but the real star had been the Kenyan math whizzkid who'd alerted Cathy – by

SMS from a $10 Nokia cell phone, ironically – to what EM radiation was doing to kids' brains. Cathy would have the bus driver as judge and jury, stamping the shit out of the cell phone and the wrongdoer. People had become so damn complacent. Perhaps the British government had the right idea all along of switching off the networks. The mealy-mouthed US administration sided with business rather than public health, and the likes of Joseph Gardiner were paying the consequences. From straight-A student to banged-up on a psych ward – with no passing go and no collecting $200. Sometimes, he wished he had Dale's capacity to distance himself from the refuse laid daily at their feet, but KCPD hadn't extinguished the inquisitive psychologist in him quite yet.

The bus pulled up just outside the driveway to Two Rivers. There was an anachronistic handmade wooden sign pointing visitors in the right direction. Steve half expected to see patients wearing straitjackets lining the road, walking with the shuffling gait of the Thorazined psychotic.

"Hi there," Steve said into the intercom at the entrance to the adolescent unit. "I'm here to see Joseph Gardiner. I phoned earlier. My name is Steve Abrams."

"Let me go check, sir," an androgynous disembodied voice said, impressively matter-of-fact.

Steve heard papers being turned. He guessed he was

through to an administrator's office.

"Do you have ID, sir?" Still chilly.

"Yes, ma'am. I have my badge." He hoped he had the sex of the voice correct.

The door clicked open without further questioning. Prominent signs read: 'No phones allowed'. He showed his ID card to a security guard and handed over his cell phone. He'd left his firearm behind in the department. Walking through a security scanner completed the check. The door to the ward lay straight ahead. Another intercom, another flash of the badge at a camera and he was in.

Bedlam would be one way of describing it. Adolescents lurched at him from every direction and speech-like sounds emerged from multiple mouths along with spittle. None of it made much sense. A sliding door opened on the left and he found himself freed from the zombie-like grasping of needy youth. A girl who looked to be in her early teens pouted her lips against the glass and then licked the surface with her tongue.

"Sorry 'bout that," the male nurse said chirpily. "We don't get many visitors these days and you must seem kinda special to them."

Steve didn't feel at all special. His shirt had stuck to his back and his hair needed a barber's attention. "If you say so." He smiled wanly.

"Friend or family?" the nurse said, inspecting

paperwork for Steve's details.

"Neither," Steve said almost apologetically, shrugging. He flipped his badge again.

"Sorry, Officer, I hadn't realised," the nurse said, straightening up. "I'll go arrange an interview room."

Steve checked the nurse's name badge. "Thanks, Nurse Elliott, but there's no need. I saw him in the ER all those months ago and just wanted to check on him. He sorta got to me, I guess."

Something akin to a light illuminated the young nurse's face. "Christ, you're one of the detectives! He reached out to shake Steve's hand vigorously. "What was your partner's name … Dale, wasn't it? He's a real cutie." He blushed. "Sorry, Officer." He reddened some more.

Steve smiled. "Yeah, he is." He paused and decided to leave it at that. "So, how is Joseph doing?"

Nurse Elliott recovered his composure. "Okay, I guess. He has his good days and his bad days, if you know what I mean. He's in the art room at the moment. I'll take you there."

Joseph was sitting at a table in what evidently passed as the ward's creative facility. A bored-looking member of staff sat in the corner, thumbing disinterestedly through a magazine. "Myra, this police officer is here to see Joseph. Keep an eye on him, will you," the nurse said.

The woman looked up briefly, mumbled "sure" and then resumed her half-hearted reading.

Steve pulled up a chair and perched next to the boy. He'd put on a ton of weight since he last saw him in the ER. Steve leaned forward to inspect what he was drawing. Joseph was sketching a peanut. Except it wasn't just any peanut. The boy had caught every indentation of the shell and it had a 3D quality. The bottom of the husk was opened up and the cavity drew the viewer into the space like a vacuum. To the right of the shell the boy had drawn the peanut itself, standing upright and supported by a realistic ear on either side.

"That's awesome, Joseph," Steve said, smiling at the boy.

Joseph said nothing and continued adding details to the left ear.

"Do you remember me, Joseph?" Steve asked. "I'm one of the police officers who interviewed you in the ER. My name is Steve Abrams."

The boy switched his attention to the right ear.

"I guess you're mad at me for putting you here," Steve said.

Back to the left ear. This isn't going well. Okay, I'll ask about the peanut.

"Why the peanut, Joseph? I mean, it's a fine peanut but …"

"Peanut brain," Joseph said obligingly, without

removing his pencil from the paper.

"Sorry, I don't get it." Steve was up to date with Rorschach but peanut interpretation was new to him. Those human-looking ears must mean something, though. Perhaps ...

"My brain," the boy said abruptly, as if reading his thoughts. "Peanuts."

Steve guessed this wasn't anything to do with the Charles M. Schulz comic strip. "Do you mean your brain is like a peanut?"

Joseph turned slowly to look at him. "Yeah, like two fucking peanuts," he drawled lazily. He mimed tossing nuts into his mouth and swallowing them. "See, now they're gone. Here today, gone tomorrow. The sun'll come out tomorrow." He turned back to the drawing. "Yeah, I remember you." There was a purposeful edge to his voice. The boy slipped his free hand inside his pants. The pencil made ever faster strokes on the paper. A look of consternation crossed his features. His left hand resumed its rather more methodical detailing of the right ear. "Sorry," he said softly, as he withdrew his other hand from his pants.

Steve left the room. Overstimulation wasn't something the boy needed. He found Nurse Elliott in the office. "I see what you're getting at. Is his brain really that bad?"

"Like in his drawing, you mean?" Nurse Elliott said.

Steve nodded.

"Well, it's certainly shrunk some, but it's more wrinkled than a peanut. He's improving, though. He's on some experimental drug developed by some guy at Caltech. I guess we'll just have to wait and see."

Steve had heard about that. The Kenyan wunderkind who'd blown the lid open on the dangers of cell phones had moved on to shaking up the pharmaceutical industry. He was on a scholarship at Caltech and he'd found a boyfriend, too. "Does that mean he's still on involuntary treatment?"

"Of course," Nurse Elliott said. "There's no way he can consent as he is. His dad doesn't like it, but he's not complaining."

"And he can't leave, either?"

The nurse shook his head. "He's here on an executive order. Only the White House can free him – " he looked towards the pandemonium across the way, " – along with the rest of these poor young suckers. God help the lot of them, I say."

CHAPTER TWO

Dai Williams, ex-Pontypridd student of the mystical practice of hocus focus, now back on terra firma after confinement in his fortress of solitude in a Battersea tower block, mulled over the events of the previous day. He glanced at the glittering insignia with its red and gold ribbon hanging at the end of the bed. An invitation to drinks at Buckingham Palace wasn't something to be passed over lightly. It also gave him a distinctly queasy feeling. Was it treasonable to view repeated contact with Her Majesty as potentially life-threatening? Particularly for her. What if she had another stroke? At least the footmen must be up-to-date with CPR – and this was hardly an assignation in the middle of nowhere. Perhaps she'd slip something in his drink and cast him into the dungeons so that he'd be at her behest for another round of space-time tinkering.

Then there was the minor problem that the Queen hadn't specified a time, so maybe he should ring her private secretary to check. As his grandmother used to remind him, old folk required their supper early to avoid indigestion and trips to the loo. She might also be testing him to see whether he'd pry into her thoughts with a ping. Or perhaps the Queen might telepathise him the details while Prince Philip helped himself to corn flakes out of the 1950s Tupperware container. Fat chance; the Queen was no better at long-distance telepathy than he was. Sandra was still the expert in *that* department.

He turned to look at his fiancée. For once, her dark hair wasn't covering her face. Her nose twitched from time to time, as if her senses were on guard, monitoring the world around her. *That goes with being a telepathic lackey for MI5*, he thought. Dai gently touched Sandra's bump. He longed to know more about the baby busily growing under his fingertips and resisted giving it a gentle ping. He'd already discovered it was a girl but hadn't told Sandra yet – or allowed her access to the thought. Antenatal ultrasound scans were such an anti-climax when one could see more than any machine.

He was still waiting to be told off for getting too close to the Queen. It wasn't his fault that he was a bit touchy-feely. Granny Betty had been rather adept at laying on hands, too. With a dying monarch just feet away, what else could he have done, for Chrissakes! It was also strange there'd been no debriefing after the Balmoral incident, but perhaps it was a royal prerogative to keep the details under wraps. As far as the general public were concerned, they'd been advised that the Queen had had a stroke and he'd valiantly come to her aid. There was no mention of the fact that they'd been sitting together on a roughly hewn bench on the Balmoral estate and that she'd transgressed the space-time continuum.

A loud noise disturbed his cogitation. Doorbells didn't come any more ear-piercing than theirs. There was a groan from the other side of the bed. Sandra was about to demonstrate her displeasure at being so rudely awakened. "I'll get it," he said to the recumbent form. It was 7:00 a.m. and way too early for the postman. He stumbled into some clothes and padded his way, bare foot, downstairs to the front door. "I'm coming," he yelled. Dai put an eye to the spy hole and saw someone in black silhouetted against the sunrise. The sight was definitely ominous with a capital 'O'. He did think MI5 could have waited until after he'd had his three Weetabix.

Dai opened the door and a tall figure dressed entirely in black thrust an envelope into his hand. A gleaming motorcycle idled on the pavement, purring loudly like an over-indulged cat. The letter was highly embossed, bore no stamp and had the Queen's distinctive curlicue writing on the envelope. It read, without any elaboration, 'Sir David Williams'.

"You work for his sirness, do yer?" the courier asked through the niqab-like gap in his flip-up visor. It was like communicating with Gort. Dai was all ready to say the phrase 'klaatu barada nikto' in case he demanded a tip with menaces.

Admittedly, Dai didn't look anything like a knight of the realm that morning; jeans and a hooded top had been the only clothes to hand when he leapt out of bed. Granny Betty had always insisted that doors should be answered whatever one's state of dress. "It could be the good Lord calling," she used to say with a wink. He'd never been partial to Pontypridd's doorstep bible bashers, but the prospect of fried leeks and laver bread for tea performed miracles for adolescent incentivising.

"I work for myself," Dai said, glancing at the courier's bloodshot eyes inside his carbon fibre carapace. Strictly speaking, that *was* true; MI5 paid him as a freelance agent with bonuses according to the assignment. Interrogation with the hocus focus paid handsomely and it was a lot less messy than waterboarding. Granny Betty wouldn't have approved, but, hey, he had dependents now.

They heard someone retching inside the house. It had started the previous evening when they'd made a flying visit to the Park Estate. He'd gone out onto the balcony to show Mrs Pigeon the shiny insignia. She'd always been ready with her comforting coo and a quick flash of avian insight. Admittedly, it had usually been about her reproductive needs. And pinging a one-gram brain had to be done very gently. Human brains were a doddle in comparison.

Sandra had ended up confined to the bathroom for 20 minutes. One bout of vomiting seemed to follow another. She hadn't been a pretty sight when she eventually opened the door. Perhaps his improvised Faraday cage had trapped some bad karma in the apartment. He really should have removed the ten-micron thick copper mesh lining his flat, but he wasn't about to destroy his bolthole in case Wi-Fi and mobile networks got switched back on.

Dai half-turned into the hallway. "Sorry, mate, I need to go. My girlfriend's not feeling too good." He turned over the envelope and noticed the Royal Crest. "Thanks for delivering my invitation to tea."

The courier reached up to remove his helmet. He blinked in the sunlight smearily reflected off the grime-covered windows of neighbouring buildings. The headgear definitely suited him better on than off. "You mean … you're … Christ!" He stood looking flustered. His batteries had to be running low.

Dai touched him on the shoulder, recalling that the Queen had done the same to him with a ceremonial sword. "That's okay, mate, I guess it's not every day you meet a knight without his suit of armour on."

The courier shook his head vigorously. "Christ, man … I mean, your *grace* … you *saved* the Queen! How the fuck did you do that?" He reddened, evidently embarrassed by swearing in front of a knight of the realm.

Dai shrugged. MI5 employees did a lot of that. Explanations were best kept to a minimum in his line of work. "Sometimes a man's gotta do what a man's gotta do," he said limply without the usual John Wayne impersonation. What he meant is, "a man with special powers has gotta do what a man with special powers has gotta do," but it didn't sound right – and required way too much clarification.

The courier reached in his jacket pocket for something. He thrust a grubby piece of paper and a leaking biro into Dai's hands. "It's for my girlfriend. She fuckin' worships the Queen. She'll never believe I met you. Her name is Sonia," he explained breathlessly. "I'd have taken a selfie but the guvnor confiscated our mobiles. 'Government's orders', he said. We have to use these bloody walkie-talkies now." He pointed at a speaker attached to his leathers that had been squawking like a strangled parrot.

There'd been a girl named Sonia at Dai's primary school. She had a limited but effective repertoire of insults that made fun of his name. It was predictable but it still hurt. If the hocus focus had been active in those days, he'd have been tempted to ping and leave a lasting impression. She'd got her comeuppance when her face erupted with pustules of acne as a teenager. Not even Granny Betty's laying on of hands could deal with that.

So, what should he write? 'Dai' or 'David'? With or without the 'Sir'? Formal or friendly? A knighthood ought to come with an induction course in using the bloody title. The sword might come in handy to beat off the signature hunters, too. 'Hi Sonia' was a friendly start. He signed 'Dai Williams' and added 'Sir David Williams' underneath as a touch of formality. He returned the paper and biro to the courier. Ink had been deposited generously on his finger-tips.

"Thanks, your *knightness*," the courier said. "Sorry 'bout the biro. It's probably being shaken about on the bike that made it leak."

Dai sympathised. He'd probably leak if he was vibrated at high speed over rubbish London roads. Filling in pot holes barely figured on the list of government priorities. They were still trying to work out what to do with all the kids who'd been locked up in old mental asylums for the common good. Occasionally, someone jumped the fence, but there were plenty of vigilante mobs out there ready to deal with the waifs and strays.

•••

As PA to the Royal Glamorgan Hospital's Chief Executive, it just wasn't in Joan Edwards's makeup to wait demurely in Accident & Emergency for her daughter and friends to be treated within the arbitrary four-hour target. Since the death of her husband in a freak accident in the National Theatre of Wales, she'd become someone on a mission, even if the assignment wasn't obvious to most around her. People saw her as a soft touch, which suited her fine.

Once Mrs Edwards had wrapped Bronwen's hideously expanding body in food wrap, she'd called 999 and mumbled the bare bones of the situation. Fortunately, an ambulance crew were enjoying a tea break in a nearby café and they were around in a jiffy. But she'd had to endure some strange looks and questions from the paramedics. And she'd never hear the end of her neighbours' tongue wagging.

"Isn't Ceri a bit young to have started that sort of thing?" one of her neighbours had asked with a smirk. The truth was, bondage that had gone amiss wasn't exactly uncommon in the Valleys. Folk needed something to occupy their idle time now that the coalmines had been closed, after all.

Mrs Edwards had done her best to look suitably in command of the situation when they arrived at the hospital. If mobile phones had been available, she felt certain their photos would have been uploaded to social media within seconds. Ceri and Dilys were still in their 'Gold Witch' costumes and far from being their normal sizes. Bronwen had been rushed into the resuscitation bay and staff were crowded around her bloated, plastic-coated body like worker bees buzzing around their queen.

Mrs Edwards was banking on the gawpers assuming the girls had got stuck in their Halloween outfits after too many treats. At least Ceri and Dilys were no longer gasping for air. She was also dreading the ambulance crew tipping off the local press and had scribbled a brief and suitably ambiguous press statement while she was waiting.

"Good Lord, Joan, what the hell happened to them?" the A&E consultant asked, scratching his head.

Although Mrs Edwards wasn't a witch, the advice given by the Cymry Wiccae Association about disclosure was clear. Complete honesty was rarely recommended, even in a life or limb situation. She'd also been complicit in allowing the girls get on with the task of bringing the cauldron into the 21st century. On the other hand, it was her daughter's health at stake.

"Well ..." Mrs Edwards said, considering her words carefully, "I think they were playing with some sort of chemistry set. The smell was something dreadful. I suppose it must have backfired on them. Ceri said it was for a GCSE project to do with potions in Welsh folklore. Perhaps it was a chemical past its use-by date. I should have checked, but I didn't want to spoil their fun. You know what children are like on Halloween night." She ended the explanation with a shrug. A&E

staff heard plenty of lame excuses for bizarre mishaps and she was sure hers would pass muster.

The doctor raised an eyebrow. "Hmm. Could they have inhaled or swallowed something?"

Along with an eye of newt, Mrs Edwards thought. "I suppose so. They were around a pot. There was smoke, but no fire that I could see." She'd almost forgotten the golden object spinning above the cauldron and what had happened when she dowsed the orb with water. Did it really enter Ceri's mouth? It had probably been a trick of the light. And it had been extremely small. Stomach acids would destroy it, probably.

"Do you know whether they're allergic to anything? Bees, wasps, peanuts, that sort of thing?"

Mrs Edwards shook her head. "Ceri isn't, but I couldn't speak for Dilys and Bronwen. You'd have to ask their parents." She looked in the direction of the resuscitation bay. "Do you think she'll be all right?"

The doctor followed her gaze. "It's hard to say, Joan. We definitely can't afford to wait until the toxicology results are back. It could be a severe allergic reaction, so we'll give them adrenaline. Your daughter and her friend don't seem too badly affected, but – "

The screech of a cardiac monitor's alarm broke through the general commotion of the department. "I should go," the consultant said, briefly touching Mrs Edwards's arm before turning to leave. "You can reach me on my mobile." He smiled wryly. "Sorry, old habits die hard. You'd better try my secretary's landline instead."

Mrs Edwards returned to the hospital, bleary-eyed, first thing in the morning. The royal visit was scheduled for 11 o'clock. A benefactor had left the hospital millions and the Queen was due to open a new medical assessment unit. Ironically, Ceri and Dilys were among the first patients to occupy its pristine beds. They'd responded to treatment and had been liberated from their garish fancy dress. Bronwen was in the Intensive Treatment Unit and they were still wrestling with how to deflate her body without compromising her breathing. She was thought to have some sort of compartment syndrome and 80 per cent of her body had been affected. The unusual case had already been lined up for the back page of the *British Medical Journal*. The vicar at St Dyfrig's Church had kindly offered prayers for her during the morning's Adoration of the Blessed Sacrament. The supermarket had been alerted to the danger of overweight schoolgirls stuffing themselves into the 'Gold Witch' costume.

The Queen's helicopter was due to land in the grounds of the nearby rugby club. The Chief Executive, the Lord Mayor and the Member of Parliament for Pontypridd were first in the line-up to greet her. Mrs Edwards had been given the task of breaking the bad news to those who'd been omitted from the welcoming committee. The name of the new unit was to remain a secret until Her Majesty unveiled the commemorative plaque. There'd been so many attempts at pulling strings – the publicity-grabbing mayor included – that Punch the bookie was accepting bets on who'd get pride of place on the wall. Mrs Edwards smiled to herself. She wondered whether she'd get an opportunity to speak with the Queen. She was a busy woman after all and probably had other engagements to go to after cutting the ribbon. They'd laid on a buffet lunch, but no one actually expected her to stay.

A flurry of activity at the entrance signified Her Majesty's arrival. Mrs Edwards thought the Queen looked amazing for her age. She didn't show any outward signs of having had a stroke. After a quick speech, which included a dedication in a dialect of Welsh unique to the Royal Household, the Queen declared the medical assessment unit open and pulled at the cord. The curtain covering the plaque started opening and then got stuck halfway. The Queen chuckled and tugged it again, clearly at home with such occupational hazards. 'THE BETTY WILLIAMS MEDICAL ASSESS-MENT UNIT' was revealed in all its bilingual glory. The Welsh slate glistened in the halogen lights. It had been a battle of wills persuading the hospital's Executive Board to agree to 'Betty' rather than 'Elizabeth'. A roar of applause echoed around the department. Mrs Edwards thought she'd prepared herself for this, but a lump was growing in her throat. She looked around and observed the mayor dabbing at tears – just as a photographer from the local press took his photo.

The Queen and her entourage made their way onto the ward. One of the doors refused to budge, and the hospital carpenter was on his tea break, so it was a tight squeeze for the outsize mayor. The procession halted right by the beds occupied by Ceri and Dilys. Ceri was scowling and Dilys had her mouth open. The photographer was already snapping away. The Queen beamed in a grandmotherly fashion at the girls. Ceri continued to glower. Mrs Edwards waggled a finger at her to behave.

"And why are you in hospital, my dear?" the Queen asked sweetly, cautiously approaching Ceri's bedside.

"Allergic reaction," Ceri said unconvincingly, fulfilling everyone's expectation of the sullen teen.

"How interesting, my dear," the Queen said, taking a quick step back in case it was catching.

"We b-b-blew up like b-b-bouncing b-b-beach balls," Dilys butted in, her mouth not quite up to speed with her brain.

"Did you indeed," the Queen said, looking distinctly uneasy.

"It was all b-because of her and the ph-photo of

D-Dai," Dilys blurted, glaring at Ceri. "The c-c-cauldron was m-manky, too."

"Shush," Ceri said menacingly.

The Queen smiled enigmatically. "Goodbye," she said with a delicate but precisely delivered wave.

"If you would care to come this way, Your Majesty," the Chief Executive said, bowing obsequiously while gesturing at a nearby door, "there's a display of photographs that should be of interest to you."

The crowd made its way into a seminar room that had photos detailing the unit's construction displayed along one wall. It was the sort of architect's indulgence the Queen must have seen thousands of times during her reign. She nodded politely as she was led towards the present day. She stopped in front of a black and white photo. The female subject had a halo of grey hair, twinkling eyes and sat half-turned towards the camera. A black cat was spread out on her lap, its obsidian eyes regarding the viewer with glacial coldness.

"Betty Williams?" the Queen asked.

"Indeed," the Chief Executive said. "She used to volunteer at this hospital, pushing a book trolley around the wards. The books were in Welsh, of course. I'm afraid *The Old Man of Lochnagar* didn't stand a chance." He chortled at his wit and turned to Mrs Edwards who'd been keeping a respectful distance. "Perhaps

Your Majesty would care to meet her granddaughter, Mrs Joan Edwards?"

"You must be so proud," the Queen said. Mrs Edwards was treated to a warm smile with crinkles in all the right places. Her Majesty displayed wondrously white teeth for an 88-year-old.

Mrs Edwards curtseyed and took the Queen's proffered hand. It was so small and delicate looking in the pristine white glove that she was worried she might crush it.

"Please don't be concerned, Mrs Edwards, we are made of stronger stuff than that," the Queen said, her eyes sparkling.

Mrs Edwards realised with a start that she was still tethered to the Queen's gloved fingers. "Sorry, Your Majesty," she mumbled, relaxing her grip slowly, anxious that it might appear she was dropping the royal limb. She felt scores of eyes on her. Grandmother would have coped far better with the etiquette of interfacing with royalty. A flash of inspiration came to her. "My neighbour, Mrs Griffiths, breeds corgis, you know, Ma'am."

"How interesting," the Queen said, with an eye on the buffet. "Actually, we are feeling quite peckish. Flying has that effect on one. Would you care to join us, Mrs Edwards?"

The Chief Executive didn't look at all pleased to be snubbed just seconds away from a lunch date with the

Queen. He turned to the mayor who was already piling his plate high. For once, the hospital kitchen had done more than overcook frozen vegetables and add lumps to packet custard. The chefs had even included one of Her Majesty's favourites, a circular jam sandwich known in royal circles as a 'jammie'. In the meantime, Mrs Edwards was trying to remember what her neighbour had told her about breeding corgis. How did they keep their legs so stumpy, for instance?

"Has David informed you, Mrs Edwards?" the Queen asked gently, in between nibbles on a Tayside salmon and cucumber slice.

Mrs Edwards was hugely relieved she didn't want to discuss dogs. But what did she think Dai might have said? A sudden thought came to her. "Do you mean about giving you first aid, Ma'am?"

The Queen paused, a frond of dill hanging intriguingly from her lower lip. "Ah, not exactly, Mrs Edwards. We were thinking more of his, er, *ability*."

Mrs Edwards wondered whether she should draw the Queen's attention to the errant greenery. She decided not. She was also at a loss to think of any particular talent. Dai had resisted all of Grandmother's attempts to get him to join St Dyfrig's Church choir. With his dislike of traditional ingredients, he'd never make it onto the Welsh edition of *MasterChef*, either. He had an encyclopaedic knowledge of science fiction and popular culture, but that never got him anywhere – particularly when he started wittering on about radiation and the like. He was also evidently attractive to impressionable young teenagers like her daughter, but that was surely of no interest to someone as important as the Queen.

"I'm sorry, Ma'am, I can't think of anything. Dai's a nice boy all right, but – " she pointed at her head, " – he's not blessed with brains. To be honest, I think he watches too much TV for his own good."

"I see." The Queen looked thoughtful and nibbled another centimetre of the chef's savoury delight. "And your daughter … Ceri, is it?"

Mrs Edwards felt herself blushing. She should have intervened earlier – or refused to buy those ridiculous costumes. Why didn't Ceri just phone Dai like normal people do when they want to make contact? "I'm sorry about her rudeness, Ma'am. You know what children are like …"

The Queen sighed. "Indeed, Mrs Edwards. Such an endless source of concern for us. We give them so much and all they bestow on us in return is heartache. And then there are one's grandchildren …" Her eyes were misting over and Mrs Edwards was all set to place a comforting hand on her shoulder. *She must miss her granddaughter something rotten,* Mrs Edwards thought. The Queen seemed to anticipate the imminent gesture and swiftly cleared her throat. She looked intently at

Mrs Edwards. Her teeth were more pointed than was apparent in photos. "Tell me, my dear, have you heard of Siandi Da'aan?"

It was Mrs Edwards's turn to display her tonsils for royal inspection. She hastily considered what the Cymry Wiccae Association would make of the question. It was probably harmless. Perhaps the Queen had been doing some bedtime reading. "Er, yes, Ma'am, she was a – " she checked to make sure no one was eavesdropping, " – a *witch*." Except that what emerged was more like 'wheesh'. Mrs Edwards counted herself lucky to have got off so lightly uttering the word in public.

The Queen leaned forward, their plates of food almost touching. "She was an adept of the Dynion Mwyn tradition, we believe," she whispered conspiratorially. "Did you know that Queen Victoria used to burn an effigy of her every Halloween at Balmoral? Her ghillie John Brown was behind that. He saw himself as something of a witch-finder. Not a pleasant man." The Queen abruptly put some distance between their plates. "Now, returning to your daughter ..."

"Yes, Ma'am?" Mrs Edwards was all ears. Maybe she'd offer Ceri a job as her private secretary if she passed all her GCSEs. She could always add 'Royal Studies' if Religious Studies wasn't sufficient.

The Queen deposited her half-eaten plate of food. "Perhaps you might rein her in, Mrs Edwards. David is important to us and we would not want him to be deflected by some silly little spell."

Mrs Edwards was dumbstruck. Both she and her sandwiches were curling up at the edges after the Queen's unexpected admonishment of Ceri's antics. How did she know? "Of c-course, Your M-Majesty," she stuttered.

And with that precisely delivered Parthian shot, the Queen and her retinue departed. The jammies remained untouched. The mayor surreptitiously appropriated half-a-dozen chocolate brownies on his exit. He possessed impressively capacious pockets.

Everyone trooped out of the main entrance and waved as Her Majesty set off in a limousine for the brief journey back to the temporary helipad. A short time later her maroon helicopter took off, heading back in the direction of London. A tiny, white hand waved to the crowd from the window but Mrs Edwards didn't return the gesture. There was a whirling sensation inside her skull and it wasn't due to the noise overhead. How dare she speak to her like that! She'd referred to Dai as 'David'. Grandmother used to do the same. And to cap it all, the Queen was informed about Ceri's ritual. Mrs Edwards felt aggrieved and puzzled. There was someone she needed to phone urgently. "Houston, we have a problem," would be one way of putting it.

•••

Dale Franklin took his first steps on English soil – and immediately regretted it. He should have suspected something would go pear-shaped when Chief Scanlon agreed so readily to his request for a week's leave. Not that they hadn't deserved it. They'd been working their nuts off for the last few months.

Dale bent over double and grabbed at Steve for support. It was a throbbing pain of the 'Jeez that hurts!' variety. The nearest equivalent he could think of was having his testicles gripped by an ex-girlfriend who had the unshakeable belief that guys enjoyed it. Okay, he had squeezed her breasts a few times, but that was almost a rite of passage for teenage girls back then.

"What's up, sweets?" Steve said, concern etching his handsome, KCPD poster-boy face. "You're not gonna kiss the ground like His Holiness the Pope, are you?"

Dale pulled himself up cautiously, wincing.

"Are you okay, sir?" someone called from behind. "Can I get you a wheelchair?"

Dale saw Steve turn. It was a member of the ground staff in a hi-vis vest. "No thanks, sir. My friend tripped. He's good now."

"No I'm fucking not," Dale moaned. "It's like someone twisting my nuts."

Steve looked down, grinning. "Well, it looks like a normal, all American package to me. Perhaps it's a horny Heathrow ghost wanting to make your acquaintance."

Dale grimaced some more. "Thanks for the support, dude."

They continued walking towards the terminal building. Dale couldn't help walking with a strange pigeon-toed gait and he sneaked a glance at his crotch every so often. Something was getting up way too close and personal for first thing in the morning. Another twinge almost had him doubled up again. *Christ almighty!* Perhaps his nuts were twisted. He ought to get checked out in an ER. There were other thoughts spinning around in his head, too: vague impressions of things happening and being out of his control – almost a sense of impending doom. *Fuck, I'm having a panic attack!* He looked back, almost longingly, at the Delta Airlines aircraft, and considered flying straight back home. *Jeez, what am I thinking of. Be a man, for Chrissakes!* Well, that's what his dad would have said. Mom, on the other hand, would have rushed over with lotions and ointments and insist on applying them herself. He cringed at the thought.

"Or it could be due to the change in air pressure," Steve added, always keen to demonstrate his superior knowledge of human physiology, and looking annoyingly bright-eyed with the excitement of being a tourist in London.

"Yeah, like I don't know my ears from my nuts? Jesus H. Christ," Dale said ruefully.

Dale and Steve found a black cab just outside arrivals. Curiously, Dale's discomfort had dissipated while they were queuing to get through border control. They'd been distracted by seeing hapless tourists have their cell phones confiscated as soon as they tried switching them on to get a signal.

"You sure we can afford it?" Steve asked after the driver quoted an exorbitant price to take them to their hotel.

Dale didn't even want to consider the alternative of the Victorian Tube train system in his delicate condition. "It's okay, sweets, I can always sell the DeLorean if we get that hard up."

Steve raised both eyebrows ponderously slowly.

"Just kidding. I'll put you on the streets to hustle first."

Steve mock pouted.

The phantom testicle grabber took that opportunity to strike again. Dale slumped, white-faced, against the cab. "Christ, that was the worst ever," he said through gritted teeth.

"Okay, driver, change of destination," Steve said authoritatively. "Make it the hospital nearest to the hotel. I need to get my partner checked over."

The cab driver's expression morphed from one of greedy disdain to solicitous concern. He levered his bulk out of his seat and opened the passenger door, supporting Dale's elbow with his other hand. "Don't you worry, guv, I'll get you there in two shakes of a lamb's tail."

Dale and Steve exchanged a 'what the fuck?' look. "I hope that's better than two tugs of a dead donkey's dick," Steve grumbled.

"Yeah, it damn well better be," Dale said grimly, lowering himself gingerly onto the back seat, as if in the throes of a third-degree haemorrhoid attack.

The driver proved true to his colloquial expression. Dale sat back with his eyes closed, trying not to register the jolts and bumps as the vehicle cocked a snook at the insolent potholes out to impede their progress. He'd been hoping for the smooth ride of an eight-lane freeway. He cupped his balls supportively and did his best to remain oblivious to the weird looks he was getting from the driver. The grinding pain had become a more manageable dull ache. He glanced at Steve who was happily feeding the driver's insatiable curiosity about their vacation plans. The driver was a mountain of expensive information, accompanied by business cards that covered every touristic opportunity. Dale released his hands cautiously, and at least the pain didn't get any worse. He reached for his cell phone in his jacket inner pocket. It came to life but it wasn't making a connection.

"You won't get anywhere with that, mate," the driver

said. "If you're not careful, they'll confiscate it, too. Government's orders, you know." He nodded sagely.

"Thanks for the heads-up," Dale said, resting the useless phone on his lap.

"If you ask me, kids have had it coming to them," the driver continued. "I mean, all those selfies and watching pornography. And what about that Kardashian bird with the huge bum?" He shook his head. "It's just not my cup of tea. Rots the brain, too."

Dale wasn't sure whether the driver was referring to the selfies, the porn or the pneumatic posterior, but he nodded anyway. It was then he noticed that the ball ache had stopped. Instead, his cell had taken over the throbbing. He inspected it. Vibrate was switched off. So, why was his phone pulsating? He powered it down and the throbbing stopped, but the gnawing at his nuts restarted. Back on, the ball ache stopped. *Christ, this is seriously weird!* He tapped Steve on the thigh.

"Er, sweets, there's something weird with this cell. Have a feel of it …"

Steve took hold of the phone and almost dropped it. "What the hell? It's sorta throbbing and warm. You must have the vibrate on."

Dale shook his head. "It's off."

"Man, that's creepy," Steve snickered. "It's just like your morning wood."

Dale swiped at Steve's ear.

"Perhaps your nuts are trying to tell you something," Steve said. "You know, like you're all bitter and twisted. You need to let it all hang out, dude."

The swipe made contact the second time.

Dale and Steve arrived at the hospital 45 minutes later, which the driver assured them was a world record for the trip from Heathrow to Central London. He clearly expected a generous tip. With his wallet depleted of rather too many Great British pounds, Dale stared at the sign that read, 'ACCIDENT & EMERGENCY'. The hospital had a parking area at the front and a janitor was busy sweeping up greasy takeout containers. The UK government had clearly been no more successful than the US administration in curbing the nation's addiction to trans fats.

Dale stepped out of the taxi and promptly crumpled to the ground, experiencing a sudden compulsion to expel Delta Airline's unpalatable breakfast. His nuts were well and truly back in the grinder. He wished he hadn't thought of takeouts and promptly barfed over his shoes. He heard Steve yell for help, but the janitor continued his pre-programmed path like some robotic vacuum cleaner. Their arrival must have been observed on CCTV, as a nurse and porter rushed to his aid with a wheelchair.

"Let's get you inside, love," the nurse said, seemingly unfazed by his pathetic condition. "We don't want you catching your death of cold, do we?"

Unlike fast food, that example of the English vernacular was definitely not shared across the pond. Dale smiled wanly and allowed himself to be hoisted onto the chair. He wondered what happened about payment. In the US, they'd be asking for a tourist's MasterCard in the next breath.

Dale was fast-tracked into a cubicle while Steve completed the paperwork. It transpired that emergencies were free on the National Health Service. He climbed uncomfortably onto a trolley, holding on to his genitals as if his life depended on them. Which it did, of course. Living without peeing would be damn tough.

"A bit of bother down there, is it?" the nurse inquired sympathetically. "We'll have you right as rain before you know it, love." She placed a blanket over his lower half and adjusted the trolley so that he was comfortably propped-up. The nurse turned her attention to Dale's jacket, which he'd let drop onto a chair. His cell phone fell to the floor with a plasticky thud. "Well, you won't be needing this nasty thing," she said disapprovingly, picking it up and holding it like dog poop she'd just scooped into a bag. "If it's all right with you, I'll take this away for disposal. A doctor will be here to see you shortly."

Steve popped his tousled head round the curtain just as the nurse was departing. "Ah, you've got Dale's iPhone," he said, observing what she was holding at arm's length. "I gave it to him for his 30th. It's an iPhone 6." Steve took the phone from her before she could object. "He'll be needing this for medical reasons." The nurse looked on disbelievingly. Steve tossed the cell phone to Dale who placed it over his groin.

"Phew, that's better," Dale said, relief crossing his features like the calm after a storm.

"Well, I never," the nurse said, cocking a well-plucked eyebrow. "What you boys get up to!" she added archly.

Dale wasn't sure what he was being accused of, but he appreciated the respite from agony. Just then, a female doctor appeared. Her dark hair was pulled back severely, accentuating her narrow face. Her glasses reminded him of a certain Ms Virginia Ironside at Staley High School. A bright slash of lipstick and a quick flash of unusually white teeth gave the impression she was ready to draw blood. Dale prepared himself for the worst.

"How do you do? My name is Dr Amelia Strutt. And you must be – " she consulted her clipboard, " – Mr Dale Franklin, if I'm not mistaken."

Dale switched the iPhone into his other hand and extended the hand that had been holding the cell. Dr Strutt looked at it uncertainly and shook it fleetingly and limply. "So, what seems to be the problem, Mr Franklin?" Her gimlet eyes were fixed on his groin – and the phone he held against it. He'd decided to keep the explanation to the point. There was no point in wasting the National Health Service's time. The phone was helping, after all. That's when it started again …

"Fuck!" Dale leaned back hard against the trolley, trying to catch his breath. He glanced through the fog of pain and noticed that the iPhone's battery had died. "Can I borrow yours, sweets?" he implored Steve, holding his hand out shakily, like some junkie desperate to source his next fix.

Steve shrugged apologetically. "Sorry, babycakes, mine's dead, too. Look, give me yours and I'll go find somewhere to charge it." He rummaged in his bag for the charger. "And make sure you tell the doctor everything," he said as he exited the cubicle.

Dale sighed. This was gonna sound screwy Louie, as his dad used to put it. When he was in a good mood. He took a deep breath …

CHAPTER THREE

An hour later, Lieutenant Dale Franklin had been poked and prodded, bled within a few millilitres of his life, tested for infections he'd never even heard of and subjected to an interrogation of his sexual history, past, present and possible future. Dr Strutt had also listened unblinkingly to his description of an intimate attachment to his iPhone. She'd paused her pen only when Dale joked that Steve Jobs might have cured his pancreatic cancer with a laying on of his own technology. The doctor didn't cope well with a cop's sense of irony. Dr Strutt's lips had quivered when he mentioned the feeling of impending doom and he could see her mentally dialling for the psych consult. But she'd definitely been convinced by the repeated spasms of pain. In fact, her upper lip had rippled like some exotic caterpillar as he cupped his testicles for the umpteenth time that morning.

Dale soon learned that torsion of the testis was top of her differential, testicular tumour a bit further down and something hideously psychogenic might be lying in the basement to snare the unwary. Torsion of the testis clearly satisfied her need to nip masculinity in the bud. Her bedside manner left a lot to be desired, but at least she'd forgone the bite. Dale couldn't stop imagining her chomping on some part of her boyfriend's anatomy later on.

The next stop on Dale's whistle-stop tour of the UK's flagship healthcare was an ultrasound scan of his testicles. Steve found Dale just as he was going into the exam room and – oh, joy of joys – he had the iPhone with him. Dale watched the screen intently as the technician glided her shiny instrument over his lubricated nuts. A spasm of pain reminded them both why he was there.

"Strange," the technician said with a frown, "they both look normal to me."

Her puzzled expression went into overdrive when Steve handed him the iPhone and he held it over his groin. The throbbing must have been audible around the block.

Dale's final destination that morning was what Steve called 'the pecker checker', generally known, in more discreet circles, as a urological surgeon, and, on this occasion, a certain Mr Featherstonehaugh. The formidable clinic receptionist made certain they were aware that he was a 'Mr' rather than a 'Dr', and that his name was pronounced 'Fanshaw'. Both seemed as weird as the British obsession with football.

Somehow, Dale's testicles had settled into a state of grateful submission and the ache was more like his anatomy reminding him of their presence than the excruciating digging in of someone's heel. His iPhone was another matter, though, as the pulsating technology had taken on a life of its own and was drumming away like a woodpecker determined to drill its way through an entire tree trunk.

"Good morning, gentlemen," the urologist said breezily, as he entered the cubicle. "So, what – "

Mr Featherstonehaugh was good looking in a gentlemen's club sort of way, all salt and pepper hair and Saville Row suit, and he wore one of those strange affectations called a bow tie. There'd been a preacher at Dale's church who wore a similar item of clothing, complete with flashing LEDs to illuminate his less than luminary sermons. The present bearer of such sartorial extravagance seemed temporarily lost for words. Dale had to admit, the phone was making quite a racket.

"Sorry," Dale said. "It's been getting louder and louder all morning. Steve's put his on charge, too, in case mine runs out."

"You're holding a *mobile phone* against your genitals?" the urologist said. He made it sound like headline news.

"Yeah," Dale said. "I don't know how, but it seems to stop the pain." Actually, that wasn't entirely true. All the waiting around had given him time to mull things over and he reckoned he had some sort of explanation. But there was still the sense of something scary looming over him, and the image of the screaming triplets in the Marshall kitchen had flashed through his mind yet again.

"Really?" Mr Featherstonehaugh said, in a tone of voice that oozed disbelief. "So, when did the pain in your testicles start, Mr – " he glanced at the notes in his hands, " – er, *Lieutenant* Franklin?"

Dale glanced at Steve for support. His boyfriend seemed busy admiring the cut of the doctor's suit. *Some things never change,* he thought. "Just as soon as we stepped off the airplane, Doctor. It was like someone had my balls in a vice." Dale made a squashing motion with his free hand. "You know what I mean, Doctor?"

Mr Featherstonehaugh picked up the rubber end of a reflex hammer and grasped it tightly. "Like that, you mean?"

"Yeah," Dale said flinching, "just like that."

"And what happened next?" the urologist asked, clearly on tenterhooks to discover more about Dale's grievous goolie grabbing.

"He bent forward until he was almost touching the ground," Steve said. "I made a joke about the Pope kissing the tarmac. I didn't realise he was in so much pain." He followed that with his oh-so-cute dumbass smile that could melt an iceberg. Not that icebergs could be bothered to venture as far south as Central Missouri, of course – even for a beer with the wizard.

Dale had to admit, this guy sure knew his way around a man's genitals. This was a palpating and probing that spoke of years of study and thousands of patients who'd lain back, closed their eyes and thought of England, hoping that he had the solution to their intimately excruciating problem. But Dale was sure Mr Featherstonehaugh had never come across ball ache accompanied by thoughts of impending doom. His exam was also mercifully quick, unlike the redoubtable Dr Strutt who'd approached his groin with all the slow, fumbling confidence of a teen at her first prom date without the benefit of liquor. Her dilated pupils and blush response had been such a giveaway. She'd obviously never fantasised about being caught in the sights of *Blade Runner's* Rick Deckard. Admittedly, in Dale's case, that had been with them both sporting helluva boners under the table.

Speaking of which, Dale was rather hoping he'd get a clean bill of health so he could enjoy a bit of R&R with his fiancé. Remarkably, everything had remained quiescent throughout the morning's incursions into the most private region of his body, but something would have to give sooner or later.

"Well …" Mr Featherstonehaugh said pregnantly, shedding his latex gloves. He'd replaced the sheet over Dale's pelvic region not a moment too soon. Dale glanced at Steve who had a hand over his snickering mouth. The gloves were dropped into a yellow biohazard container. Dale didn't immediately see why and then it hit him between the eyes. Dale prepared himself for the thunderbolt to end all thunderbolts. No quality time with Steve. Instead, he'd be locked away in a decontamination unit with a Geiger counter for a bed buddy. Time to fess up to Mr Featherstonehaugh. He took a deep breath.

"… I don't believe this is torsion of the testis," the urologist said. "It's true that your condition shares some of the characteristics of torsion, but the sudden onset, in the absence of trauma or any previous history, makes it extremely unlikely. If you were younger and a rugby player, then it could well be torsion and I'd want to admit you for observation, with a low threshold for surgery." He turned to make his exit. "However, if the pain doesn't resolve or gets worse, then I would advise you to come back to A&E."

Steve was nodding in agreement – and completely missing the point. Dale's gonads were still aching, which put their vacation in jeopardy as well as their sex life. He sure didn't fancy firing on one cylinder for the rest of his life. And what if they wanted to have kids at some point? No, man, this was serious. He had to put the question, come what may. He took another deep breath. "Er, Doctor, could it be due to radiation?"

"Radiation?" the urologist said with an arched left

eyebrow straight out of a James Bond script. "What makes you think that, Lieutenant?"

"Well, it's just that I've got this DeLorean DMC-12 and I bought a replica flux capacitor for it on eBay. I mounted it in the console and plugged it into the lighter socket. It didn't take anything like 1.2 gigawatts. The light tubes were just like those in the movie. The box had a radiation symbol on it. I thought that was a joke … but it was made in China … and I'm just wondering …" Steve was rolling his eyes and Dale knew he was digging himself into an ever deeper hole. Mr Featherstonehaugh shuffled uneasily on his feet.

"Interesting …" The urologist looked serious. Dale flinched in anticipation of the blow. "Well, if you'd suggested Wi-Fi and Bluetooth – " Mr Featherstonehaugh gestured at the iPhone still in Dale's hand, " – you wouldn't be too far off the mark, Lieutenant. We've been aware for 10 years that mobile phones can affect sperm production. Not surprisingly, manufacturers have tried to block the research. Tight jeans and alcohol can also affect fertility in young men, but I believe phones are the main culprit. With the government's kibosh on telecom networks, perhaps that will improve, but vulnerable young bodies may have already been damaged in ways we don't even know about."

Dale and Steve shared a 'well, I never' look. That was some soapbox he'd just climbed onto.

"Sorry about that," Mr Featherstonehaugh said. "It's become a bit of hobbyhorse for me. I'm afraid my son is detained under the Mental Health Act because of …" He turned away from them to clear his throat.

"Unilateral cerebral atrophy?" Steve said unexpectedly.

"'The screaming'?" Dale said almost simultaneously.

The urologist was staring at them open-mouthed. "Good Lord. How come you're so well informed?

Dale looked at Steve who nodded for him to continue.

"Well, you could say we broke the case," Dale said.

Mr Featherstonehaugh frowned. He wasn't getting it.

"March 2014, Kansas City and a 17-year-old named Brandon P. Marshall who shot his parents and then himself," Dale said.

"In front of their three kiddies at the breakfast table," Steve said.

"And triggered by hearing the sound of a child screaming," Dale said.

"In other words, the index case," Steve said.

"Of course!" the urologist said. "I must have seen you on the news. Well, well …" He leaned forward, looking at them intently. "You know, Officers, I thought the current situation with children mainly affected the UK."

"That's because of what your government wants you to think and what our administration chooses to believe," Dale said with a perspicacity that seemed to have arrived right out of the blue.

"So, the problem is just as widespread in the States?" Mr Featherstonehaugh said.

"Probably worse," Dale said. "We lock affected kids up and it's not entirely lawful – "

"They call it an 'executive order'," Steve said.

"Meaning there's no get out clause," Dale continued, "and there are still no limitations on networks or Wi-Fi. Which means that the CDC's perfect storm hasn't moved on and neither has our beloved president."

"So, how the hell are you keeping a lid on it?" The urologist looked puzzled.

"Mass brain scanning, curfews, whistle blowers, 'no cell' signs and all that sort of thing," Dale said. "It's like Prohibition all over again."

"Plus a low threshold for depriving kids of their liberty, of course," Steve said.

"Christ," Mr Featherstonehaugh said, rubbing his eyes, "perhaps we're better off here, after all."

"Returning to my problem, Doctor," Dale said, repositioning his cell phone for maximum therapeutic effect, "is this a radiation thing or not? After all, proximity to metal seems to ease the pain and some metals can block radiation."

Dale's iPhone took that opportunity to spur on the discussion with a healthy thrumming noise.

"Well, Lieutenant, the one thing I've learnt in the last year is never to discount the impossible," the urologist said. "Believe it or not, there've been rumours of strange happenings at Buckingham Palace, including telepathy and the like. My wife is one of the physicians to the Royal Household. She's signed the Official Secrets Act, but she passes on a few snippets from time to time. They're pretty mean at paying for her services, so you can't blame her." He sighed. "So, returning to your question, Lieutenant, a) I don't know, and b) I suppose it could be."

Steve didn't look convinced by Mr Featherstonehaugh's answer. "But if the UK has stopped Wi-Fi and cell networks, surely that means there should be less EM radiation in the air."

"Go on," Mr Featherstonehaugh said. He pulled up a stained and generally much abused plastic chair.

"Well ..." Steve took a breath, "back home, there's EM radiation everywhere and Dale never had aching balls. Here, you've cut EM radiation and he gets an ache as soon as he steps off the plane." He shrugged. "I don't get it."

Dale agreed. Whichever way you looked at it, it wasn't adding up. There was also the minor niggle of thinking something bad was lying in wait for him round the corner. He didn't believe in hauntings, but his nerves were being jangled by something lurking in the vicinity. He was sure he could hear a child screaming in the distance. He was starting to think he should never have followed through the 911 call to the Marshall household that fateful spring morning.

"Well ..." Mr Featherstonehaugh's patience was clearly being tested. "Look, chaps, I'm just a humble surgeon. There are limits to what we get taught in medical school. All I'm sure about is that it isn't torsion of the testis. As to radiation ... well, I'm afraid I can't say." He paused and fumbled in a jacket pocket. "I just remembered this card. It's someone my wife had dealings with. He's an eccentric, but he's a good doctor by all accounts. My wife says he's on the lookout for subjects with problems that are unusual. His name is – " he squinted at the card, " – Dr Petros Kyriakides. He's in private practice, so you should find his rooms somewhere on Harley Street."

Dale took the card. He'd forgotten about the wild, bearded Greek doctor until then. Dr Kyriakides had stunned his audience at an early morning conference call by displaying the teenage homicide-suicide cases from around the world on a *Minority Report* type display. Spelling out that the combination of Wi-Fi, 3G, fast food and copper had shrunk teenagers' brains had taken guts – and been a helluva bitter pill to swallow.

Perhaps he should give the doctor a call. On the other hand, the ache wasn't that bad and there was a lot of sightseeing Steve wanted to do. And they thought they'd try tracking down Dai Williams, assuming His Sirness could find time in his hectic schedule to see a couple of lowly US cops.

•••

Dai left Sandra behind nursing her nausea. The journey to Green Park took longer than he'd anticipated as some idiot kid insisted on jamming his foot in the Tube train's closing doors at every stop. Dai gave in to his better judgement and unleashed a disabling ping, courtesy of the hocus focus, as well as a telepathic *"Fuck off!"*, which left the kid stunned and drooling at the mouth. His fellow passengers wouldn't have been aware of his intervention, but they'd burst into spontaneous applause once he'd been immobilised. *Yet another one destined for the funny farm,* Dai thought.

The light was fading when Dai emerged out of the Underground station. He looked for a friendly bobby, but the only one in sight was busy removing wads of gum from the soles of his boots. "Bugger ... shit ... fuck," he whinged in an angry mantra, hopping on alternate feet and poking at the offending substance with a stubby, police-issue biro. The air was turning colder and bluer by the second. Passers-by tutted about the declining standards of law enforcement.

Dai strolled across Green Park. By the time he

reached Buckingham Palace it was well and truly dark. The Queen was clearly one to keep the home fires burning, as all the windows glowed from the inner radiance of old-fashioned light bulbs. Dai imagined it was all about keeping up appearances. He waved cheerily in case Her Majesty was taking a sneaky peek at the outside world while going from room to room to adjust the dimmers.

It felt strange walking into the Palace forecourt unaccompanied. He wondered whether he was being monitored on CCTV. If he hadn't worn his suit, he'd probably have been suspected of planning to climb into the Queen's bedchamber. The footmen greeted him as Sir David, although he didn't feel remotely like a knight. He should have commandeered a police horse and ascended the red-carpeted steps on a white charger in full regalia. Sorry, wrong millennium. And he'd never mastered riding a horse. Knowing his luck, the beast would probably use the opportunity to shit on the carpet – and he'd find himself stuck to the saddle by chewing gum. The red carpet had been replaced, so an equine accident could have already happened. Or the Queen might have been cantering along the grand corridor to demonstrate her miraculous recovery from the stroke. It had certainly been something of an *annus mirabilis* so far. And the year wasn't over yet …

"Enter!" came the curt response to the footman's

tap on the door. It sounded so formal, and not at all as Dai remembered from his first visit to Her Majesty's inner sanctum. Perhaps she'd been catching up on her paperwork, concentrating hard, drink in hand, and had forgotten their assignation. He needed to watch protocols this time – no pinging of the royal brain as well as no touching of her personage.

The Queen was standing by her desk when Dai entered her private study. He smiled, bowed and took her extended hand. She had on an elegant powder blue dress with a string of pearls and wore a silver broach on her left shoulder. She studied him closely. He blushed and felt overdressed. Jeans and a hooded top would have been much better for a drink with a mate. Except she wasn't a mate, she was *the Queen*. And he'd forgot to bring her some flowers. He reddened again. Her Majesty sat and smoothed her dress. She gestured him to take a pew.

"Do you always let your mind wander so much, David?" the Queen asked with a glint of amusement Dai hadn't expected so early in the evening. But she was right – using Sandra's thought boxes to keep his musings private from fellow telepaths didn't come easy to him. He lacked discipline. Perhaps MI5 would knock him into shape with a boot camp or two. He glanced at the table between them: it was totally bare. So, where were the drinks? A knock broke his reverie.

"Come in!" the Queen said, still looking pointedly in his direction. "Well, David?"

A footman entered bearing a tray laden with bottles and glasses – and, if Dai wasn't right royally mistaken, a bowl of Pringles. They were always produced on special occasions in his grandmother's house. "Sorry, Ma'am, I have been a bit distracted – " she must have been prying inside his head although he couldn't blame her, " – and I guess I haven't quite mastered Sandra's thought boxes."

The footman retreated and the Queen mixed their drinks: two parts of Dubonnet to one part of gin, with a slice of lemon and some ice, served in a cut glass tumbler. Dai sipped warily. It was strong stuff. Rather medicinal, too. He felt sure he was being softened up for something important.

"How is it?" the Queen asked.

"Hmm, interesting," Dai said, hoping he was sloshing the pink liquid appropriately without appearing a total prat. "Unusual, too. There's something in it that I recognise but can't put a name to."

"Quinine," the Queen said triumphantly.

"You mean the stuff for malaria?"

"Indeed. We always take a few cases of Dubonnet with us when we're travelling to – "

"Bongo-bongo land?"

The Queen smiled. "You might say that, but we couldn't possibly comment."

"Touché, Ma'am."

They sipped their drinks. A trio of corgis appeared from somewhere and sat obediently at the Queen's feet, their ears pricked forwards and noses sniffing at the air. There probably wasn't an organism on the planet that didn't drool at the smell of the hyperbolic paraboloid called the Pringle. Dai was slavering, too.

"We visited Wales today, you know," the Queen said abruptly. Her eyes were all aglint again.

Dai inclined his head. "Oh?" He see-sawed in the opposite direction to prevent a drop of pinkish spittle landing on the magnificent Axminster carpet.

"We went by helicopter. So useful for a round trip and being back in time for tea."

They continued to sip their drinks. There was definitely an agenda afoot. The dogs were waiting with bated breath.

"We opened a new unit at the Royal Glamorgan Hospital," the Queen continued.

Dai's jaw dropped. This was getting too close to what he used to regard as home.

"It was modern. Charles would have hated it. He'd have the patients in long, cold dormitories, with nurses running around in starched uniforms handing out laxatives and bedpans. Still, we met some interesting people – " she paused for a drawn-out swallow, " – what was I saying?"

This was psychological torture. "You met some interesting people, Ma'am," Dai said impatiently.

"Yes, indeed we did." She held out the bowl of crisps. "Would you care for a Pringle or two? The sour cream and onion variety are our favourite. Most deserving of the royal warrant, we believe."

Dai took a handful. This was exactly the sort of delaying tactic Granny Betty used. He crunched three chips in quick succession. The corgis had their beady eyes on him. The penny dropped. "This is to do with my grandmother, isn't it, Ma'am?"

The Queen deposited her glass on a side table. "Of course, Dai. They named the new unit after her."

"Really?" he said incredulously. His eyes had turned strangely watery. "I don't understand, Ma'am. She was only a folk healer, after all."

The Queen's expression was inscrutable. She would have made an excellent sitter for a certain Venetian artist circa 1503.

"Wasn't she?" Dai said, wondering whether his mind was about to be blown wide open yet again.

"Under the radar I think, Dai," he heard inside his head. Her Majesty was learning the tricks of the trade fast. She was able to switch into telepathic mode in the blink of an eye. Perhaps the walls had ears. He glanced around the room. Where to start? Listening devices in lamps were old hat. He tried to recall his MI5 training:

something about Occam's razor and going for the bleedin' obvious. Three of the obvious were staring him in the face – and panting heavily. Christ, she believed that the dogs were bugged!

"Indeed they are," the Queen retorted telepathically. *"If you look inside their ears, you'll see for yourself."*

Dai bent down and inspected an ear of the nearest corgi. There were things like tiny peas attached to the soft fleshy lining. One of them moved. The other ear had even more of them. *Ear mites*, he thought. Having five dogs in the same household must be a recipe for all manner of canine infestations. But he wasn't about to argue with Cruft's chief patron. And he hoped he'd kept that thought to himself. He looked up at the Queen. *"I see what you mean, Ma'am. They look Chinese to me. Probably powered by body heat."*

The Queen gave a little grunt of approval. *"Does the name Siandi Da'aan mean anything to you, David?"*

Dai shook his head. It sounded like something served in a pub.

"She was a witch. In fact, a very famous witch. And she came from Pontypridd."

Dai mouthed, "Granny Betty."

"Yes, David. Your grandmother, Elizabeth Williams, was a direct descendant and even more powerful than Siandi Da'aan."

"Gosh, I had no idea." He really didn't. His grandmother had been tight-lipped to a fault and she'd kept her

credos to herself. There'd been occasions when things happened that she couldn't explain, but she'd smile and then look serious and say, "The Lord moves in mysterious ways, Dai." And with no response to that, he'd return to his bedroom without questioning the wisdom of an elder. But that left a nagging question no amount of pinging of brains could answer: if Granny Betty really had been a witch – assuming witchery worked – was that an explanation for the hocus focus? And was that the only thing she'd bequeathed him, hidden away until the time was right?

"That's exactly what I've been wondering," the Queen said, sneaking herself back inside his head. *"And I don't believe I'm the only one who wants to know."*

Dai almost choked on his drink. It was all making sense. Something weird had happened back in the Park Estate flat, and Sandra had got the brunt of it. Witchery was definitely an explanation for her sudden bout of morning sickness. Could the mesh have protected him from some spell? But that would mean witchery involved EM radiation, which was 100 years out of Granny Betty's comfort zone. He'd better book an appointment with Dr Kyriakides to get checked out. But that still left the nagging question of who was behind it.

Her Majesty smiled ruefully. *"We have an idea."* She blinked an eye. "Would you care for another drink, Sir David?"

Green Park on a chilly autumn night was rather forbidding for those of a nervous disposition. The Victorian street lamps cast ominous shadows of the gnarled black poplars, their spindly branches ready to snag the unwary, including those who'd consumed one too many Dubonnet and gins. Dai was vaguely aware of the trees' resemblance to witches with or without broomsticks, but his mind was also on the lookout for chewing gum, dog poo and other watch-where-you-put-your-feet inconveniences. The Queen had offered to call for a cab, but he needed to clear his head before he faced Sandra's interrogation.

Dai had also been thinking about his first encounter with Tania Goldman. He remembered as clearly as yesterday going out onto his 20th floor balcony with the feeling that something was about to happen. If he hadn't put on his metallized fabric protection and ventured downstairs into the murky shadows of Battersea Park, he'd never have seen the teenager hunched over her laptop with sizzling sounds leaking from her earbuds. That wouldn't have stopped her EM radiation-frazzled brain from hatching the plan to murder her parents, but at least he wouldn't have been part of it. Then he'd have been left with Mrs Pigeon and her brood for company. No saving of the Queen's life. No knighthood. No fiancée or baby. No Dubonnet and gin. Back to his mind-numbingly tedious existence of dodging EM radiation.

So, who was really pulling the strings? His actions still felt predestined and doomed to repeating themselves over and over, at the whim of some omniscient puppet master who got his kicks from watching people squirm. *Gosh, did I think that? I've got Q on the mind again. And not the cuddly MI6 sort with a soft touch to cover up the gruesome reality of killing people.*

But how did his family fit into all of this? Had Ceri been put up to it by someone? And what the hell had she been trying to do to him? If he hadn't conveniently returned to the Park Estate, would he have turned into a golden beach ball? And why was the Queen so interested in witches? He'd never heard of Siandi Da'aan, but it sounded as if she belonged in the footnotes of some scholarly tome rather than someone with a connection to his grandmother. And Granny Betty a witch? It was getting way too complicated for a boy who didn't have much of a brain. *"Sorry, Ma'am, I had to ping to find out what that cow said about me."* Actually, he'd put that in the draft thought box to send later.

Dai crouched to tie a shoelace just as an illuminated flying disk soared past where his head had been. He stood up, wondering who'd thrown it. It could have been a miniature UFO. *Christ, I feel strange! Woozy. Light-headed. About to keel ... feel ... peel ... over. Oh fuck, my brain's affected, too! Or is it those bloody witches? And there's something strange happening at foot level: the grass has turned*

*translucent and I can see down into the earth. My God, it's full
of stars!*

•••

Dai came to with Green Park greenery in his mouth
and a tenacious tendril worming its way up a nostril.
His outstretched fingertips were resting on a blanket of
grass that was cool and comforting. It reminded him of
a park in Pontypridd where he used to lie flat on his back
and look up into the sky, hoping that a friendly spaceship would beam him up, up and away from the land of
leeks and laver bread. A bright light had just appeared
to his left. Perhaps the time had finally come for his
departure. He hoped they wouldn't require his passport.

"Are you all right, sir?"

It was a friendly male voice. English born and bred.
Educated up to GCSEs, Dai decided. A hint of authority,
but also a bit out of breath. Dai turned his head. The
owner of the pleasant voice crouched by his side and
his torch illuminated his face. He was still panting. And
he wore a helmet. With a spiky thing on it.

"I saw you fall, sir, so I came running. I was just
about to go off duty, or otherwise I wouldn't have seen
you. You were lucky."

On the basis of how he currently felt, which was
like having the grey matter immediately behind his left
eyebrow pulsed sadistically in a blender, Dai wasn't so
sure about that epithet. He also wondered why so many

policemen were overweight if they were required to run across England's green and pleasant land to rescue those afflicted with a sudden compulsion to hug the earth. Except his wasn't some common or garden, back-to-grass-roots lurgy. Two options crossed his troubled mind, and they weren't mutually exclusive: firstly, that the government had bowed to the might of the telecommunications industry and switched Wi-Fi and mobile networks back on; and secondly, that someone was flexing their witchy muscles again.

"I'm all right I think, Officer." That didn't come out quite as he intended. It sounded more like: "I'm all righ' I thin', Offisher." Dai sensed wheels of logical deduction at work even without using the hocus focus.

The policeman harrumphed. "Er, sir, do you have any identification on you?"

Dai reached for the back pocket of his trousers. His wallet wasn't there. *Shit! I've been attacked by a flying disk of unknown origin and then mugged by a Good Samaritan!* Then he remembered the invitation. He pushed himself up – *Christ, my head hurts* – and rummaged inside his jacket. The thickness of the paper was strangely reassuring. He handed it to the police officer.

"Dai Williams at your service, Officer: soothsayer and lifesaver to Her Majesty the Queen of England, Scotland, Northern Ireland, and last, but definitely least, Wales." He'd said something similar before, but he couldn't remember where. Such loquaciousness was usually the sign of an attack of radiation sickness. The policeman tut-tutted and shook his head.

"You wouldn't be taking the mickey, would you, sir?" the officer said as he unfolded the sheet. His index finger carefully traced the words on the page and then came to a halt, hovering with a quiver above the Royal Coat of Arms. "Jiw, jiw!"

Dai shouldn't have judged a book by its cover: the policeman was as Welsh as he was – and his jaw had just dropped a good few inches. He hoped he wasn't about to burst into song with one of Bryn Terfel's greatest hits.

"Not quite God," Dai said, touching his forehead gingerly. Despite a half-hearted attempt at some therapeutic self-pinging, it still throbbed like a front row forward's cauliflower ear. Actually, it had made it worse, so he'd probably set up a feedback loop. "I don't suppose you've got some aspirin on you, have you?"

The bobby on the Green Park beat chuckled and reached into one of the multitude of pockets in his uniform. "A few too many is it, sir? I've heard Her Majesty is partial to a tipple." He handed Dai something white and aspirin-like covered with blue fluff. Dai inspected it and put it into his mouth despite its unknown provenance. Curiously, it hadn't crossed Dai's mind that he'd had too much to drink. When the Queen is mixing the best cocktails in the land, it's easy to lose track.

"Er, yes, Officer. Dubonnet and gin," Dai said ruefully.

"Dubonnet and gin?" the officer said, rubbing his head in sympathy. "I'm not surprised, sir. Dangerous stuff." He glanced towards the park exit. "I'd better be on my way, sir. Are you all right to get home? I could order a car, but …"

Dai guessed what he was going to say. It would be embarrassing for both sides. He could see the headline: 'ROYALLY DRUNK KNIGHT ROLLICKING IN ROYAL PARK.' It'd probably become known as the 'Parkgate' scandal. And Sandra would never forgive him for misusing the public purse – not to mention the Privy Purse, if he'd had *that* much to drink. Rumour had it that a bottle of Dubonnet was as expensive as the best champagne now that it was manufactured solely for the Royal Family.

"No, that's okay, Officer. I can find my way home," Dai said, pulling himself to his feet. "I don't suppose you've seen my wallet lying somewhere, have you?"

The policeman fished something out of another capacious pocket. "Well, I found this, but it can't be yours. It belongs to someone with an MI5 ID. He looks a bit down at heel. Needs a haircut, too."

Dai put up his hand. "That's me, Officer. Soothsayer,

lifesaver *and* scruffy spook, although I've probably broken the Official Secrets Act telling you that." He should get the photo replaced. It still showed him wearing the mesh to shield him from EM radiation.

The police officer stood up and saluted, his wobbling belly barely contained by his uniform. "I'm honoured to make your acquaintance, Sir David. Are you sure I can't get you a car?" he asked solicitously.

"No, Officer. I'll be fine now," Dai said, pulling his jacket around him against the chill in the evening air. "Noswaith dda." He extended his hand for a parting handshake.

"Noswaith dda, Syr Dafydd," the policeman said, shaking hands rather too lingeringly. "Noswaith dda, Dai bach."

Now, that was puzzling. Why had an officer of the law I'd never met before call me 'Dai bach'? Whoosh. Crash. Ouch, I'm prostrate again. Memo to self: never trust a total stranger who can't decide whether he's English or Welsh and gives you a white pill covered with pocket fluff.

CHAPTER FOUR

Sandra Evans's first realisation on waking was that she was alone in bed. Her second thought, just a second or two later, was that she no longer felt nauseous. She placed both hands on her bump to reassure herself that she was still pregnant. Yes, all present and correct – and warm, well-nourished and growing surprisingly fast. The baby stirred and gave her two sharp kicks. She resisted the temptation to send a quick message of love and encouragement. And an apology for spewing her guts up throughout most of the previous day. That had been strange, occurring so out of the blue. And why in Dai's old flat of all places? But with all the bizarre things happening recently, the notion of reverting spontaneously to how she was six months ago didn't seem that farfetched. The reality of life with Dai was still far from ordinary, and even normal meant him being summoned by MI5 at any time of the day *or* night. She sighed, but it was with a wry smile on her face.

Sandra wasn't exactly run-of-the-mill herself: a survivor of abuse who ended up held captive by MI5, in some mysterious country house, just because she became speechless and then telepathic. Okay, she had sabotaged the brakes on her father's car. And her mother died as well. Big mistake. Then, to complicate things, she couldn't even mutter 'no comment' when interviewed by the police. Some crazy lady. 'Psychogenic aphonia' was the final diagnosis. Her emerging paranormal ability wasn't even mentioned, although it was experienced by a few who came too close. Major Chisholm had been adept at hiding indiscretions and making people pay their keep. What would have happened if she hadn't met a reluctantly Welsh Welshman named Dai Williams? She'd probably still be in The Manor and going round the bend. She certainly had enough to be bitter and twisted about.

Sandra thought of her parents. She'd give anything to turn the clock back and see the look on her father's face when he learned of her new title: 'Sandra, Lady Williams' – once they'd tied the knot, of course. So many years of belittling her and telling her she'd never do anything significant with her life. It was ironic that his end had become her new beginning – or at least, a new chapter in a pretty weird book.

Like Dai, she'd had her head probed electronically in the Brain Lab. Dr Kyriakides had told her they were on the same wavelength. Such a cliché. And then it turned out that there were many more people like them, all freed to communicate telepathically when Wi-Fi and mobile networks got banned by the government. The initial flurry of flirtation with freedom didn't last long, though. The restaurant they started, called 'Ψ', didn't have a chance in hell amid the paranoia following 'the screaming'. Telepathic ordering of food was always going to be a fad.

Dai had been part of 'the screaming' – or, more precisely, he'd helped to identify what lay behind teenagers going berserk and then killing their parents and siblings. And he'd saved the Queen's life – with her assistance, mind you, as it was with her telepathic ability that he'd been able to call for help and get Her Majesty transferred to hospital. So, all things considered, Sandra thought she was rather deserving of the title of 'Lady Williams'. And they'd be getting married soon, once the royal diary had been consulted and the right church found.

Sandra looked at the bedside clock: it was just after 6:00 a.m. So where exactly was her fiancé? His invitation had been just for drinks, not drinks, dinner and a prolonged drinking session with Prince Philip. He might have a habit of slipping out of bed in the middle of the night, but he'd always leave a note or send her a thought as he closed the front door. She pushed herself up and swung her legs out from under the duvet. Pausing to catch her breath, she sat on the edge of the bed and glanced around. It was just as it had been when Dai left for the Palace in his suit. He definitely hadn't been back. She pulled on a dressing gown and padded heavily into the living room, one hand on her swollen belly. Her eyes darted around, looking for one of Dai's trademark messages. Nothing caught her eye. He hadn't written on the mirror with one of her lipsticks, either. That used to annoy her, but even 'Dai woz ere' in pillar box red would have been better than nothing.

"David, are you nearby?" she communicated as forcibly as she could. She was shouting the thought. If Dai was close by, he'd come running into the flat with both hands clamped to his head. And he'd be angry.

Nothing came back. The front door didn't open. There was no darkly attractive Welshman with spiky hair shouting at her. *Okay, girl, get your thoughts together, where else might he have left a message?* She gave a little whoop of glee when she remembered the jokey birthday gift of alphabet fridge magnets. They had a running contest to see who could write the longest sentence with the twenty-six letters. Neither were particularly good at it and it usually read, 'LETS FUCK'. Sandra half-ran, half-wobbled into the galley kitchen. The message hadn't changed. She rearranged them to read 'TUCK SELF', which seemed more appropriate given her condition. She'd replace it with 'LUCK FEST' when Dai returned. Then she noticed that the kettle was cold. Dai always had a coffee before he went out.

What should she do? Logically, her best option would be to ring MI5. Shortly after they moved to London,

Dai had given her a piece of paper with an emergency phone number. It was useless given her handicap, but she was certain it was still in a kitchen drawer. Perhaps someone could ring it for her. She yanked at all the handles in sight, desperate to find her prize. She didn't give a shit about the contents tumbling to the floor. *Oh God, did I throw it out the previous week?* A wave of panic threatened to engulf her and then she remembered that she'd put out the rubbish too late for the council truck. *Perhaps it's in the wheelie bin after all!*

It took scarcely a minute for Sandra to deposit the contents of the bin onto the pavement, tear open the black bags like a ravenous fox and then locate the all-important digits. The slip even had MI5's crest and the motto 'Regnum Defende' at the top. *Thank-fucking-God*, she thought, holding it up as if it was a lottery win awaiting the attention of some perma-tanned twat on primetime TV.

"Well, really," an elderly passer-by groused in disgust, not realising that the wild-haired bin scavenger hadn't even opened her mouth.

What next? Sandra thought, as it dawned on her that the 11 numbers were only the start of her Sisyphean task to locate her fiancé. Perhaps one of her neighbours would help. She pressed all the entryphone buttons to the flats in the house, but it was like trying to raise the dead. Sandra's heart leaped when she noticed a young man walking on the other side of the road. Disregarding the green cross code inculcated in her formative years, she waddled across and accosted him with the grimy piece of paper. "Sorry, missus, the fuckin' government's got my phone, innit," he said with the terminally despondent tone of the permanently out of luck.

Safely back on the rubbish-strewn pavement outside their flat, the well-being of her fiancé dug away in Sandra's mind like a score of JCB diggers. A flash of inspiration came to her when she saw a black cab turn into the road: *I'll go and see that nice Sergeant Slocombe at Battersea Police Station! Dai's always saying how helpful he'd been in his time of need.* She'd completely forgotten that she was barefoot, still wearing her dressing gown and had no money. And that the front door had closed behind her.

Sandra's journey to Battersea Police Station took less time than she'd anticipated. She used the driver's biro to scribble where she wanted to go on the slip of paper, and had to jab at it several times to dissuade him from taking her to the nearest maternity unit. "Okay, you know best, love. Hang on to your horses and I'll get you there in a trice," he'd said with a wink. Even at her destination, he'd accepted her less than convincing mime of being penniless. "That's all right, ducks, you just take care of yourself and the little 'un." Sandra's faith in humanity had been fully restored when she walked up to the police station entrance at shortly after 8:00 a.m. That proved to be short-lived, as she was almost knocked to the ground by some inebriate lurching through the doors in search of his first bottle in a bag of the day. And he didn't even say sorry.

"Bill, there's someone who wants to see you," the desk sergeant called through to the back office.

Sergeant Bill Slocombe groaned wearily. He'd just come off desk duty after a night of drunks and the mentally-challenged, and he was enjoying his tea in the souvenir Arsenal mug that he intended to see him through to retirement unchipped. He lived for the day that Jack Wilshire came through the door with complimentary season tickets. "Who is it?" he called out with the reluctance of the near dead to consider their epitaph.

"Well, she's not able to say, although she has written it down," the sergeant said. "You'd better take a look for yourself."

Bill Slocombe's first glance at his uninvited guest suggested the worst. The woman was wild-eyed and her head appeared to be sprouting snakes. She was barefoot and dressed more for the boudoir than the local nick. His hackles were all set to rise when he noticed something significant: the crest on the slip of paper she held up for inspection. The fact that she was pregnant had lodged itself in the folds of his brain for subsequent processing.

One of the sergeant's hobbies was collecting crests and the more ornate the better. What he detested were those made up by some Towie upstart living in an over-extended bungalow who thought he could inveigle his way into the House of Lords by waving a coat of arms. The future King of England was almost as bad, and Bill Slocombe's ire had been exceptionally irked when he caught sight of the Cymry Originals logo: giant leeks and harps, for goodness sake!

But as soon as Sergeant Slocombe saw the MI5 crest, with the motto 'Regnum Defende' beneath it, he couldn't help going all gooey inside. It took a lot of willpower for him not to genuflect spontaneously in the waiting room. This was a crest with class, a crest above all others, la crème de les crests … Above all, it was about defending the ruling monarch and he'd fight to the death with anyone who thought differently.

"Would you like to come with me, miss?" Sergeant Slocombe called to the woman. "There's an interview room over here."

The two of them sat down on cheap plastic chairs that'd had their fair share of being hoisted aloft as weapons. He prayed that a mental health assessment wasn't on the cards, as his stomach was rumbling in anticipation of his wife's full English. He harrumphed and took a closer look at his interviewee. She was good looking, although her hair could do with a brush. After half-a-lifetime on the force, he thought he'd become reasonably adept at sussing people out. On this occasion, he saw concern, not madness. He took out his pocket book and pen.

The woman grasped his hand before he could even start writing. His eyes drifted to the red panic button – he tried to recall when it had last been tested – and back. She seemed to be making a 'no' sign with her fingers. Then she grabbed the pen. Sergeant Slocombe bent across the table to see what she was writing, all the time keeping a watchful eye on the biro should it head in the direction of his face. Christ almighty, she'd just written 'Dai Williams'!

Bill Slocombe's bizarre encounters with the man from the Park Estate came flooding back. Dai's unusual insight into how a football reacted to being kicked meant that he hadn't looked at a football in quite the same way since. Dai called it using his hocus focus. Bill's wife had called him a silly old fool when he recounted the story, but he'd been there and knew what happened. Thanks to Dai, he'd finally come to accept the improbable, even if it was a bit late in the day to actually make him a better copper.

So he'd been as chuffed as a … well, a chuffing choo-choo when he saw Dai collect his knighthood from the Queen on TV. He cleared his throat again and extracted a tissue from a pocket to wipe away a tear.

And then it dawned on him where he'd seen the woman before.

"Christ, you're Dai's wife! I saw you on TV!"

Sandra smiled shyly and shook her head. She was mouthing something. He'd always been rubbish at lip reading, despite the compulsory, equal opportunities, twice-a-year training.

"Sorry, I meant *girlfriend*," he said, wishing that the blooming obvious was more obvious to blooming him.

And so it came tumbling out … well, slower than tumbling and actually rather laboured, but, putting two and two together, he discovered that Dai had gone for drinks with the Queen; that his girlfriend had developed morning sickness at a stage of pregnancy when such a thing was unheard of; and that Dai hadn't returned, or in other words, had gone missing. Meaning that an MI5 agent had gone AWOL, which was big business for Battersea nick.

After making Sandra some tea and promising her he'd do his best, Sergeant Slocombe found an unencumbered and relatively hygienic phone in the back office and proceeded to dial the numbers on the paper. Most police work was boringly tedious, so the opportunity to ring the Thames House HQ came as manna from heaven, even if he should have gone off duty 45 minutes ago to enjoy a lesser food from the gods. Maybe his wife could make brunch instead. The phone was answered on the first ring.

"Good morning, is that MI5? ... Oh good. Sergeant Slocombe here from Battersea Police Station ... Slocombe ... no, not Soaken, *Slocombe* ... As in blue rinse and pussy? ... Yes, that's it ... Now, look, I have a young woman here in the station with your telephone number on a piece of paper ... How did she get it, we're ex-directory, you're saying? ... Well, she was given it ... Yes, I know about the bloody Official Secrets Act ... You're taping the conversation to be used as evidence in a possible prosecution? ... Oh, for goodness sake! It's Sandra Evans and she's just reported that her boyfriend Dai Williams has gone missing! ... Yes, *Sir David* Williams ..."

•••

Steve read aloud from the pocket guide to London: "Trafalgar Square is home to Nelson's Column, iconic stone lions, the famous fourth plinth and a lot of pigeons." On initial inspection of the landmark, Dale wouldn't disagree with any of that. In fact, the pigeon population seemed to exceed the number of tourists by several fold. Back home, they'd have exterminated the lot of them. By 9:00 a.m., he guessed the public space would be invaded by coachloads of fellow Americans, and the square's inhabitants would be swooping down on high calorie carryouts, leaving gloopy white poopouts in generous exchange. Still, at least it was a traffic-free zone.

Dale made a beeline for the fourth plinth without knowing what was on it. Steve had to run to catch up. "What's the rush, Dale?" he yelled breathlessly. "It's only pop-up art by some jerk with an inflated ego."

They read from the inscription on the side of the plinth that the installation illustrated humankind's fragile dependency on technology. Some critics viewed it as an ironic gift from the Chinese for all the millions of phones exported from their factories. Most saw it as a shrine of remembrance for those who died as a consequence of 'the screaming'. The art work, entitled 'Gone Phishing', comprised a transparent tank, measuring about twelve feet by six, full of hundreds of deadly but redundant mobile phones suspended in clear jelly. Dotted between the phones were the names of factory workers who'd died doing their jobs.

Dale stared up at the unusual aquarium and felt a compulsion to scale the plinth and commune with the technology. His nuts had started aching again, despite the protection he'd added inside his boxer briefs. They'd found a sports store near their hotel selling a space blanket that Steve had fashioned into a metallic diaper. It wasn't comfortable and it definitely wasn't sexy, but it took the edge off the gnawing.

The image of the triplets from the Marshall

household's kitchen flashed suddenly into Dale's mind, except they weren't sitting at a table waiting to be fed. Their mouths were open in a silenced scream, as if witnessing something and unable to respond. An icy chill slithered slowly up Dale's spine and stopped at the base of his skull to hammer the message home.

"Dude, you're looking rather weird," Steve said.

Dale whipped his head around. A young family had just appeared from nowhere and the mother was pushing a trio of infants strapped into a triple berth stroller.

"Shit!" Dale said under his breath.

The triplets looked at him as one and started yelling their heads off. The tortured sound reverberated around the square and the pigeons scattered to the sanctuary of nearby rooftops. Dale sensed tendrils of disapprobation sneaking out at him in the early morning mist. A fat crow landed on top of the plinth and added its raucous squawk to the general commotion. It was like a scene in a John Carpenter movie. All it needed was the noodling electronic soundtrack.

"Let's get away from here," Dale said, wincing painfully.

"What the fuck?" Steve mouthed. He plainly wasn't getting the B-movie vibe.

They moved away from the exhibit. Dale felt sure the parents were staring at him. He glanced back. The man was looking around suspiciously, as if seeking a reason for the infants' disquiet. Dale imagined him turning into a vengeful fisherman with murderous hooks for hands. The kiddies were like wailing banshees. He had to find somewhere to sit and get his bearings. *For fuck's sake, what's happening to me?*

"Eh, what's up, Doc?" Steve said playfully, making rabbit ears with his hands.

Jeez, I knew he was going to use those words!

Dale grasped Steve's hands and looked him squarely in the eye. "Why the fuck did you say that?"

Steve shrugged. "I don't know. It just sorta came to me."

"Steve, I could tell you were going to say, 'Eh, what's up, Doc?'"

"And make the rabbit ears, too?" Steve showed his incisors. They were far too orthodontically perfect to resemble rabbit's teeth.

"Yeah." The chill at the base of Dale's skull was digging ever deeper with sharp ice-picks. The sort that got used for lobotomies, in fact.

Steve raised his shoulders again. "So what? It's just a phrase."

"One more thing: I knew that family were going to appear."

"Okay …" Steve had lost his wide-eyed, tourist-on-vacation look.

"And I know what you're going to do next."

"Look, sweets, if this is you practising your magic trick for the Christmas party, it's not amusing." Steve wrestled his hands out of Dale's grasp and crossed them over his chest.

"You just did it," Dale said.

"You're fucking scaring me, dude."

"I'm fucking scaring myself," Dale said, shaking his head. "Let's go find a coffee. I need to do some thinking."

They found a coffee shop just off Trafalgar Square in St Martin's Lane. Dale left Steve sitting at a table on the sidewalk while he went in to order their beverages. Away from the family from hell, he already felt some semblance of equilibrium returning.

"I'll take two medium skinny lattes, decaf and hold the sugar," he called to the barista over the hustle and bustle.

"Sure, sir. Can I get you anything to eat? I can recommend these healthy doughnuts." The barista pointed at a stand of garishly coloured pastries on the counter. "We bake them from a special recipe we got from a deli in the States. They're quite special."

Dale caught the price. It was displayed in dollars and euros, as well as pounds. "Phew!" he whistled through his teeth.

"Anything wrong, sir?" The barista looked disgruntled.

"No, no," Dale replied swiftly. "It's just that we know the deli owner. In fact, he's my boyfriend's ex." He decided not to mention they were half the cost back home – or that he'd need to take out a second mortgage to keep KCPD supplied with oxynuts at this coffee shop's jacked-up prices.

"Way cool!" the barista said. He leaned across the counter. "Actually, we modified the recipe. It seemed a bit weird, if you know what I mean?"

"A hint of brie?"

"Yeah ... like, well ..." he spluttered. "Anyway, we had to change the label, too. Would you believe, we had some tourist return a half-eaten doughnut saying she couldn't taste the oxygen. I mean, Christ!" His tongue clicked in exasperation. "What did she expect? A cooling waft of mountain air from inside a fucking pastry, huh?"

The barista's hands hovered over oxynuts festooned with the Stars and Stripes and the Union Jack, but he settled on two with the Rainbow Flag. "These are on me," he said with a wink.

Dale walked back to Steve with the lattes and doughnuts, wishing their vacation could start all over again, bypassing landing at Heathrow, taking a rain check from the high-speed journey to the emergency room and leaving out Trafalgar Square and its goddamn pigeons. There were more tourist traps to come, though, and he didn't fancy their chances at Madame Tussauds, which was the nearest to a museum of haircuts that London had to offer. Families with screaming kids in strollers were clearly best avoided.

Traffic on the street outside was moving fast and the sidewalks were full to bursting with people scurrying to work, pushing past stationary foreigners trying to decipher miniscule maps in all the languages of the world. Dale heard the sound of an ambulance, the pitch of its siren dropping suddenly as it reached its destination close by. A squad car screeched past just in front of the coffee shop, its blue lights flashing. Dale recognised the look on the driver's face: that tell-tale combination of fear and excitement, fuelling the adrenaline rush of the cop in the hot seat. He carefully set the carryouts on their table. He didn't want to cause someone to slip in a spill, after all. And he started running ... and running. The ache in his balls propelled him on. He was dimly aware that someone was following him, calling his name. It must have been Steve. Perhaps he'd picked up one of the lattes and was trying to drink it on the run. He smiled at the thought of it; he'd trained him well. Then he remembered that the oxynuts were rainbow striped. That made him grin, too.

Dale reached the end of St Martins Lane where it met William IV Street. The sirens had stopped but he continued running towards the flashing lights. A vacuum seemed to have descended on the street that sucked away the sound of everything other than his heartbeat and his pounding feet. Passers-by had stopped dead in their tracks to stare. The ghouls were sure out in force this crisp November day. The mangled remains of the stroller lay in a store's window display amidst chocolates, candies and shattered glass. He wondered whether there'd be a half-price sale of the tainted goods. With Thanksgiving in three weeks, and gifts to buy for Steve's folks, that sure could come in handy.

Burly paramedics crouched over the three tiny bodies forcibly separated from each other by the SUV. The driver must have taken the wrong turn down the one-way street. Perhaps someone had messed with the sign. That sort of vandalism was happening back home. Turn it through 180 degrees and make life do an about-turn. There was way too much blood for such small people. Dale recognised the triplets' parents huddled together on the sidewalk, shivering and crying, trying to focus on anything other than the carnage that was their kids. A police officer offered blankets but the father pushed him away. Dale knew that macho stance well. Hell, it's probably what he'd do if he had children. That's when the man noticed Dale and stared at him.

Dale came to an abrupt halt in the middle of the street. He stood there, rooted to the spot. He was just another dumbass cop in the wrong place at the wrong time – and the squeezing of his man parts hadn't let up. A manhole cover was directly beneath him and he wished he could just vanish from sight. Life as a sewer rat would be a whole lot better. He felt utterly sick to his stomach and crumpled over. Gentle fingers touched his shoulders. He turned slowly and looked into Steve's pools of blue. Perhaps he should just get lost in them. He saw love, fear and something approaching understanding.

"Steve, I knew that was going to happen," he said, forcing the words through frozen lips. "I could have stopped it."

The parents were pointing out Dale to police officers. They were coming towards him. "It might as well have been me that killed them," he heard himself saying, far too loudly.

The triplets' father opened his mouth and it wasn't to scream silently.

•••

Charing Cross Police Station wasn't usually included on the London tourist trail, although it was a fine example of late Georgian architecture and had been a teaching hospital until 1973. Those tourists who did enter under the impressive portico were usually there to report a mugging while sightseeing in the West End. With the government's draconian ban on mobile phones still in place, there were rich pickings for thieves on the lookout for handsets that could be sold on the black market. Clandestine mobile phone networks had sprung up around the country and Operation Bloodhound had been established to stamp out the illicit operations. TV license detector vans had been seconded to identify transmitting premises. For those who could remember that far back, it was like the clamping down on pirate radio stations in the 1980s. The Metropolitan Police Service was in the thick of it and Charing Cross Police Station was the centre of the operation.

Behind the impressive frontage, huge echoing wards had been transformed into large open plan offices that were universally disliked. For some working on Operation Bloodhound, there was a bitter sweet quality to their endeavours: it was satisfying bringing to justice those misguided enough to cash in on other's misfortunes, but it was damn painful if you had a child languishing in hospital while the government decided what to do with their frazzled brain.

•••

"Sammy, have you got a minute?" DS Choi said, turning towards a colleague a couple of workstations away. His associate's face was just inches from a monitor, which made it look as if she was sniffing out criminals. Which, in essence, she was; DS Sampson's nose was bifurcated at the tip and years of merciless taunting had tuned her skills as a detective. She was fast-forwarding through mugshots of suspects and cursing beneath her breath as she scrolled. DS Choi appreciated that this was deeply personal, as her son was detained in an adolescent unit in South London because of psychopathic creeps misusing the internet and leading him astray.

"Eh?" came the response, eventually.

"I said have you got a moment."

The detective turned reluctantly from the display of malignant criminality. "No, you didn't. You said 'minute', not 'moment'."

"So what?"

"Well, a minute is precisely 60 seconds, whereas a moment could be anything." She glanced at the screen and jabbed at the space bar a few times. "Shit! I thought I'd found him just then." She glared back at the questioner. "Thanks a bunch, Mike. You've made me lose a serial killer in the making."

DS Choi shrugged. "Tell me something new. Dropping cases is all we seem to do these days."

"Well, for some of us, finding criminals means something."

DS Choi raised his hands placatingly. "Sorry, sorry. It's been a bit of a day." He frowned. "Look, the thing is, I've got these guys in the interview suite. They say they're American police officers on vacation, but they've got no ID on them. One of them took out a mobile phone to take a selfie – "

DS Sampson groaned. "And it got confiscated by a concerned passer-by, I suppose."

"Yeah, how did you know?" DS Choi grinned. "The weird thing is, the other guy claims he had knowledge that a road traffic incident was going to happen before it did. You may have heard about it. A SUV with some oligarch in the driving seat went the wrong way down a one-way street and carved up a kid's buggy."

"Was that the one in St Martins Lane?"

"Almost. William IV Street. The Russian is causing quite a rumpus and trying to cite diplomatic immunity. He says he just obeyed the sign. Unfortunately, some bugger had vandalised it, so it was pointing in the wrong fucking direction."

"Christ, not that trick again!"

"Yeah. Kids are certainly coming up with some creative ways to pass the time."

"Where do I come in, then?" The left side of DS Sampson's nose twitched in anticipation.

"Well, while I was interviewing them, the guy with the premonition grabbed his balls and went berserk. He started going on about people being in danger."

"His *balls*?"

"Yeah."

"That's not so bad, then. They could have been yours. What happened next?"

"His friend started complaining about homophobia."

DS Sampson wrinkled her nose. "What's that got to do with the price of fish?"

"Well, the two of them were wearing that Banksy 'kissing coppers' T-shirt and – "

"Someone took exception."

"You got it. The desk sergeant wasn't having a good day. The taller one got put in cuffs."

"Fuck! You mean, someone put handcuffs on an American police officer who was just trying to be helpful?"

"Yeah. I know." DS Choi paused and did his best to look imploringly. "So …"

"You mean can I help defuse the situation?"

DS Choi fiddled with his shoe laces. "Yeah, something like that. A hand across the pond sort of thing." He wriggled uncomfortably. "Er, there's something else."

DS Sampson's eyebrows rose.

"When I asked whether they had someone who could vouch for them, they mentioned Dai Williams."

"What?!"

"Yeah, I thought that was strange. Trouble is, MI5 have confirmed he's gone missing. His girlfriend reported it to Battersea nick. And to complicate matters, that was just after he had cocktails with the Queen."

●●●

Charing Cross Police Station's 'interview suite' sounded rather grand, but the reality was dismal and would barely rate a single star on TripAdvisor. Jacuzzis and mini-bars were out of the question. Bleak, windowless rooms, with grubby furniture fixed to the floor, were as far as it went. Smoking was banned, but it happened anyway. Stale sweat and a whiff of urine completed the depressing picture. The interview suite was also situated exactly where the mortuary once ruled the roost over departures to the great beyond. Its only saving grace was that most of the characters passing through the cheaply refurbished doors left breathing spontaneously.

DS Sampson took a deep breath as she opened the door to the interview suite. She found that a long, hard sniff was the best way of sussing out the department. Today, there was plenty of adrenaline and a touch of testosterone, which was just as she liked it. She wasn't tall, but she commanded respect and appreciation. Smiles and the occasional "Hi, Sammy" greeted her as she approached the front desk – and the redoubtable desk sergeant. He was on the phone and displaying his annoying habit of repeating everything the caller said. She waited until he'd finished. The problem was, the Great British public were too ready to complain. If it wasn't someone whingeing about a bobby swearing in public, it was an evening stroller moaning about the police using unconventional means to transport those who were worse for wear from drink.

"I hear you've got some colleagues from across the pond for me," DS Sampson said, leaning her elbows on the counter to goad the sergeant.

The desk sergeant looked up momentarily from the desk to put a face to the voice and arms. DS Sampson wondered when the keyboard had last been disinfected. The same could be said of the sergeant himself. His ginger beard looked in need of some TLC, or, at least, disengagement of stubborn food particles. She resisted the temptation to sniff out the contents of his last meal.

"Yeah," he said, his fingers not deviating for a second from their laboured jabbing at the filthy keys. "They make a handsome couple." The corner of his upper lip curled up ever so slightly. Perhaps he'd been on equal ops training, after all.

"Mike Choi thought I might be able to help with the interview. You know, break the ice somewhat," DS Sampson said almost tactfully.

"Room Three," the desk sergeant said. "They asked for some water. You can give it them."

DS Sampson turned away from the desk in search of the water cooler.

"Oh, Samantha," the desk sergeant said, ominously engaging in eye contact.

"Yeah?" She hated being addressed by her real name.

"Being gay's one thing, but that T-shirt is taking the piss."

DS Sampson shrugged and followed the trail of spilt water. The cooler beckoned with its choices of tepid and lukewarm water. It hadn't been the same since a mouse breathed its last on the condenser. Her nose had come in handy tracking the smell. She approached the interview room holding three full cups and pushed the door open with a foot. Two faces looked up at her. The happy couple were certainly cute. Jeans, smart jackets and Banksy T-shirts went a long way in her professional estimation. The older, taller cop had a slightly battered look to him, as if he'd been round the block a few times and still had an axe to grind. He reminded her of that *Indiana Jones* actor. The other one was pure sex-on-a-stick. She couldn't resist those puppy dog eyes. And then there was that hair … Jesus, it'd be tough to go bald with him around.

"So, gentlemen," DS Sampson said, after introducing herself and handing out the water, "I gather that you are police officers on vacation. Is that correct?"

"Lieutenant Dale Franklin," the older one said, leaning forwards to shake hands. He winced and glanced at the mobile phone on the table. "Shit, it's run out of power again." He raised his hands apologetically. "Sorry, Sergeant, that wasn't the best of starts."

"You seem to be in some pain, Lieutenant," DS Sampson said.

"Yeah, you could say that," he said, "but I guess I'm learning to live with it. It sorta comes and goes. The phone helps, though – when it's got a charge." His sheepish expression was something else to die for.

"Sergeant Steve Abrams," the one with all the hair said. His smile would have melted the hardest of hearts.

"Was it your mobile phone that got stolen?" DS Sampson said, torn between wanting to bury her head in his luscious locks or drown in his eyes.

"Yeah," he said. "I was trying to take a photo of the crime scene and some guy grabbed the cell out of my hands. He'd disappeared into the crowds before I could do anything about it."

"Hmm, you were asking for trouble displaying a phone in public," she said. She realised she'd tutted reflexively and felt like a schoolmistress. That was just the sort of thing her ex-husband used to tease her about. "They're banned here, as you probably know," she continued. "Still, you may be able to claim on your travel insurance. I'll give you a crime reference number. Meanwhile, make sure you inform your network provider. Your phone could be on its way to just about anywhere in the world by now." She turned to look at the lieutenant. He was still in some discomfort. "Are you okay to answer some questions, Lieutenant? I can come back later if that would help."

Lieutenant Franklin smiled wryly and looked her in the eye. "Yesterday, I spent all morning in a hospital with my nuts in a twist; today, I've been put in cuffs because of some T-shirt. It's not exactly a great way to start a vacation. So, if you don't mind, Sergeant Sampson, I'd just like to answer your questions and then get the hell out of here."

"Yay! Way to go!" his friend said, punching the air coltishly.

Okay, DS Sampson thought. *The lieutenant's balls may be painful, and he's at risk of getting on my tits, but he's still got balls – and a sexy mid-west twang.* She decided to disregard the sergeant's lack of respect for the interview process.

"Very well, Lieutenant," DS Sampson said, swiftly locating her pocket book and pen. She leaned back and considered her interviewee. "So, what exactly happened this morning?"

Lieutenant Franklin shifted his weight on the chair. He was definitely nursing something uncomfortable down below. She wondered whether they still had that rubber ring in the lost property cupboard. "We walked to Trafalgar Square," he said. "Steve thought we should get there before the coachloads arrived. I got this urge to climb the plinth. It was something about the cell phones that did it. Next thing, there was this family with three kiddies in a stroller." He paused and tears welled up. "Shit!" he bleated beneath his breath. His friend placed a hand on his shoulder. The lieutenant smiled wanly. "Sorry, these things get to you. The point is, I knew something was going to happen to them. I can't tell you how, but I just knew it." His voice was getting huskier by the second. "You'd better take over," he said, turning to his friend and brushing away tears.

"There was a case back home, Sergeant Sampson," Sergeant Abrams said. "A multiple homicide-suicide witnessed by triplets of a similar age. Dale seemed spooked by seeing the family, so we went in search of a coffee."

"We found a Starbucks and I went to order," Lieutenant Franklin continued. "I started walking back to our table and then – " DS Sampson could see he was perspiring, " – well, everything just went crazy. I heard a siren and a squad car went by. I started running. I knew something had happened. And that's when I saw ..."

DS Sampson didn't need his description or Sergeant Abrams's mobile phone to show her the bloodbath. The photos were on the wall in the incident room. Poor little mites. They simply had no chance against a 2 tonne vehicle in the hands of someone who'd blindly followed a street sign and thought money could buy immunity from prosecution.

The lieutenant's buddy was comforting him. Touching scenes like that weren't exactly common in the machismo-driven Metropolitan Police Service.

"Er, there was something else, Sergeant Sampson," Sergeant Abrams said tentatively. "When we were in Trafalgar Square, Dale guessed what I was gonna say and do. It was freaky. I joked he must be practising magic for the department's Christmas show."

"If only," Lieutenant Franklin said. He looked as if all the cares of the world had been dumped on him. Even his gelled hair had flattened. She readied herself for the jolt of disclosure. "I get these premonitions. It's like being in front of a screen with all these aircraft up in the air and knowing they're gonna crash and you're powerless to do anything about it. Sometimes it's more than just letters and numbers, as if it's got a real identity and I think I can reach out to save it, but then it vanishes again – " his voice tailed off, " – or fucking crashes." He thumped his hands on the table.

DS Sampson wondered what to write. She'd been doodling as he spoke and the drawing looked uncannily like a plane with three small passengers. At least hers was still in the air. "You mentioned Dai Williams to my colleague," she said to the lieutenant. "How do you know him?"

The lieutenant looked up. Perhaps she was back on safer ground. Then he shrugged. Maybe not.

"We worked on a case," he said.

"Loads of cases," Sergeant Abrams added. "You

might have heard of them. Collectively, they were called 'the screaming'."

DS Sampson glanced from one police officer to the other. She'd seen them somewhere before. "Yeah, I've heard of that," she said wearily. "So has my son – a first-hand experience, you might say."

It didn't take much for the tears to well up. Her bastard of an ex-husband didn't like that, either.

DS Sampson left the lieutenant and his friend to consider her options. Fact is, it was all rather Captain Jack Harkness – with more than a hint of Batman and& Robin. There was the mobile phone business, but they were just tourists. And rushing to the scene of a crime, knowing what he'd find? Tricky. Was it premonition? Her nose left her feeling uncertain. There were some things she was still rubbish at sniffing out. It was the business card that the lieutenant showed her that finally decided her actions. Fast track to MI5 and The Manor. She reached for the phone.

CHAPTER FIVE

The end-of-terrace clapboard house still took pride of place in the street, presiding over a municipal park donated by some benefactor who believed in the rejuvenating effect of fresh air. Glimpsed from the generous expanse of greenspace, the house must once have had the no-nonsense elegance of a family residence with well-to-do owners. The windows were shuttered, allowing the occupants to see out, but not for passers-by to see in. The front door was large and imposing, with stained glass panels, approached by half-a-dozen steps. Plenty of separation from the hoi polloi.

Now was different. Decades of neglect gave the impression of a dowager long past her prime, lost in her memories and shrouded in gloom. The clapboards were filthy and falling away, the shutters hanging askew like broken teeth, the stained glass cracked. Children out with their parents would point and ask, "Who lives there, Mummy?" The answer would be along the lines of: "I don't know, darling, but it looks rather sad, doesn't it?" Mother and child would briefly wonder who *did* live in the house, but a few yards later, something more mundane – typically, dog poo or an antisocial skateboarder – would have diverted their attention.

Inside, the house's sole occupant was currently preoccupied with making space on a wall in the over-stuffed back parlour. The aspidistra respired desperately beneath a thick deposit of dust and cobwebs. Grubby, fraying antimacassars had reached the point of no return many years ago. Old family photographs had been dumped unceremoniously in a corner. Shards of glass glinted menacingly in the light squeezing through a chink in the curtains. Another smaller collection of photos had been afforded more respect and placed in a neat pile on a low table. The topmost picture showed a man in an outdoor scene with the surprised look of an animal caught in a spotlight. He was heavily bearded and held a rifle. It looked as if he'd been caught unaware by the camera, although the reality was that he'd probably had to stand unblinkingly still for many minutes. The room's guardian of the past bent to touch the glass over the man's face and sighed. A few taps of a hammer later, the photo was fixed to its place on the wall and the photographer's subject appeared to gaze through the gloom.

Two bare feet continued to pad around, sending ancient dust particles to join the motes drifting lazily through the air. "Fuck!" The owner of the expletive extracted a piece of glass from an incautious big toe. A pearl of blood oozed. It was surprising how much a small cut could sting. The figure dabbed at the blood with a finger-tip and then licked it. The bitter ferrous taste was strangely comforting.

Sometimes, there was nothing better than a blank canvas. A fertile imagination usually filled the void. This time, that wasn't the case. The moment had come to settle the feud. After so many years of losing the battle with technology, the airwaves had suddenly become opened up. Amazingly, their powers seemed greater than before. But it was still a jigsaw that required the right pieces in place. That stupid girl and her friends had almost ruined months of planning.

The figure turned to the table in the centre of the room. It had been fashioned for strength and stability, and, allegedly, dated back to the reign of George III. It was even rumoured that the mad king once used it to divine his future with Tarot cards. The floorboards had been strengthened to support the table, although it would never be groaning under the weight of a banquet fit for royalty. It all came down to ensuring that the table wouldn't budge even a nanometre when it was under stress. Pride of place went to the receptacle in the centre. Its present day keeper leaned forward to inhale the intoxicating aroma derived from centuries devoted to fulfilling its tradition. The cauldron needed feeding.

•••

Dai didn't care for the dark and he'd woken up in a place

that was like looking up at a night sky with all the stars gone out. *In space no one can hear you scream.* Thanks for the reassuring thought. He'd never been down a mine, but the coalface had to be just as unremittingly black. Perhaps if he closed his eyes and counted to three, a light would come on when he opened them. One ... two ... three ... Nope, if anything it seemed darker. Wherever he was, it was deadly quiet and the only thing he could hear was his breathing. There wasn't even the hum of electrical equipment. He was sure he was on his own – unless someone was holding their breath in an attempt to spook him. He couldn't smell anything, either. A canary in a cage would have been a welcome companion. What would he call it, though? A bird that worked for its food in a pitch-black hellhole deserved a name. And, please, please, don't let it be fucking Tweetie Pie.

His father had died in a mining accident and he could imagine what went through his mind when the tunnelling stopped and he realised the rescue attempt had been abandoned. Perhaps he'd have sensed vibrations from the church bells tolling away for the men trapped underground. Did his father's canary die before him? Imagine hearing the bird sing its last song and knowing that your turn is next. Shit. His dad had a fine voice, although that was usually when he'd too much to drink. Maybe he sang a duet with the bird. His mother went to pieces following the body-less funeral. They'd put bricks in his coffin. Dai shivered even though he wasn't remotely cold.

"Help! Is there anyone out there?"

Dai's voice didn't exactly echo around the room, but he was sure he heard reflections. He tried moving his limbs, but whatever was tying them to the chair wasn't about to give. The chair didn't move, either. His heart beat faster. *Stay calm and carry on, Dai bach.*

So, what was that police officer's part in his abduction? The white pill didn't taste remotely strange, after all. Perhaps it was some top-secret knock-out drug that looked like pocket fluff. Surely it had to be someone playing a joke on him. Didn't it? He inhaled, exhaled … inhaled, exhaled …

At least nothing was hurting. They must be using duct tape – as found in every Hollywood movie kidnapper's kitbag. He'd almost bought a reel of it from Treforest hardware store when he was living at Granny Betty's. He had some whim of wanting to know how it would feel to be helpless. It was probably the sound of church bells that had triggered it.

Fava beans and a nice Chianti. It's bloody inconvenient when one's worst nightmares come back to haunt you and there's fuck-all you can do about it. Did Hannibal Lecter use duct tape? He'd call it something pretentious in Italian. He imagined the bad doctor's sensitive fingers applying it over his mouth … precisely … More likely, he'd cut out his tongue with a scalpel and then sauté it with garlic. Perhaps that was coming next. If someone wanted him to feel fear, it was working. His bladder felt near to bursting.

"Please, whoever you are, I need to go to the toilet!"

Silence.

Okay, take a deep breath, Dai … there's a way out of this. Remember you're a superbeing. *You might think so, but I couldn't possibly comment.* Very funny. All right, you're a boy from the Valleys with an extremely weird ability and green kryptonite for an Achilles heel. *Good one – and I'm sitting here waiting for something to happen, with my bladder about to explode.* Focus out and zero in, boyo! *It's all very well for you to say that. What would I zero in on, anyway? Walls don't have much to say in my limited experience.* Try a bit of telepathy, then. *Long distance stuff never works that well.* What about Balmoral? *Okay, but Sandra was there to receive my thoughts, and it was only a mile or so to the castle.* Dai, you're being a loser. Think of MI5. Think of Sandra. Think of your unborn child.

That was a bit below the belt, but nothing Granny Betty hadn't tried on him before. Her favourite was: "What would your mother have said if she was still alive?" She wouldn't, of course; boo to a Welsh goose was as far as it went. So, what about the Queen's motives? Maybe she'd decided that a knight who drinks one too many Dubonnet and gins belongs in the Tower of London, after all. On the other hand, it couldn't be the Tower because there was no echo, it didn't smell dank and musty, and no princely ghosts had come to haunt him, their severed heads tucked under their arms. What about Diana, though? He shivered all over again.

"Please, is there anyone out there?"

Still nothing but silence – and his thumping heart-beat. And the pressure in his bladder. It was funny how his voice sounded more Welsh when he tried to make himself heard.

Okay, I'll try a ping.

Mastering the hocus focus had taken some doing. Mrs Pigeon would have attested to that if she hadn't worn herself out, pursuing her prodigious reproductive need. So, too, would Tania Goldman, Lady Leandra Windsor and the unfortunately, but appropriately, named Randy, except they were no longer alive, either. They'd all been pawns in a sick game and now he was just as trapped as they'd ever been.

The doctor in the Brain Lab at MI5's country pile had explained his superpower in terms of high frequency waves emanating from the pineal gland. He'd discovered that by wiring him up to an electroencepha-lograph. Then there was something called 'wave particle duality' for the trip back to his brain, which was all to do with quantum mechanics and had to be explained in a robotic voice, with reverential deference to the Large Hadron Collider.

Just as with a pigeon, a ping from the pineal needed to come home to roost. It was somewhere between a cuckoo taking over another bird's nest and a snake biting its tail. His brain worked like an FM radio, with the cranium acting as a waveguide, but it was able to receive at the same time. Which was all rather mind-boggling. Like the policeman of dubious provenance in Green Park, his grandmother would have said, "Jiw, jiw!" And then she'd have made a nice pot of tea. With bara brith as an accompaniment.

'Focusing out' and 'zeroing in' was the way Dai put it when asked to describe what he did – to someone like the Queen, for instance. With a reasonably evolved central nervous system, the ping from the hocus focus made the neurons release what had been stored in memory. The problem was, recollections could be anything, so it wasn't the most reliable way of extracting information. MI5 seemed happy enough, even if pornographic images were only occasionally what they were after.

So, faced with a pitch-black room of unknown dimensions, and only the vaguest echo, Dai felt unsure where to start and was back at the drawing board. His grandmother used to tell him to gird his loins when someone bullied him at school. It always sounded vaguely erotic. That was well before realising he had a weapon of mass destruction at his disposal. Being taped to a chair made girding anything rather impractical, but he imagined doing it anyway, ready to do battle with his adversary.

Okay, I'm focusing out ... imagining a tunnel ... zeroing in ... engaging the hocus focus ... letting loose with a gentle ping ... Ouch! Shit, fuck! That was painful! I can see stars ... and light ... and floating things ... and Granny Betty smiling at me ... and showing me her teeth ... and they're pointed ... very pointed ...

Dai came round feeling as if his head had just been pummelled by Joe Calzaghe when he was pissed off about something. He was the only Welsh boxer he could think of and he didn't even have a Welsh-sounding name. While his frontal lobes attempted to remind themselves which was left and which was right, he tried to work out what the hell had gone wrong. If no one was doing anything to him, then they must be wanting him to do things to himself – like letting loose a ping so that it would bounce back. He'd been in a MRI scanner once and the hocus focus had caused mayhem with the delicate machinery. Perhaps he was in a lab where they were analysing every move in order to find his weak spot. But that puzzled him. It was common knowledge that EM radiation was his green kryptonite. He decided to up the ante.

"Where are you? Where are you, you fuckers? Let's

be 'avin' you! I'm not scared of you, you fuckers!" He'd elaborated that a bit. This was a life or death situation rather than a Norwich City football match.

The response was immediate and not unexpected. Someone must have had their fingers on a switch labelled 'Wi-Fi'. It was almost comforting to be reminded of the excruciating visceral discomfort that had been his world when EM radiation was still coursing through the English skies. His trainers wouldn't have agreed with that sentiment, as the contents of his stomach had just landed on his feet. He imagined the vomit was pink with fragments of chips. The sickly odour of sour cream and onion simmered in 37.4 Centigrade gastric juices threatened to turn his stomach upside down all over again. And then there was the feeling of being assaulted from both ends. Someone certainly enjoyed turning up the agony. Then suddenly, it stopped.

And started again.

Then stopped.

After that, Dai lost count. Hyperbolic paraboloids on an empty stomach had been a bad idea.

•••

Dale hadn't factored in a chauffeur-driven trip to the Oxfordshire countryside on their travel agenda. It was a pleasant countryside, too, with patchwork fields of hay all bundled up for the winter, church steeples poking up with the desperation of the starving clamouring for food and the occasional farmer driving his cattle along the middle of the road with a blind indifference to traffic. But it wasn't a patch on rural Kansas. It was a matter of scale. Rolling plains and the baking sun were more his kind of thing. The occasional twister helped, too; he appreciated some drama in his romantic idyll. His dad's call of "Batten down the hatches!" had never failed to engage his thrall. He even used to enjoy his mom's thrice-cooked pot roast in the rapidly growing darkness. But his dad did used to get as drunk as a *Mephitis mephitica*.

Fact is, being driven anywhere was a rarity for him. Relinquishing control to someone else in the driving seat just wasn't part of his make-up. *Yeah, I'm such a mucho macho guy,* he thought with a grimace. And that had been true. Ask any of his colleagues in KCPD and they'd have said, "Yeah, a right-on dude. A bit heavy on the vino, but a regular kinda guy." That would've been followed by: "He just needs to find himself a nice little wife." Ouch. Yup, that hurt. And now here he was all set to nab himself a nice little *husband*. Well, large rather than little, and very damn nice. He'd kicked the wine habit, too. Connubial bliss with Steve was healthy to a tee. It was all decaf this, hold-the-sugar that and jogging to work. French cheese was his new weakness, and a nice ripe brie in particular. It was curious how much his tastes had changed. And that had been in a scant six months. Jeez.

So, everything considered, he'd been surprised to find himself drawn to the sleek outline of the back of Deborah Jenkins's head. It bore a disconcerting resemblance to Darth Vader's helmet. She had a sultry dark voice, too. Every now and again she turned to say something, giving him the benefit of her aquiline profile. He hoped Steve hadn't noticed his momentary crossing back to the other side. Perhaps all the stimulation had done something to his testosterone levels. He discreetly felt his beard. Yup, definitely more growth than usual. He also realised that his nuts had stopped being all gnarly with him. Maybe it was some process of adaptation – or the limousine providing protection. He'd never been that into beards before, but he guessed it was a small price to pay for having a superpower bestowed on him. Now, if only his nuts would play the game.

After all those years of being told he knew nothing by teachers who knew even less, it was pretty damn weird to suddenly become a know-it-all. Well, not *all*, but definitely the potentially interesting bits. Gruesome stuff, too, as he'd discovered in the street near the coffee shop. Problem was, it was still all too random and non-specific – rather like being a fly on the wall in a clearing house of thoughts, having to focus a thousand lenses on a million streams in multiple languages simultaneously. It had to be some sort of payback time for all those bible classes he'd had forced on him. A sort of transaction of knowledge in reverse, if you like: 'to thee that had, thou shan't; to thee that didn't, thou has.' It was a tad biblical, but the idea sure had validity.

"We're almost there, gentlemen," Ms Jenkins said. Dale had already noticed that she'd been watching the GPS closely.

The driver slowed the car until it was barely crawling along the narrow country lane. Dale looked at the hedgerow and tried to remember when he'd last been out of town back home. They'd planned to go to some line dancing festival the previous weekend, but work had intervened and they'd ended up doing the cowboy boogie at home instead. All of a sudden, a massive lion entered Dale's field of vision.

"Christ! What the fuck was that?" Dale said with his customary directness of expression.

There was a stifled squeak of surprise from the other side of the limousine. Steve pointed at an identical stone sculpture. He'd shown a keen interest in artistically carved bodies back in West Hollywood, but these ones ended at the shoulders.

"Welcome to The Manor," Ms Jenkins said proprietorially. "Those fine specimens are our guardians, otherwise known as Patience and Fortitude. Watch carefully, gentlemen. You should find this interesting."

As they continued slowly, but inexorably, down the driveway, the immediate landscape seemed blurred, as if covered by a shifting haze. The colours were also constantly on the move, greens becoming blues turning into reds. If Dale concentrated on something that had appeared solid, it then vanished altogether. Anything in the distance stayed where it was and in focus. He rubbed his eyes and turned to Steve: "You know, sweets, I think I need to get my eyes checked when we get back home."

Ms Jenkins chortled. Dale thought it incredibly sexy. It reminded him of being back on the farm. His dad's pigs used to do that when he tickled them behind the ears. "That's our little party trick," she said. "I know it's childish, but it never fails to impress our visitors."

Dale and Steve looked at each other. They didn't get the nature of the amusement. "Sorry," Dale said, "but are we missing something?"

"Everything, actually," Ms Jenkins said with a twisted little grin. "As you'll see now, if you care to look to your right."

The limousine came to an abrupt stop and they found themselves at the bottom of steps to a large and extremely grand house that looked straight out of *Downton Abbey*. But the bizarre thing was, they hadn't seen it coming. It had literally appeared out of the blue.

Ms Jenkins neatly anticipated Dale's next question.

"The answer is stealth technology, Lieutenant. A combination of Heisenberg's Uncertainty Principle and a superfast quantum computer, which enables our defences to anticipate encroachment. You ought to try visiting us in a helicopter. It's quite something." She grinned seductively. Dale imagined her using the 'come ride with me' smile to lure customers at a defence exhibition. "Her Majesty the Queen is rather proud of her little baby," she added surprisingly.

As they exited the car, Dale wondered how many more bombshells MI5 had up its bountiful sleeve. He had a small surprise to give them, too. A small thought had arisen out of thin air as he imagined stroking the nape of Ms Jenkins's neck, and it had progressed to one of monstrous proportions. He was trying to decide how much of it was real and how much was wishful thinking – plus his raised testosterone level.

The sign on the door had announced that it was the 'Brain Lab'. Entering involved the high security combination of an iris scan and a fingerprint reader – but applied to all three of them. Dale couldn't immediately recall where they'd had the scan done, but then he remembered the airport. Clever – and deviously illegal without informed consent, get-out clauses, Miranda rights, etcetera, etcetera. The lab was large and full of expensive-looking equipment. Dale noticed the huge display as soon as they'd entered the room. He'd seen it before, but close up it was even more impressive. But it wasn't showing much activity. MI5 had to be having a slow news day.

"Welcome to my lair," a man in an oversized lab coat boomed abruptly. Dale wasn't sure whether he was being greeted by the monster or the doctor. He couldn't see signs of a bolt through his neck. The ID on his lapel read 'Dr Petros Kyriakides'. It didn't indicate his specialty, but he was definitely the guy who'd stunned everyone with his revelations of teenagers running amok at the MI5 conference call. In the flesh, the doctor was large and impressively bearded, going on 240 pounds and six feet two, but probably packing more muscle than fat. Dale thought he'd deliver quite a punch. He was the sort who would never do well should he switch to a life of crime: far too easy to pick out in a line-up – unless the other suspects were all Greek restaurant owners. The front pocket of his white coat was stuffed with pens, some of which had leaked. Dale thought that added a ring of poetic authenticity. Fact is, life was just plain goddamn messy and no cop could resist a leak.

Dale could see Steve was right at home. His eyes swivelled like the turrets of a chameleon as he checked out the hi-tech joint. He'd graduated summa cum laude in psychology, which meant he had awesome observational skills. More to the point, Steve seemed on the cusp of asking a question Dale hoped would resolve why his testicles had turned informant and become harbingers of doom. Puzzlement had crossed his fine features and he'd opened his mouth to speak.

"Er, Doctor, why is it that Mr Fanshaw calls himself a 'Mr' when he's a doctor, and 'Fanshaw' when his name is Featherstonehaugh?"

Ms Jenkins and the doctor shared a look with simultaneously raised eyebrows. "The first bit is easy, Sergeant," Dr Kyriakides said. "In past times, barbers used to be surgeons, so surgeons hang on to the title of Mr. It's logically illogical, but that's medicine for you. As for the name, well you'd have to ask Deborah about that. I don't understand it, either. You might say it's all Greek to me." He convulsed with laughter. Dale hoped the foundations would hold up.

Ms Jenkins raised her finely contoured eyebrows some more – and then followed through with a prosaic shrug. "Don't ask me. English customs confuse the hell out of me as well."

Dr Kyriakides looked delighted not to have been found wanting. Dale's nuts took that opportunity to request an introduction. "Ouch," he winced. The vehicular protection had to be wearing off. He fumbled for his cell phone and positioned it discreetly. True to form, it started throbbing. Dale decided to check the doc's credentials before submitting himself to a repeat set of indignities. There was only so much palpation a man could endure. The bearded guy could be a veterinarian with aspirations above his station – plus a penchant for sticking his hand in dark places.

"Most interesting," the doctor said, observing his patient and stroking his beard in the manner of a certain coke-addicted quack.

"Excuse me, Doctor," Dale said, "but what exactly are your qualifications?"

"MB BS, that's a medical degree from Athens and London; MAs in psychology, physics *and* nuclear physics, all from Cambridge University; then a PhD in theology from Cardiff; oh, and I speak half-a-dozen languages fluently," he finished with a flourish.

Steve was shaking his head, his IQ reduced in a flash to lower case proportions, like a bug meeting its end as a splat on a windshield. Dale had nothing to be belittled. Okay, he had done a tech course in car mechanics, but he doubted that counted in the grand scheme of things. But where did religion fit into MI5's activities? It was news to him that British spies had morals, but hey, at least someone was looking down on them.

"Ask him about the diploma in chocolate," Steve whispered teasingly in his ear. Dale glanced at him quizzically. *Er, whatever, dude,* Dale thought.

"Didn't you forget your diploma in chocolate, Doctor?" Dale asked naively.

Even his beard and olive complexion couldn't disguise the change in colour.

"What was that about?" Dale hissed out of the corner of his mouth.

"It's just something that Dai told me when you were in the restroom at the Burn Center," Steve said not nearly so innocently. "Apparently, he likes having chocolate licked off his – "

"Gentlemen!" Ms Jenkins said. "We need to proceed. Over to you, Dr Kyriakides."

Dale thought that sounded ominous. He'd already taken note of the large drum-like machine at the back of the lab. One of his weaknesses that Steve didn't know about was his fear of being trapped in small spaces – particularly ones involving whirring machinery. His DeLorean was the exception: it purred rather than whirred. Even now, the odour of certain washing powders put him into a cold sweat. It hadn't been his fault that the inside of his mom's giant Westinghouse washer had looked so enticing. He needed closure on the past, but the thought of putting a lid on anything was enough to send him back to the goddamn *vino de la casa*.

Okay, in for a dime, in for a dozen. Dale started peeling off his pants. The zipper got stuck half way. Steve was grinning. Deborah was smirking. The doctor's hands looked XXL large. And he wasn't wearing gloves. *Oh Christ!*

"No! No!" Dr Kyriakides said, waving his hands manically. Dale concluded that he'd never do well in court exhibiting that level of emotional arousal. "That won't be necessary, Lieutenant. Mr Featherstonehaugh has provided all the details I require. The results of your examination are over there."

Dale followed his pointing appendage and saw an A4 manila folder with his name at the top in large letters. MI5's surreptitious data collection seemed disturbingly similar to that of the FBI. Dale swiftly restored his dignity, took a deep breath and waited for the next bombshell to drop.

"So, what exactly is the nature of your problem, Lieutenant?" the doctor asked in a kindly tone.

The divine Deborah was still smirking. She'd obviously read the report. Dale decided to cut to the chase.

"It's a matter of knowing," he said meekly.

"Knowing?" Dr Kyriakides said.

"Yeah. Knowing this, knowing that, but without the when, how, where or fucking what."

"That's not entirely true," Steve chipped in sweetly. "After all, you knew the accident was gonna occur and also what I was gonna say."

"You mean, the triplets in the pushchair?" Ms Jenkins said.

"Yeah, the *stroller*," Dale said. As if he could forget …

"So, what was Steve going to say?" she asked.

"'Eh, what's up, Doc?'" Dale said.

Ms Jenkins and the doctor looked puzzled.

"As in *Bugs Bunny*," Steve said, making rabbit ears to illustrate the point.

"I knew he was gonna do that, too," Dale said smugly.

"Any other examples of this, er, precognition?" Dr Kyriakides said, looking less than convinced by Dale's superpower.

Dale considered his timing. He didn't have anything else that was immediately tangible, but it was rather letting the cat out of the bag and risking a helluva scratching. Knowing his luck, Ms Jenkins could be armed with a light sabre. Still, what the hell, she'd know about it soon enough. He cleared this throat and looked at his prospective precognitee. "Tonight, Deborah, your boyfriend will cook you a delicious birthday meal, you will make love and you will become pregnant." That sounded straight out of *Live Your Dream*. He'd even gotten the intonation right.

Ms Jenkins's facial transitioning should have been videoed for posterity. Pink became puce became ashen. Her lower lip seemed to be trembling. "H-How did you know?" she eventually squeaked out of her shrinking, but still highly desirable, frame.

Dale shrugged. "That's the point. I just knew. A bit like a parcel all wrapped up in ribbons, ready for lil' ol' me to do whatever I choose to do with it. But it came to me. And I opened it. And it will happen."

Dr Kyriakides looked equally stunned. "Is that true, Deborah?"

Ms Jenkins shifted uneasily. She was sitting on her hands. "That was the plan. The dinner was meant to be a surprise, but I found a list of ingredients in his forward planner. You know, champagne, oysters, steaks, pommes frites, chocolate nemesis – " judging by the change in his skin colour, Dr Kyriakides's undoing seemed stuck on repeat, " – all the usual things for a romantic dinner. And it is the right time of the month …"

Dale started humming. He had no idea why. The song had just popped into his head. And as Steve would agree, he usually whistled rather tunelessly.

Dr Kyriakides looked horrified. "You're humming 'Knowing Me, Knowing You' by Abba".

"Am I?" Dale said. He'd honestly never heard of the song or the group. Country and Western was more his cup of tea, as the British would say. "I guess I just knew it was a song you liked."

"Very well, Lieutenant," the doctor said, pulling his considerable self together with a seismic heave out of the long-suffering plastic chair, "it's time for some tests …"

CHAPTER SIX

"We need to talk, cariad," Ceri heard her mother saying through the dense musical fog emanating from her earbuds. She didn't feel like talking to anyone after her visit to the hospital to check on Bronwen's progress. Her life seemed to have been sucked out of her and she'd stared at Ceri uncomprehendingly. A psychiatrist had been to assess her because the doctors thought she was in a state of shock. She'd said nothing to him, either. The nurse had mentioned about transferring her somewhere for rehabilitation, although Ceri doubted it would make much difference. The footnote in her great grandmother's potions book had made it clear what could happen if a hex failed to find its target: 'Warning about the Divination Hex: this will transmute into a Lifedrain Hex if misdirected.' One thing was for sure: Bronwen wouldn't need to go on any more cabbage water diets.

Ceri had been trying to conjure up reasons why Bronwen's plight wasn't her fault, but she'd failed at every turn. She'd disregarded the skull and crossbones, and had then compounded her guilt by laughing off the footnote. If only Miss Donn hadn't put her up to the project in the first place. The teacher had also gone on indefinite sick leave, so it probably wouldn't even get marked. It all seemed so unfair and she knew her mother wouldn't understand. Dilys's mam was on the warpath, too. And then there was Dai. Why had the hex gone astray? Perhaps the knighthood insignia conferred some sort of protection on the bearer. She wished Granny Betty was around to lead her through the minefield of modern witchery.

"I'm busy," Ceri shouted. She also had her eye on the news, although she couldn't quite say why. There was something niggling at her that made her think she shouldn't switch off quite yet.

Ceri saw her mother enter the living room out of the corner of her eye. She closed the door slowly behind her. That stealthy action and her mam calling her 'cariad' were the warning signs of her wheedling approach, which usually involved a dive for the jugular by the end of the conversation. Her mam gestured for her to pull out the earbuds. Ceri yanked at the cable and her ears popped annoyingly. She glared at her mother, her hands crossed defiantly over her chest. "What's it about now?" she asked, a dark cloud crossing her face.

Ceri's mother forced a smile and was about to say something, when she seemed distracted by something she noticed to Ceri's right. Her mouth remained open. "Oh my God!" she said, putting a hand to her face.

Ceri turned her head to look at the TV. The breaking

news banner at the bottom of the screen read: 'NEWLY-KNIGHTED SIR DAVID WILLIAMS MISSING.' The screen showed the image of Dai and his girlfriend outside Buckingham Palace, and the newsreader was reading solemnly from a press statement released by his workplace. His employer wished to remain anonymous for reasons of national security. The report mentioned that Dai had disappeared after attending an audience with the Queen. She was said to be distraught and had offered the Palace's resources to help locate him. Ceri and her mother listened silently until the news moved on to the next item. Her mother reached for the remote control and switched the TV off.

"You've got some explaining to do, young lady," her mam said sternly.

"Well, you're a fine one to talk," Ceri huffed. "You know you could have stopped us." She'd never considered her mother as weak before, but now she saw a similarity with Dracula's dogsbody, Renfield. They'd been reading Bram Stoker's book for GCSE English. She'd better check for flies in the soup at supper.

Her mother looked taken aback. "Well ..." she spluttered.

Ceri smiled sweetly. "It's all right, Mam, I won't tell anyone – particularly Bronwen's and Dilys's parents," she added archly.

Her mother seemed to shrink in stature before

her eyes. "Cards on the table?" she said, shrugging in capitulation.

"Okay, Mam, but no sneaky stuff," Ceri said. "Remember I'm the witch in this household." She impressed herself by how emboldened she'd become.

Her mother's mouth opened and closed again slowly, as if she was allowing entrance to a large fly. "You know?"

"Of course," Ceri said.

"How?"

"Dunno. It just dawned on me. Perhaps it was something about the cauldron."

A half-smile came to her mother's face. "Oh yes, the awful smell. That was an indication the cauldron recognised you for what you were. Grandmother should have patented her witch finder trick. The smelling-in period is always the worst part. The burning-in is easy in comparison. Someone who wasn't a witch would have thrown the cauldron out with the rubbish."

"And someone who didn't suspect that their daughter was a witch would have done the same," Ceri said.

"Very true." Her mother smiled more warmly. "You're learning fast, cariad."

"Nos galan gaeaf," Ceri said, as if on autopilot, although puzzled by the words she'd just spoken unwittingly.

Her mother raised an eyebrow. "Hmm, 'spirit night'.

So, you knew about the Halloween ritual all along?"

Ceri shook her head. "It just seemed the right thing to say, Mam. I'm not sure why …"

"Well, well, you really are the chosen one, *Caridwen*." She leaned forward to grasp Ceri's hands. "But never in a million years would I have believed it'd be my daughter." She brushed away tears.

"Why did you call me 'Caridwen'?"

"That's your witchery name, Ceri. Caridwen was one of the Gwyddon gods, and said to be keeper of the Cauldron of Knowledge, with the power of magick and prophecy. She was also known as 'The Crone'."

"Are you serious?" Playing at being a witch was one thing, but getting named after some hideous old hag was the last thing she wanted to hear. She'd be developing warts on her nose next.

"Of course, Ceri. It was your great grandmother who suggested the name when you were born. She must have known even back then."

"So, what can I do if I'm this awesomely amazing witch? I don't even have a bloody broomstick."

Her mother smiled enigmatically. "Don't swear, dear. Your great grandmother wouldn't have liked it."

"Okay, I get it. Broomsticks don't work, right?"

"Not usually, dear, although some witches claim to have hovered a few inches above the ground. To be honest, it's on a par with yogic levitation."

"What people choose to believe in, you mean?"

"Something like that. A bit of hysteria goes a long way, too. There was a girls' school where an entire class fainted at the shock of seeing witches flying across the sky, with black capes billowing behind them. It was actually a flock of crows, but someone had low blood sugar and an overactive imagination, and her classmates chose to believe her."

"So, is there anything I can actually magick?" Ceri wasn't sure why the 'k' got added, but it looked good on paper. Perhaps it was to distinguish real witchery from the magic tricks performed at kids' birthday parties.

"Darling, you've already demonstrated that you've got the gift." Her mother looked towards the TV screen. "A divination hex, if I'm not mistaken."

"Er, yes, but it didn't quite work out – " Ceri looked at the carpet, " – as you know."

"Yes, dear."

"But I didn't have anything to do with Dai disappearing!" Ceri shouted.

"I never thought for one minute that you did, dear. Whoever was responsible for that is a lot more sophisticated than a schoolgirl attempting her first incantations."

Ceri glared. She should have seen that put-down coming.

"So, Ceri bach, what exactly happened with the

divination hex? The orb was clearly rather … er, *energetic*, so you must have got most of it right."

Ceri hadn't banked on home tutoring to develop her witchery skills, but her mother's knowledge was the nearest she'd get to acquiring her great grandmother's wisdom. She took a deep breath. "Well, we found most of the ingredients for the potion, although a couple were from the back of the cupboard and the rest were freeze-dried."

"Oh, you mean, eye of newt, toe of frog, wool of bat, tongue of dog, testicle of kitten – "

"Mam, no!" That must have been why it had gone so horribly wrong. But where would she find a kitten's testicle? Mrs Griffiths's moggy was well past having kittens. Perhaps the vet would pop some in a bag for her if she smiled nicely.

Her mother reddened. "Sorry, darling. Just a little joke. Unfortunately, Shakespeare's *Macbeth* has a lot to answer for. None of those things make any difference. They're just setting the stage. It's the witch's relationship with the cauldron that's important."

"So, what about the hairbrush, toothbrush, photo and Christmas card? Were they a waste of fucking time as well?" Ceri blurted angrily.

Ceri's mother tutted. "Remember a hex in haste is worse than – "

"A spell at speed. Yeah, I know, Mam. I read the book."

Her mother looked thoughtful. "You used all four, did you?"

"Yeah, so what?" She could see another put-down coming. Her mother was a lot more cunning than bloody Renfrew.

"Two samples of DNA, plus images of Dai and his home, amount to overkill, darling. You're not giving the hex any freedom to take its own path. It's like tying someone up in chains and expecting them to read a book by turning the pages with their tongue. I'm not surprised it turned nasty. Still, it is strange it didn't find its target."

"Could the knighthood insignia have been the reason?" Ceri said eagerly. "Perhaps it protected Dai in some way."

"Hmm, I'm not sure, dear. I've not heard of that before, although it's an interesting proposition. Amulets used to be used as protection from black magic in the Middle Ages. But perhaps there's another reason why Dai was immune to the hex."

"Well, he lived on the 20th floor, so the hex could've got bored waiting for the lift," Ceri said with a grin.

Her mother raised an eyebrow. "On the few occasions we spoke on the phone, he seemed preoccupied with there being too much radiation around him, so that's something else to consider."

"I suppose so." Ceri was trying to remember what

Mr Ellis their physics teacher had said about radiation. Wasn't there a radiation belt around the Earth that stopped people from being fried by the Sun's rays? That sounded like the effect of an obliteration hex. "Mam, if radiation can stop a hex from getting through, is there more magick happening now that mobile phones aren't working?"

Ceri could see the wheels turning as her mother considered the question. "Jiw, jiw! I think you might be right, darling," she said excitedly. "It was only last week that the Cymry Wiccae Association reported a big increase in the purchase of cauldrons. We thought it was because they were being used as ornamental planters. But if the people buying them didn't know what they're doing – " she shook her head, "… well, it's a dangerous business."

Ceri wondered where her mother fitted into the witchery business. She'd mentioned an 'association', so could she be its chairman? She felt guilty for regarding her as inconsequential as the fictional Renfield. Keeping witches in order was probably even more difficult than running a hospital.

"Now, returning to the matter of your cousin, what *were* you trying to do?"

Ceri sighed. She knew her mother would go for the jugular sooner or later. "It's complicated, Mam," she said.

"I'm sure it is. He's a good-looking young man, too. It was so nice to see him in a smart suit. I'm pleased that he dressed up to meet the Queen. He used to be rather untidy, as I recall."

Her mother's smile reminded Ceri of the meddling school counsellor. "I wanted to find out more about him. There's no law against that, is there?" Ceri said petulantly.

"You mean, 'open up his mind'."

How did she know? They hadn't written anything down. "Er, you could put it like that."

"And you thought he might be using witchery himself?"

Ceri wondered whether the term was warlock or wizard these days. Perhaps it was just 'witch', regardless of gender, so as to keep everyone politically correct. "Sort of," she mumbled.

"And you were jealous of his girlfriend."

Her mam had missed her true vocation. There had to be a vacancy for a life-sucking phlebotomist in the hospital. "Not really," she protested. *Oh fuck, it was pointless resisting.* "Well, perhaps a little."

Her mother looked relieved. "Well, at least that's a little clearer. Still, it's a shame you roped in Bronwen and Dilys – particularly that poor wee Bronwen. I don't know how her parents will cope." Her mother had thrown her a censorious look, but she'd blown it by describing her friend as wee. Ceri would never understand why Scottish words had entered the Welsh vocabulary. "That was overkill, too," her mother said. "A good witch does her magick on her own."

Ceri was impressed by her mother's wisdom. But there was still Dai's strange disappearance to explain. "So, why should someone want to kidnap him? I mean, there's nothing that special about him."

"Well, he is a knight of the realm …" Her mother looked thoughtful.

"Gosh, Mam, do you think he might have been taken for ransom?"

"It's possible, but …" Her mother frowned, as if trying to make sense of something. "You know, Caridwen, the Queen spoke with me after you were so rude to her." Ceri groaned out aloud, anticipating the bite on the neck. "I didn't like her tone, and it's making sense now. She asked me to rein you in."

Ceri would have fallen off her chair if one of her great grandmother's feather dusters had swung in her direction just then. "You mean she knows about witchery?" Ceri stuttered.

Her mother nodded. "She mentioned Siandi Da'aan, too. Then there was a strange moment when I was worried about taking hold of her hand. She said, 'We are made of stronger stuff than that.' It was almost as if she knew what I was thinking."

Ceri remembered Siandi Da'aan's name from the book they'd borrowed from the library. She couldn't wait to share all this juicy information with Dilys. "So, what do you think it all means?" she asked breathlessly.

Her mother leaned closer. "I think there's more to Her Majesty than meets the eye, so we'd both better be careful."

•••

The last time Lieutenant Dale Franklin was stuck in some high-falutin', high-tech machinery, it was as a volunteer having his body scanned at the felons' entrance to Kansas City Police Department. The idea had been Chief Scanlon's, who'd been banking on technology identifying hidden weapons before they inflicted damage on his officers. Two things conspired against his munificence that mid-summer day: firstly, the fact that the scanner was a prototype without all the requisite safety features; and secondly, predictably unpredictable power surges were afflicting downtown KC owing to its love affair with air-con units. The long and short of it was that Dale was both captured in 3D and captured in reality, as the electrically-powered scanner door refused to let him out. His desperate clawing for release was recorded in perpetuity on half-a-dozen departmental cell phones. The irony of his cell now being his new best friend wasn't entirely lost on him.

Currently, Dale was doing his darndest to distract himself from the mother of all claustrophobic attacks while the MRI scanner was leisurely detecting the up-down spin of his cerebral nuclei. He had headphones on, so the clanking was more like wrenches hitting a metal door than sledgehammers striking the gates of hell, but it was still enough to give him a terminal case of the heebie-jeebies. The doctor had explained the machinery carefully, so he'd just about accepted he hadn't time-tripped back to being stuck in a washer. But not being able to scratch his nose put him right back in the firing line of a certain Sunday school preacher who was rather too fond of keeping his young charges in order.

Fact is, he had to consider the off chance that he'd return to US soil with his curiously cursed cojones exactly as they were – not to mention the bizarre relationship they had with his befuddled brain. Steve had suggested that he gave whatever was happening to his brain a name. It seemed like some crazy old phone exchange, with callers clamouring for attention, so he'd decided to name it 'Ma Bell'. In fact, the network had carping away like niggling ants ever since he succumbed to the tomb-like embrace of the machine. It hadn't helped that his iPhone was now 20 feet away, out of the destructive reach of the scanner's seven tesla magnetic field.

First off, he'd need the right attitude if he was going to impress folks back home with his newfound wisdom. He reckoned a few sessions of cognitive refocusing might help him get back on track. Not NLP or anything flaky like that, just some purposeful encouragement to accept his new status as the fount of all knowledge. Something like: 'Dale Franklin, Man of Prophecy'. Then, perhaps, beneath that: 'Have thought, will travel. Imminent family tragedies a specialty.' He'd need to factor in Steve as his sidekick, too. His mode of transport was already sorted, although he should probably ditch the replica flux capacitor. The gull-wing doors would make rapid exits a cinch. Then there was the costume to consider.

So, what were his choices among the current batch of superheroes? The blue and white costume of Captain America had the right allure, but it was way too high school and serious. Hazing and initiation rituals had never appealed. Going around with a huge 'D' stamped on his forehead wouldn't do much for his credibility, either. Now, Thor had the right idea. Sun-burnished hair, hairless pecs, rippling abs and a mighty great hammer was … well, *manly* … not to mention the leather tunic … his heart was already thumping away in anticipation …

"Okay, okay, Lieutenant, you'll be fine now," Dr Kyriakides seemed to be saying from a distance. "You've had a bit of a panic attack, but that's to be expected.

Anyway, we've completed the scan of your brain."

Dale felt as if he'd been through a wash cycle without the spin dry. He was more than just sweaty. And everyone seemed to be staring at him. He wanted to shout, "Fucking go away!" but the words seemed to have defeated him. Yup, that sure was a mother of a panic. Worst of all, they'd witnessed it.

"Lieutenant, the scan is most interesting," Dale heard dimly. Dr Kyriakides seemed to be on the cusp of a stereotypical eureka moment. This was a transitional moment in Dale's life that he should be savouring, except he was shit scared and embarrassed.

"Dorso yadda-yadda-yadda," the doctor seemed to be saying.

"You don't mean the DLPFC?" Dale heard Steve say excitedly.

Dr Kyriakides was glowing with delight. Put two psychologists together and they'll spout abbreviations as if they're the keys to some ancient religion. It was just like the KCPD. Dale eased himself into a sitting position and glanced across at the screen they were glued to. He'd seen a few brain scans in recent months and reckoned he knew his frontal cortex from his cerebellum. Steve and the doctor were busily fingering some spots on the display that glowed a bright yellow like the sun in Missouri's high summer. If he didn't know better, he'd have thought his brain was on fire.

"Yes, Sergeant, his DLPFC is all fired up," the doctor was saying keenly. "I've never seen anything quite like it."

"Excuse me," Dale said, swiftly regaining lucidity. If there was a fire to put out, he'd need his wits about him. "Being the owner of that fine grey matter, am I not entitled to know what you're looking at?" But even before he'd asked the finely phrased question, he'd guessed the answer. His heart was going pitter-patter all over again.

There was a momentary silence while the doctor stroked his beard and Steve dragged both hands through his hair. It was as if they were transacting their analysis by semaphore, leaving him to fester in the hot seat. That's why he would never allow Steve to drive his DeLorean. He needed assertive. He needed definitive. He definitely didn't need fucking analysis. Ms Jenkins reached over to reassure him with her long dexterous fingers. That was a nice touch. And Steve had witnessed it. He was staring at him suspiciously beneath his long, dark eyelashes.

"That is your brain, Lieutenant," Dr Kyriakides said with compassionate simplicity. "It's a damn fine brain, and hot, if you'll pardon the expression. Which means that – " Dale could see the rub coming at him like an express train, " – the DLPFC is showing intense activation."

Dale considered that carefully. "That's where every-thing is sorta gathered together, right?"

The doctor and Steve nodded in synchrony. When-ever his boyfriend did that, Dale couldn't help but imagine him on the back shelf of a car. He was so good at that repetitive movement. That was the only way he resembled a dog, of course.

"Correct," Dr Kyriakides said, clearly impressed. "The DLPFC is also thought of as the precognitive area. Essentially, its role is to receive sensory input and pass it on to the frontal cortex. But in your case, there was little sensory input while you were in the scanner, meaning that the activation had to be coming from – "

"Something unknown and invisible?" Dale offered with a partially educated guess. Being stuck inside the Chester's Mill dome had to be his worst nightmare. It was the same old issue of out of control situations coming back to haunt him. Without any means of escape.

Steve had stopped bobbing his head and was looking straight at him. The doctor had just mouthed, "Yes."

"So, how?" Dale hardly dared to ask. He'd seen too many movies involving alien takeover and didn't fancy trying sleep deprivation as a way of keeping the bastards out of his head.

Dr Kyriakides threw his hands up in frustration and grinned sheepishly. "I don't know, Lieutenant, but it is rather intriguing. Perhaps it's all due to EM radiation." He'd said that with a shrug, so it was hardly a definitive diagnosis, but it gave Dale an idea worth pursuing.

"The strange thing is, Doctor, I seemed to be getting more random thoughts when I was in the scanner," he said. "And my nuts were aching, too."

"Nuts?"

"Oh, you know, nuts, balls, bollocks, cojones …"

"Ah, yes, the testicular pain, as mentioned in the urologist's report." Dr Kyriakides reached across for the file and started thumbing through it. "Hmm, that's interesting …"

"I thought he gave me a clean bill of health," Dale said. He didn't like people reading stuff about him that he had no knowledge of. It just wasn't cricket.

"Well, yes, but not exactly," the doctor said confusingly. "The point is, Lieutenant, that some of your blood tests came back abnormal. DHT, TSH, FSH, LH … they're all elevated and by some margin."

Dale knew that should have worried the hell out of him, but it made sense. His nuts had been trying to tell him that sort of gobbledegook all along. He'd always been useless at listening to his inner self. The simple message was: he'd been under attack, and it had been sneakily below the belt. "And the thoughts I'm getting?"

"Well …" the doctor was messing with his beard again, "I think the testicular pain and the precognition are somehow connected. We know from studying children affected by 'the screaming' that EM radiation causes cerebral atrophy like with Alzheimer's disease, so other parts of the body could be vulnerable, too. Any organ with high rates of cell division, such as the gonads, would be particularly susceptible. MRI uses resonant frequencies up to 85 megahertz, so that's probably where we should be investigating. As to where the thoughts are coming from – " his hands shot up again, " – well, I'd put my money on some fundamental particles having a few tricks up their sleeves." He paused, looking self-conscious. "Sorry, that was stupidly anthropomorphic and a bit of a lecture, but it's what MI5 pay me to do. You know, inwardly digest, cogitate and, hopefully, spew out something that makes sense to the average layperson."

"Sorta makes sense to me," Dale said. Getting his head around his latest trip into *The Twilight Zone* might be a tad complicated, but it was a walk in the park compared with the horror of 'the screaming' – so far, at least. It was the doctor's mention of spewing that had him worried. When he threw up, he really tossed his cookies. And the incident with the stroller still had him spooked. If it was simple stuff, with a bit of personalised divination here and there, no problem. He could book a booth at the Kansas State Fair. The mighty Thor would have to chill out until he'd gotten his bearings.

Anyway, the hammer wouldn't fit with KCPD standard operating procedures. But he might borrow the leather tunic for the season.

"Me, too," Steve said, "or, at least, the first part. One thing that's bugging me is why Dale was only affected when we arrived at the airport. I mean, is it something about the UK that's different to the US?" There was a subtle shift in his features. "Jeez! I've got it! We haven't switched off the cell networks."

Dale had said it before, and he'd say it again: his boyfriend was way too bright to be a cop.

Steve's blinding insight galvanised Dr Kyriakides into action like the frog that kicked its legs in the name of science. He leaped out of his chair, at a speed Dale would normally have deemed impossible given his bulk, and dived for the wall-sized display, his fingers reaching out as if to phone homes in multiple galaxies. The screen came to life with what appeared to be a weather map of the UK, dominated by a mass of multi-coloured clouds. It was more like *The Wizard of Oz* than the nightly news bulletin and Dale was on the lookout for the yellow brick road.

"That's the EM spectrum for the UK before Wi-Fi and mobile networks were switched off," Dr Kyriakides said. "The bright green colour represents the 2.4 gigahertz band of Wi-Fi and the dark yellow is the 2.1 gigahertz used by mobile phones. If I change the orientation of the display, it should become a little clearer."

The doctor wasn't kidding. As the map shifted into 3D, the chaotic tapestry of overlapping clouds turned into stratified ovals littering the length and breadth of the UK. It was a tad too Jackson Pollock for Dale's taste, but there was no doubt about the widespread take-up of Wi-Fi and cell phone technology across the country. He figured that the Outer Hebrides must have been the safest place to be if you were a teenager. Kids probably weren't allowed to consume trans fats there, either.

"Jesus!" Dale said. "Are those really all different frequencies?"

"Absolutely," Dr Kyriakides said. "There's EM radiation wherever you care to look. Between 118 and 137 megahertz, there are 1,000 channels used by civil aviation. The TETRA system used by the police force operates in the microwave region, at 380 megahertz. Our friend over there – " he pointed in the direction of Dale's idea of a dryer from hell, " – is responsible for the wispy magenta cloud of frequencies between 15 and 80 megahertz you can see lying low over cities with hospitals."

Dale had never liked the colour magenta even as a child. Perhaps that had been a subtle alert to his current predicament.

"And now," the doctor continued, "here's the picture

from just a week ago, with Wi-Fi and mobile networks switched off."

This time the colour separation of the 3D display was essential. Although the bright green and dark yellow had disappeared, other colours had appeared as blobs across the landscape. Dale's knowledge of UK geography was hardly extensive, but even he couldn't miss the rainbow hued colours hovering ominously over South East England.

"What's curious is that we're seeing new frequency bands that weren't there before," Dr Kyriakides said. "It's as if Wi-Fi and mobile networks were preventing other frequencies from getting a look in."

Dale and Steve exchanged glances. "We get that the whole time in the US," Dale said. "One gang jams another gang's communications. There's a massive black market for the technology and it's coming from the same countries making cell phones in the first place. It's like a pit bull chomping on another dog's balls. Alpha male bullshit, in other words." He smiled wryly. *Been there, done that,* he thought.

"Do you have an equivalent map for the US?" Steve asked sensibly.

"Actually, we do," the doctor said, "although the detail is rather basic. We have to rely on third parties for the data."

Dr Kyriakides danced his digits again and Dale gazed

at his homeland rendered in a way he could never have imagined. He pondered on what the Department of Homeland Security would make of the multi-coloured hotspots that littered the US. *Time to apply my well-honed deductive reasoning,* Dale thought. He cracked his knuckles.

"So, what you're saying, Doctor, is that there's a mess of radio frequencies out there, but something's happening in the UK that isn't occurring in the US because we didn't go for the switch off. And somehow, I seem to be caught in the middle of it."

"That about sums it up," Dr Kyriakides said. Dale glanced at Ms Jenkins, who'd been nodding away with the wisdom of a sage. He'd even noticed some grey hairs defiling her glossy carapace.

"And then there's my iPhone," Dale continued. "I guess it must be blocking some of the radiation."

"I imagine so," the doctor said thoughtfully. "May I take a look at your phone, Lieutenant?"

Dale passed his iPhone reluctantly to the doctor. The cell was still thrumming as Dr Kyriakides took it … and then almost dropped it. "Sorry, I didn't expect it to be so warm," he said with an apologetic grin. He touched the back of the phone with his fingertips. "Yes, it's definitely throbbing." The doctor handed the phone back to Dale who was already developing separation anxiety.

Dr Kyriakides teased his beard and a grain of

something fell onto his lap. Dale wondered whether he washed his whiskers. "Normally, mobile phones use cells to receive and transmit calls," the doctor said. "But cell networks are inactive at the moment, apart from a few clandestine operations that have sprung up."

"Hence the Met's Operation Bloodhound," Dale said, musing on what a police dog would discern from a sniff of the shaggy beard.

"Exactly. And if I'm right about the frequency that's affecting your testicles, I think it's somehow caused the iPhone to form its own cell, which seems to be in a feedback loop and transmitting an inverse of the original signal."

"Like noise-cancelling headphones," Steve said.

Dr Kyriakides nodded. "So, in other words, your mobile phone is protecting you from EM radiation by emitting yet more EM radiation."

"Dale, you'd better watch out your iPhone doesn't burst into flames while you're holding it against your nuts," Steve said, cringing and giggling simultaneously.

Dr Kyriakides squirmed. "Yes, that would be most unfortunate. I'd recommend using your phone in short bursts for optimum therapeutic effect, Lieutenant."

Ms Jenkins's derisive snort indicated what she thought of the doctor's advice. "That all seems somewhat ironic considering that mobile phones caused the bloody problem in the first place," she said huffily. "It's a pity Dai didn't learn that trick with mobile phones. He could have saved himself a lot of discomfort."

"Dai is rather different, Deborah," Dr Kyriakides said. "He – "

"You don't need to remind me, Doctor," Ms Jenkins said sharply.

"In Dai's case," the doctor continued, apparently unperturbed, "it's his entire body that's sensitive to EM radiation, so only a Faraday cage could have protected him. Anything fabricated from a hollow shell of conducting material makes a good Faraday cage – a plane or car, for instance. Dai used a metallised fabric for his whole body protection, which was almost as effective."

Dale was trying to put two and two together, but something still didn't fit. "Okay, so why was I still getting pain in my nuts when we were in the cab coming from the airport?"

Dr Kyriakides paused for a moment. "That's easy, Lieutenant. A London black cab might be a car, but many of them are fabricated out of fibreglass, so the bodywork isn't conductive and doesn't actually constitute a Faraday cage. The limousine that brought you here is constructed of steel, which is why you didn't experience any discomfort."

"Dai was wearing his protection when we met in the Burn Center," Steve said keenly. "It looked really uncomfortable, though, and he said he always had a problem finding the right grounding."

"*Sir David*, if you don't mind," Ms Jenkins said. Her nose twitched condescendingly, as if to the manor born.

"So, perhaps Dale could wear something similar to the mesh Sir David – " Steve smiled saccharine sweetly in Ms Jenkins's direction, " – used to block out EM radiation."

"I suppose so," Dr Kyriakides said with a hint of wistfulness. "In fact, we developed a rather nice nano-fibre version for him. It might even fit the lieutenant. And I believe it's fire retardant."

Dale noticed Steve sniggering into his hand. The notion of the mighty Thor in a nanofibre body costume didn't have nearly the same allure. Perhaps the doctor could rustle up a pair of hi-tech briefs. They had to be more comfortable than a metallic space blanket fashioned into a diaper.

"Doctor, going back to the precognition bit of it," Dale said, "I'm still trying to get my head around how I can know things before they've happened. I mean, I'm not exactly like your quantum computer."

Dr Kyriakides chuckled. "No, if you were, Lieutenant, you'd be deep frozen by now, as it's in a box cooled by liquid nitrogen. All the computer does is predict using trillions of observations. For instance, there's usually a one in 20 chance I'll cook moussaka for dinner. The odds go up if I've missed lunch and I'm particularly hungry. If I go swimming, the chance goes higher. So, taking all the potential variables that describe my eating behaviour, the quantum computer would be accurate 99 per cent of the time at predicting what I'll have for my evening meal."

Dale thought cryogenic menu planning sounded a waste of resources, but he got the picture. He tried to imagine the doctor in a pair of Speedos. He sure wasn't a Tom Daley lookalike. He'd bet a hundred bucks on him having a hairy back. Judging by the smirk on Steve's face, his thoughts had been heading along similar lines.

"Yup, that makes sense," Dale said, "but that's hardly gonna set the world alight. Let's say your quantum computer existed back in 2001. Would it have been able to predict the 9/11 attacks?"

Dr Kyriakides shifted his bulk. The chair creaked under the burden of the enquiry. "That's an interesting question ... a little unfair, but still interesting." His droopy moustache twitched at the corners. "The answer is a probable yes, Lieutenant. We ran a simulation with data feeds available back then and the computer predicted a number of events. The actual targets were hidden inside the terrorists' brains. The limiting factor is the intelligence, not the machine. Of course, if we could tap into peoples' minds ..." He raised his heavy-weight shoulders.

"Which is why Dai Williams is so interesting to MI5," Steve piped up.

Ms Jenkins waggled a finger. "Naughty boy," she said.

Dale wasn't finished quite yet. "So, returning to my brain, Doctor, what do you think is going on? Ms Jenkins mentioned something about some Heisenberg whatchamacallit, but I don't get how something that's uncertain can be an explanation for future events dropping into my head."

Dr Kyriakides nodded. "I agree that it requires a leap of faith … a *quantum leap*, one might say." He chuckled. "Let's say it's part of the explanation. To put it bluntly, current theories about time only going in one direction may be wrong." The doctor knotted his fingers behind his head and the chair lurched backwards alarmingly, as if to illustrate his remark.

Steve was already raising a hand to comment upon the doctor's unstable seating arrangement. He'd always been top of the class when it came to health and safety.

"I know, I know, it sounds ridiculous," Dr Kyriakides said, "but please hear me out, Sergeant."

Steve mouthed, "This better be good," crossing his arms huffily.

The doctor took a deep breath. "Okay, there's a strange behaviour of subatomic particles called quantum entanglement, whereby something done to one particle affects the entangled particle at a speed faster than light, even if the other particle is a distance away. Einstein referred to this as 'spooky action at a distance'. Some researchers have speculated that this might be a way of communicating over vast distances. But, in one experiment carried out in Japan, the change in the remote particle actually anticipated the first. Conventional wave theory expects one-way causality; the Japanese experiment suggests it might be bidirectional under certain circumstances. I'd wager the recipe for my grandmother's moussaka that your brain is tapping into this quantum entanglement."

Moussaka was a lot to swallow at the best of times and Dale couldn't match the doctor's appetite for the strange world of particle physics. A deep rumble from Dr Kyriakides's stomach, conveyed at sub-light speed, hinted that a lunch break was next on the agenda. Dale suddenly realised that the last sit-down meal he'd had was courtesy of Delta Airlines two days ago. At least their action-packed schedule was helping him retain the lean and hungry look that Steve appreciated so much. He hoped that MI5's cafeteria was superior to KCPD's and that projectile vomiting wasn't an involuntary sauce on the side.

CHAPTER SEVEN

As the four of them walked down The Manor's grand staircase, Dale's attention was caught by the paintings lining the wall. Most of them must have been centuries old, but that didn't diminish the piercing intelligence of the subjects' faces. A few of the pictures included scientific instruments that looked like they were straight out of an alchemist's laboratory – or they could have been distilling hooch on the side. Perhaps the idea of stuff going backwards in time would have seemed a tad less heretical in those days.

A few steps from the bottom of the stairs, he was intrigued to see a painting of a woman in a folk costume wearing a tall hat and with a large black cat on her lap. She looked out of place alongside her sternly-suited male colleagues. The sitter and her companion seemed intent on outstaring the viewer, and no matter which way Dale turned his head, the four eyes followed him. He wondered what insight they'd have had into the comings and goings inside MI5's secret research establishment. The old woman might even have had an entangled particle or two hidden under her hat, itching to tell a story.

"Dale, whatya doing?" Steve called out impatiently

from 20 feet away. "I'm hungry." He mimed putting a fork to his mouth, his perfect teeth flashing in the gloom of the hall.

Dale floundered momentarily. He was caught between examining the painting further and assuaging his hunger. "Coming," he said. The picture's occupants wouldn't be going anywhere, after all. He descended the remaining stairs, glancing over his shoulder. The old lady was still watching him and he could have sworn the cat licked its lips.

"Is that gorgeous chick a distant relative?" Steve asked Dale, grinning broadly. "I heard the Franklin menfolk have a reputation for spilling their seed far and wide."

Dale punched Steve's shoulder playfully. "Do you still wanna go to that Madame's place? I'm thinking it'd be good to go straight back to the hotel. I'm feeling kinda churned up inside, if you know what I mean," he said, making a circular motion with his head.

Steve pondered that for a moment in mock serious- ness. "Okay, agreed. Who cares about a load of old haircuts, anyway?" He slipped his fingertips behind Dale's belt. "I've been getting rather horny watching all your intimate exams."

"Come on, please, gentlemen," Ms Jenkins called out from the nearby corridor. "The cafeteria isn't open all day."

"I guess we'd better put our entanglement on hold until later," Steve quipped teasingly, disengaging his fingers after a quick tug on the belt. They followed Deborah's crisply black silhouette to a door that was already open.

"Jeez!" Dale said, as they entered the canteen. "This sure beats KCPD." He reckoned the spacious room had been the formal dining hall before MI5 took charge of the building. In contrast to KCPD's sweaty cafeteria, with its buzzing fluorescent tubes, The Manor's restaurant had calmly twinkling chandeliers. Three sides of the room were panelled with wood up to the ceiling and there were yet more gilt-framed paintings. Clouds of steam and tempting odours emanated from dishes of food under bright lights along most of the fourth side. Only a handful of tables were occupied, and the atmosphere was of calm enjoyment rather than wolfing food to sustain an afternoon of squad car chases and interrogations.

"The food is free, by the way," Ms Jenkins said, "or at least, the government pays for it."

Dale piled his plate high, oblivious to the admonishing looks Steve gave him. Hell, he deserved it! Predictably, Steve had taken the salad option. So, too, had Ms Jenkins and Dr Kyriakides. Dale paused mid-mouthful, cocking his head with an inquiring look at their plates.

"I'm training later," the doctor said. "Better not to overload with carbs."

"I'm watching my figure," Ms Jenkins said. Dale couldn't understand why; it looked perfect to him. He shrugged and continued shovelling food as if he was clearing snow from his parents' driveway. It certainly tasted a damn sight better – and healthier, too – than anything on offer back in the KCPD cafeteria.

"You can't have had much of a holiday so far," Ms Jenkins said benignly, glancing up from her plate at Steve. "Most of London is one big tourist trap. Places like Madame Tussauds and Harrods are the pits. And Number 10 is so boring now one can't go up to the front door." She carefully forked a cherry tomato to avoid being splattered with juice. "What are your plans, then, Sergeant?"

"Oh, we thought we'd try Madame Tussauds and Harrods, followed by Number 10," Steve said, not missing a beat.

"Oh," Ms Jenkins replied, choosing a less risky morsel for her next mouthful. "Why Tussauds, anyway? There's always a mile-long queue to get in, particularly when the weather is bad."

"Steve has this thing about haircuts," Dale explained. "He wanted to go to a museum of hairstyles. Madame T's seemed the next best thing."

"Hairstyles?" Ms Jenkins pondered. "That's

interesting. I'd never have thought of Tussauds as a place to see haircuts, but I suppose it is ..." She reached out to touch Steve's glistening locks. "What conditioner do you use? I'd kill for that hair."

Dale had no doubt she would, given half the chance. All the talk about hair had made him feel queasy and he eyed his half-emptied plate uneasily. Or perhaps his nuts were trying to tell him something. And then, wham bam, thank you, ma'am, they did: a snippet of knowledge had just plonked its goddamn irritating self in his frontal cortex. It couldn't have been more unambiguous. He could try shaking it off, but he knew it was there for the duration and would keep on niggling away like his fucking cojones. *Oh shit,* Dale thought. *They're not gonna like this.* He put his fork on the table and stared into the distance.

"Are you all right, Lieutenant? You look as if you've seen a ghost," Ms Jenkins said, her eyes glinting with amusement. She glanced around the room and leaned forward. "You should try coming here in the middle of the night. It gives me the shivers."

Dale was shivering himself. Steve put a hand on his shoulder. "Is it happening again, sweets?" he whispered.

Dale nodded. He felt like he was back in bible class, with everyone wallowing in his ignorance and unremitting psychological abuse, all dressed up as the fucking lamb of God. Amen.

"Er, Ms Jenkins," Dale said timidly. "I've had another thought."

Ms Jenkins inclined her head. A delicate pea shoot had just passed her lips en route to the transitory bliss of her gastrointestinal tract. If only it was so damn simple. There was no easy way to put it. "Dai Williams has been taken prisoner," Dale said bluntly.

"How the hell did you know?" Ms Jenkins said, her face turning ashen. "We only learned he'd gone missing this morning. We certainly hadn't reported anything to the press about him being abducted ... Oh my God!" She put a hand to her mouth. "You really know that he's been taken, don't you?"

Dale bowed his head. He wished he could dive under the table and stay there for good. *Please, dear God, don't let them put me back in that fucking scanner!*

Ms Jenkins stared at him with her deep, dark eyes. "So, where is he, Lieutenant? Who's taken him? You must know, for Chrissakes!"

Being shouted at in the middle of a cafeteria was one thing, but having nothing useful to say made him feel like such a fucking dipshit. He could well imagine Chief Scanlon's dismissive sneer if all he could report was that some VIP had gone walkabout. He'd be bellowing his head off with the accompaniment of flying doughnut fragments. His dumbass ability certainly gave a new slant on prick-teasing. Jeez, it was like ordering a T-bone steak and then having it taken away before he could attack it with a fork! He stared back reluctantly into Ms Jenkins's eyes. Damn, she was frightened. "I just wish I knew," he said pathetically. He felt like tearing out his remaining hair. "But I don't. I've no idea who took him or where he's gone."

Ms Jenkins seemed to be lost in a world of indecision. She got up and wandered around the dining room, going up to the paintings to stare at them and touching things at random. The other diners were staring at her. Dr Kyriakides was just watching and stroking his beard. Dale half-expected security to enter and lead her away. Even the best of MI5's battle scared had to fall apart every now and again. Eventually, Ms Jenkins returned to the table. She'd been crying and black rivulets of mascara had run down her cheeks.

"So, Lieutenant, what do you suggest I do?" she said in a tone of utter exasperation. "Go home for a birthday meal I'm not meant to know about, and make love with a purpose in mind my boyfriend has no knowledge of, or join in the search for Dai?"

Dale shrugged. "I'm only the messenger, Ms Jenkins."

"Well, it would help greatly if a whisper of information arrived in your brain that we could actually make use of," she said archly. She sniffed. "Sorry, I shouldn't have said that, but you know ..." A look of desperation flittered over her finely-boned features. She reached to grasp his hands. "Please – just tell me, Lieutenant."

Dale smiled ruefully. "You want my advice?"

Ms Jenkins nodded.

"And as someone who's always been lousy at sorting out priorities?"

She bobbed her head again.

"Best to have sex first, so that you can enjoy the meal." He was still crap at making decisions for other people. And if he was gonna get into personal divination services, he'd better be prepared for plenty of laying on of hands from Missouri's womenfolk.

"Christ almighty!" Ms Jenkins said beneath her breath. "Will someone just tell me what the fuck to do!"

Dr Kyriakides put his hand up. "Let me try. It's an interesting conundrum, Deborah. If the lieutenant had a device that could take him forward in time, and he found evidence that you gave birth to a son approximately nine months from now, who just happened to meet all the requirements to become our next Prime Minister, then doing anything that might jeopardise this evening's dinner could have repercussions extending far into the future. But, in fact, all he's describing is an event that he believes will happen today, rather than anything beyond that. I don't think it's too dissimilar to the quantum computer predicting I'll cook moussaka and me deciding at the last minute to order pizza. The other way of looking at it is that time has a way of correcting small deviations along the way, so the grand plan remains unaffected."

Ms Jenkins sighed. "Okay, so do I go with head – " she looked at Dr Kyriakides, " – or heart? Hell, I don't know." She turned to Steve. "What do you think, Sergeant?"

Steve looked to Dale for inspiration. Dale shrugged. He had to admit, it was a helluva conflict of interest for Ms Jenkins. If he hadn't opened his big mouth, they'd probably already be on the way back to their hotel. Dale wondered what Steve would pull out of his hat to sway the discussion this time.

"There was a psychology professor at school who was always disagreeing with me about everything," Steve said, fixing Ms Jenkins with his puppy-dog eyes. "One day, we were arguing about nature versus nurture. We were getting nowhere. I'd cited all the research I could think of. In the end, I just said, 'I am what I am. And what I am needs no excuses.' The class applauded and I walked out feeling great. He'd never heard of Gloria Gaynor."

Dale would also have applauded if it wasn't for the snippets of information clambering for attention inside his head. It was definitely peaking. He readied himself for the next lacerating insight. Suddenly, it went quiet again. Maybe someone up there had decided he'd done his bit as a latter-day saint.

At least Ms Jenkins seemed relieved by Steve's intervention. She was nodding and looked at peace with her conscience. "Okay, that's decided. You're invited to the christening. But first, I need to get you – " she looked piercingly at Dale, " – back to London so that you can let MI5 know if you receive an update from Petros's entangled particles."

What the fuck? Dale thought. *She's bought the doctor's explanation hook, line and sinker, but where does that leave me? Am I doomed to be left dangling for the rest of my goddamn life?*

Dale turned to Dr Kyriakides just before they left the cafeteria. Physically, he felt as if he'd been dragged feet first by horses along a rocky path. Mentally, the day had been like a prolonged session of waterboarding. His brain needed oxygen and time to think without interruptions.

"So, Doc, what will happen when I return to the US? Will I still have these thoughts dropping into my head like Beelzebub's idea of fortune cookies?"

The doctor shrugged. "It's hard to know, Lieutenant. You'll just have to see. It could be something that's been unlocked in your brain like Dai's ability to peer inside peoples' minds. There've been plenty of soothsayers or savants over the ages. You know, The Oracles of Delphi, Nostradamus, Old Moore's Almanac ..."

"Not to mention, our esteemed Chief Scanlon," Steve said. "He knows all the baseball scores."

"Really, Doctor?" Dale said, glaring at Steve. "I thought all that was a load of hooey."

"Well, I think you're proof it isn't, Lieutenant, so welcome to the club," Dr Kyriakides said, patting him firmly on the back.

•••

Dale almost smiled. He didn't mind the exclusivity of the establishment, but there seemed to be a high price to be a member. Ma Bell was mighty busy and she spoke with forked tongues. The bizarre thing was, sometimes his ability felt so fan-fucking-tastic that he wanted to shout it out to the world; the rest of the time, he wanted to crawl away like a cur that'd been banished for good. Insanity had to be lurking just round the corner.

Fortunately, madness had decided to take a rain check for the time being. Instead, a couple of hours later Dale and Steve found themselves back in the hotel. It didn't exactly feel sane being in some interior designer's idea of rural Sweden transported to urban London, but at least Dale felt in control of his faculties. Not much else, though. He was still being bombarded by what passed as wisdom, 19 to the dozen. In their room. In bed. An early dinner seemed a better option than trying to push water uphill. Mutually decided, of course.

At least the menu wasn't Scandinavian. And the dining room was a welcome oasis of calm after being cocooned in the scanner. Dale wondered whether the magnetic field had rubbed off on him, but no, the cutlery had resolutely stayed put. Steak and salad seemed the best option after the excesses of The Manor's cafeteria. Together with a bottle of *vino de la casa*. The waiter served the food with a smile. A knowing smile. Or was it leering? Either way, it didn't seem Scandinavian.

Scandinavian was clean and unadulterated – apart from way too much pine. Pine reminded Dale of air fresheners: something to cover up the shit and the bad stuff that was going on beneath the surface. And Christ, there was so much of that! Whichever way he bent his lil' ol' internal ears, it wouldn't stop. Perhaps if he just concentrated on chewing ... He could see the blood oozing from the beef ... red, amber, green ... red, amber, green ...

"That's it, darling, eat slowly for Mommy, so you'll get all healthy and strong." She was hovering over him, too close, that sickly smell of cheap fragrance.

"What the fuck d'you think you're doing, chewing like a girly?" His dad had a bottle of bourbon in his hands, as usual. He stank of sweat and piss and God knows what else.

But he wasn't in Missouri now; he was in London, UK (Northern Hemisphere), 51.5 degrees latitude, -0.14 degrees longitude, to be precise, just as he'd say in a court of law. He'd always appreciated the sense of order he'd gotten from the geography class. Battle lines were best drawn on the battlefield rather than across the kitchen table. He'd always been lousy as a peacekeeper.

"You're thinking too much," Steve said with calm concern, looking up from his plate of food. "You should eat."

Eat, piss, shit, fuck, all those things and more. Their eyes connected briefly. Dale glanced at his steak. His knife had slashed it open and the oozing juices were sickly red. And then it came to him, like a fist slammed into the solar plexus. He reeled back into his seat, gasping for breath.

"Christ, Dale! What the fuck is it?" Steve looked scared.

"Gimme your cell!" He could be oh-so commanding when it was needed; leading an army of mutants might be fun.

Steve reached into his pockets for his phone. The screen remained grimly dark under the brutally insistent restaurant lights. Scandinavia must be a helluva dark place in the winter. Steve glanced up, looking apologetic. "Sorry, sweets, it isn't charged up. Is it your nuts again?" His cuteness wasn't going to sway him this time.

"I need a phone. Now." Dale checked around the dining room and gesticulated wildly at a nearby waiter.

"Sir, I need to borrow your cell phone," he said, grabbing the waiter's arm.

The waiter backed off. Surprise skittered across his

face like an ice skater with two left feet. He pointed to the signs on the wall: 'Free Wi-Fi spot' had a slash through it. 'No mobile phones' was displayed alongside it.

"Fuck!" Dale moaned beneath his breath. His hands juddered against the table, clattering cutlery against porcelain. It was as if his 'knowing' needed a feed. His eyes flicked around for a potential source. What was that flat screen doing in a hotel dining room? They should have gone three star, for Chrissakes! Some guy was going on about freak storms back in the US. The video showed green plains lashed by torrential rain and twisters, the trees uprooted from the spot. It had to be connected with EM radiation, or so the weather anchor thought. He was a good looker, good talker and came from some place called the 'Met Office'. Where they used maps. Dale's thoughts clicked into place like a combination of 'I'll be back' and 'Here's Johnny!'

Dale plunged his hands into his pockets, pulling out everything he could find: gum, candy, ticket stubs, receipts, more gum, more stubs – *fuck, it had to be there* – skitter-scattering on the floor and the table … finally, the Golden Ticket was in his hand. He leaped out of the chair and streaked across the room. Hunting his target. Thank God he was fit. There was nothing like an old-fashioned chase on foot. Target acquired. Never had something attached to a length of wire looked so enticing.

Steve had been watching Dale closely, trying to maintain clinically detached while feeling he should be doing something. Damn, Dale could be single-minded. It had to be some clinical syndrome: not exactly 'The Man Who Mistook His Wife for a Hat', but more 'The Man Who Wished His Wife Wasn't a Goddamn Hat.' And then there was that weird thing he did with his steak: tearing it apart and then staring wide-eyed as the bloody juices spread across the plate. *An American Werewolf in London* sprang to mind, in for the kill. *Should I have intervened? Yeah, but what the fuck would I have done? Ask for a straitjacket? The UK probably didn't even use those anymore!* And now he's on his way back. He sure looks exhausted. He'll probably say he's plum-tuckered out. So cute. Perhaps he'd been burying his head in a waiter's neck. Preferable to a waiter's groin. It's been a helluva day. Okay, fingers crossed that it's actually *Awakenings*, after all. *PS: I still love him.*

•••

Dai came to with Green Park greenery in his mouth and a tenacious tendril worming its way up a nostril. His outstretched fingertips were resting on a blanket of grass that was cool and comforting. *Whoa! Haven't I experienced this before?* He turned over and pushed himself up into a sitting position. The sky looked exactly the same. The lights in Buckingham Palace still shone just as brightly.

He checked his watch: 7:00 p.m. *That's weird. Had time stopped while I was being tortured at the hands of some fucking sadist?* Oh, get real Dai! You're not in a movie now! Okay, so there were two other options to consider: a) that he'd imagined the whole thing and had just had a micro-nap; or b) that he'd been up-up-and-awayed into the lab of a passing spaceship and returned in the twinkling of an alien's lizard-like eye. He explored his teeth with his tongue for tell-tale holes where transmitters might have been implanted: nope, nothing. He examined his wrists and ankles for signs of physical restraint: nope, no marks or stickiness. Could something have been put inside him? That would need an X-ray. *So, could I use the hocus focus on myself?* For Chrissakes, Dai, get a grip! A ping let loose in his brain would bounce around in an infinite feedback loop and cause him to start speaking Welsh. And liking rugby.

Suddenly, the sky seemed to explode with light. There was a feeling of burning heat on his face and a loud whoosh-whooshing noise slammed at his eardrums. *Oh Christ, they're back to finish me off!* There was only one thing for it: he'd use the hocus focus to ping their neural network just like Jeff Goldblum did when he uploaded a computer virus in *Independence Day*. It could go horribly wrong, and he might end up with his head chopped off by a laser, but, hell, he was a knight of the realm and he might as well go out with a bang. That'd teach those who still thought he was a brainless boyo from the Valleys.

So, Dai stood up, raised his hands in the air, and focussed out … clearing his mind … whoosh-whoosh went the noise … imagining a funnel … it was hard to concentrate … zeroing in with a precisely delivered ping right in the centre of the alien computer constructed from human brain tissue … whoosh-whoosh-whoosh … and now there are figures coming for him … they're skeletally thin, holding out pincer-grip appendages to crush the last ounce of his life force …

"It's okay, sir, you're safe now," a male voice shouted. It was hard to make out the words against all the noise, but it was definitely English. Aliens were so fucking devious. They'd obviously learnt the language from YouTube broadcasts.

"Cut the searchlight," another voice yelled. "You're blinding the man."

Green Park suddenly looked like Green Park again. Buckingham Palace hadn't moved an inch and its windows were burning with light as usual. *Her Majesty obviously wasn't on dimmer duty tonight,* Dai thought. Then he realised that someone or something was shaking his hand vigorously.

"I'm Major Struthers, Sir David," the humanoid said. "It's good to have you back."

Dai tried to say something, but it came out sounding

like 'howzat', and it was the wrong time of the year to be thinking about cricket. But at least he was back on Earth. His nose registered the curiously reassuring odour of freshly deposited horse droppings nearby.

"That's okay, sir," the human said. "You're bound to be a bit disorientated. Thank God someone told us where to find you. You could have died from hypothermia, you know. Now, be a good chap and put this blanket over your shoulders."

Dai decided it was rather pleasant being looked after. It took him right back to Granny Betty's kitchen, where she'd feed him a slice of bara brith and pour out sweet, milky tea as soon as he got home from school. Sometimes there'd be a metal pot on the table. It was a huge great thing and he liked staring into it and imagining he could see the future. The major was right, though: it was cold in the park and his teeth were chattering. He allowed himself to be led towards the welcoming glow of the helicopter's interior. Someone put a flask of steaming coffee into his hands.

"Buckle up, Sir David, and we'll be on our way," the major said. "We've got orders to take you in for a quick check-up and debriefing. I expect you'll be wanting to get home to your girlfriend. She must've been going frantic with worry."

Dai didn't register much of the short flight to the hospital in the East End. He tried drinking the coffee, but it just didn't taste right. Still, the flask warmed his hands. It must have been official MI5 issue, as 'Keep Calm and Carry On' was written on the side beneath a crown. He was starting to appreciate the dangers of working for the Queen. It was all a bit too James Bond for comfort. Dinner with Delia Smith would have been an awful lot safer. He might even have tried leeks again. But not sautéed in butter.

The helicopter soon landed on a rooftop helipad and he was escorted down a flight of stairs. The décor was swish, with corporate-style art lining the walls, so he guessed it was a private wing in the hospital that MI5 had a contract with. The room they entered was nothing like his grandmother's cosy parlour, but at least he recognised the welcoming face. Emma Jones was a medic he'd first encountered at The Manor. She'd been instrumental in introducing him to his fiancée, so she'd become a friend as well as a colleague.

"My goodness, David, you've had us concerned!" Dr Jones said cheerily, swiftly popping a stethoscope into her ears. Dai smiled weakly, stripped to his underpants and let her get on with her job. There was something reassuring about the way a doctor went about their business, methodically examining parts of the body. She was taking photos, too, so at least there'd be evidence to show for his ordeal. By the end of the examination, Dr Jones was frowning and Dai expected the worst.

"Well, if I didn't know better, I'd say you've been lying on the grass for the last 24 hours. I'm surprised no one found you before. For the life of me, I can't find anything wrong. And there are no marks on you, either."

Dai examined his wrists and then bent forwards to look at his ankles. He shook his head. There had to be a sign of something. If not, why couldn't he get the idea of duct tape out of his head? He glanced at the floor. Even his shoes looked squeaky clean, as if someone had deliberately wiped them. But everything was still so hazy. He scratched his head. "So, are you telling me I imagined it all?"

"It?" Dr Jones said, a question mark hanging portentously on her breath.

Dai felt himself blushing under her interrogation. He looked at his feet. *Are my toenails really that long?* "Well, I did have some weirdly pervasive ideas about being abducted by a UFO."

Dr Jones raised an eyebrow, highlighting her strangely mismatched green and blue irises. "And?"

Dai explored his teeth with his tongue. "Well, they're rumoured to drill holes in teeth to implant their devilish devices."

Dr Jones sighed. "Okay, I'd better take a look."

Dai leaned forward and submitted himself to the doctor's careful probing. *Why is my mind so blank, for God's sake?* he wondered. It was as if someone had zapped it clean. But that was more like what the Men in Black got up to. *Oh fuck, perhaps it was an inside job!*

Dr Jones sat back and considered her findings. "Clean as a whistle, David, although you've got some fillings that need attention."

Dai wasn't surprised. Wales hadn't gotten around to fluoridation. No one would have dared add anything artificial to drinking water when his grandmother was alive.

"So, David, what do you actually remember?" Dr Jones seemed to be having a tough time hiding her exasperation.

Dai furrowed his brow. "I remember leaving the Palace. The Queen offered to organise a car, but I said I preferred to walk. She looked doubtful, but she didn't try and stop me."

Dr Jones nodded. "It wouldn't be the first time someone's had too much to drink at the Palace. Some celebrities have even taken drugs there." She tut-tutted disapprovingly. "And then?"

"I was walking through the park – near the lake, I think – and I almost got hit by one of those flying disk things. It had lights around it, so it could have been a UFO with tiny aliens." Dr Jones raised an eyebrow. "It sailed past me, though. I'd probably ducked just in time – or perhaps the navigator was having a bad day.

The next thing I remember is someone shining a torch in my face."

"Constable Pritchard, you mean?"

Dai felt his jaw drop. "He was a real policeman, then?"

"Oh yes, and he remembers the encounter. He's one of the few people around who still believes in the Royal Family. He's made sure Green Park remains his patch."

"So, he didn't give me a pill to knock me out?"

Dr Jones seemed taken aback. "What pill?"

"I asked if he had some aspirin and he offered me a white pill out of a pocket. It was after that that everything went blank."

"And you swallowed it?"

"Er, yes," Dai said shamefacedly. "I did have a headache, after all."

Dr Jones groaned. "Christ almighty! No matter what I say, agents just won't read the bloody health and safety manual. And to think of the hours I've spent updating the poisons section. If it was up to me, I'd dock their salary until they did."

Dai hung his head. "Sorry, Dr Jones."

"Anyway, the damage is done now." A look crossed Dr Jones's face. Her green eye blinked, followed a split second later by the blue one. "The constable said that when he looked back, you'd gone. So, the question is, where did you go, and if you were taken, why were you put back where you started?"

"Well, I'd still say it was aliens," Dai muttered.

"Yes, well ..." Dr Jones took a deep breath. "Look, David ... er, how would you feel about going in a scanner?" she asked hesitantly. "It might just help us to know whether you've been affected internally."

Dai's grimace must have said it all. The hocus focus had an unfortunate habit of causing mechanical mayhem whenever he was exposed to EM radiation. And the private sector would charge a hefty mark-up on the repair bill.

Dr Jones heaved a sigh of resignation. "Very well, I'll take blood for some tests. You never know, David, you might have swallowed something that disagreed with you."

Specimen tube followed specimen tube. *Do I have eight pints in me?*

"So, how are the plans going for the wedding?" Dr Jones asked to pass the bloodletting time.

"We're still waiting on the Queen's diary," Dai said, trying to stop himself adding up the many millilitres of blood accumulating on the stainless steel trolley in front of him. "Will you be coming?"

Dr Jones shrugged. "Oh, I don't know. It's not easy juggling being a mother, working in the NHS and the demands of MI5."

Dai nodded sympathetically. "So, how is your daughter these days?"

Dr Jones rolled her eyes. "Up to her usual tricks, I'm afraid. She's been trying to outstare her classmates, so there've been plenty of nosebleeds. I do wish she'd stick to dogs. They can just yelp off into the undergrowth. Still, she has to learn the ropes somehow."

Dai pondered on her words. It couldn't be easy caring for a child that was a chip off the old block. And in his and Sandra's case, their daughter would have a double helping of strangeness.

CHAPTER EIGHT

After the drama of the previous day, Steve was at a loss to understand Dale's insistence on paying Number 10 Downing Street a visit before they caught their afternoon flight back home. TripAdvisor ranked the Prime Minister's official residence a dismal 757 out of 1,272 things to do in London. As far as Steve was concerned, one set of security gates was like any other. Even if tourists had been permitted to venture along the street to gawp at the 300-year-old house, all they'd see was a black-painted door with a police officer on duty 24/7 – plus Larry the Cat, Chief Mouser to the Cabinet Office, sitting on his haunches, if they were lucky. Just like the occasional White House *faux pas*, repeat instances of the marginally interesting 'Plebgate' scandal had been sanitised out of reality.

Steve felt sure Dale had some other motive for venturing out, but he wasn't letting on this crisp November morning. Steve accepted that he needed a little head space to resolve a few issues. There was also the possibility that he didn't want to spook him, given his manic attack on the meat. There was only so much running amok someone could endure – hotel staff included. When they'd arrived in the breakfast room, the waiters had grouped in a pack for safety. And the maître d' had almost jumped out of her skin when Dale asked for a table. To cap all, Dale hadn't even divulged what the episode had been about. In fact, he'd been dead to the world as soon as his head touched the pillow. Great end to their vacation.

The fact is, when Dale spoke his mind it got them into trouble, and Steve wouldn't willingly tolerate spending hours in another Metropolitan Police custody suite on this vacation. Yes, he'd go along with The Mighty Thor aspiration, and he'd even jump into the DeLorean DMC-12 as his obedient Robin, but his partner and boyfriend sure as hell needed some fine-tuning. Coarse-tuning, actually. In fact, he could do with an injection of some major mojo to get him back firing on all cylinders.

And that was only part of it. Dale had become moody, too. That morning, he'd ordered 'the full English' and mumbled darkly about needing to prepare himself for the day. It was the sort of cardiotoxic disaster Chief Scanlon would order and then tell his specialist he was scrupulously following the diet. Except the chief wouldn't have used the word 'scrupulously'. Hell, he wouldn't have been able to spell it. Perhaps it was a testosterone thing – and Dale seemed just as afflicted as the chief. Steve had noticed Dale mentally undressing Ms Jenkins. Flipping back had always been somewhere on the agenda, but his timing sucked. *Okay, I'll blame it on the EM radiation,* Steve thought rather generously, given how much it had pissed him off.

"That guy was checking you out," Dale said, staring gloomily at the plate, drawing his fork through the luridly orange yolk. He'd ordered easy over, but that had got lost in translation by the short order chef.

Steve was impressed by Dale's unexpected shrewdness so early in the day. He'd enjoyed the attention. "So what?" he said, daring him with his eyes.

"You took way too long choosing your granola," Dale said testily. "And you were doing that jiggy-jiggy thing with your hips. You were practically inviting him to bed, for Chrissakes!"

Wow, that was below the belt. But I'm not gonna rise to the bait, Steve decided.

"Well, it's not easy choosing between pecan with cranberries and country crisp chunky nuts." Steve said. He paused dramatically. "And I think you mean 'jiggling'. 'Jiggy-jiggy' is having sex. And, anyway, I wasn't jiggling my hips. I was contemplating our wedding."

Dale looked up, wide-eyed, putting on hold his doodling in the pool of tepid deutoplasm. He hadn't even drawn a smiley face. "Are you serious?"

Steve smiled sweetly. "Sure, babycakes. I mean, do we do lunch, dinner or just forget it ever happened?" That was a tad bitchy, but it had to be said. He didn't mean it, of course.

Dale seemed ready to buckle. "Oh Christ, sweets, I'm sorry. I'm being such a klutz."

Steve agreed. "So you don't fancy Ms Jenkins, then?"

The change in Dale's facial colouration betrayed him. "Er ..." was as far as he got before crumpling over, narrowly missing smearing his face with yolk. It could have been worse; he could have retorted, "I knew you were gonna say that."

"I'll make it up to you. I swear," Dale said as soon as he was back in an upright position. He looked uncomfortable. The phantom testicle grabber had evidently struck again.

The cute guy at the cereal bar chose that inauspicious moment to pass by their table. He wasn't smiling. He was smirking. And he had crumbs of granola in the corners of his mouth.

"I know your sort," the cute guy said. "You come on all available, shaking your tush, and then run back to your boyfriend, pretending nothing happened. You're a fucking prick tease, that's what."

Steve considered his options, one of which was to hide under the table. Correcting the guy's English was another.

"He wasn't and isn't ... *mate*," Dale said, tempting providence with that unique touch of British, but brutal, informality.

"Huh?" The raised eyebrow made the cute guy look lopsided.

"In fact, he was rehearsing dance moves for our wedding," Dale continued with impressive extemporisation.

The guy raised both eyebrows. Deep furrows of confusion completed the simian look.

"Oh, and by the way, you'd better hightail it back to your room if you want to prevent your bit of rough from running off with the contents of your wallet."

Mr Cute almost left his eyebrows behind on the ceiling. They could do with a trim, too. His departing "f … u … c … k!" lingered in the air. Steve was lost for words, but a wetness in the corners of his eyes said it all.

"I knew that, you know," Dale said.

Steve blinked.

"I think I'm starting to understand how to control it. If I get angry, a thought breaks free and comes to the surface." He glanced in the direction of the exit. "Like just then, for instance."

Steve reached across the table. "I guess that's gotta be better than you going all green and turning into The Incredible Hulk."

Their hands grasped tightly for a brief moment. It was England, after all. Tongues might wag. The flat screen on the nearby wall chimed for attention. Where there's breakfast, there has to be *Breakfast,* and the

British Broadcasting Corporation did it better than most. Dale had moved on to buttering toast. Steve sat mesmerised until the news bulletin was over.

"Christ! You knew he was back!" Steve hadn't expected that bolt out of the blue. And a helicopter rescue, too. So, that's why Dale needed his cell phone.

Dale shrugged. "Yeah." He was spreading strawberry jam out of a cute, silver-topped pot. The Queen probably did the same. It had to be her crest on the jar. Her Royal Highness sure got around.

"But how?" Steve asked cautiously. Dale was back in his dormant state and Steve didn't want to tempt providence.

Dale chewed a bit. "It just came to me," he said.

"Came to you?"

"Yeah. Well, it took some work. It was as if it didn't want to be discovered."

"You mean, like someone was trying to cover up Dai's disappearance?"

Dale's eyes lit up momentarily, but he went back to buttering another slice of toast. The guy needed sustenance after all the hard graft.

So, Dai had been returned, 24 hours after he'd gone missing, but in the same spot, apparently unharmed and just a stone's throw from Buckingham Palace. And Dale had known it all along and kept it secret. Amazing. Definitely one to tell their grandchildren.

"Come on, let's go to Number 10," Dale called out, leaping out of his chair even before he'd had his customary coffee.

Steve noticed the maître d' making the sign of the cross as they left. He recalled something about Polish people believing that God used Satan for his unsavoury messages, so he could see her point. There was no sign of Mr Cute in reception. Steve wondered whether they'd be making a detour to 221b Baker Street for tea with Mrs Hudson. Or perhaps she'd do two medium skinny lattes, decaf-and-hold-the-sugar as a special favour for two fellow crime fighters on vacation.

But there was no stop-off to meet some fictional landlady. Instead, it was a fast walk to Downing Street, dodging traffic and dawdling pedestrians. Steve checked around guiltily before taking a selfie of them in front of the famous street sign. It didn't quite work, though; Dale insisted on looking away from the camera, as if he had more important things to do. At least they seemed to be the only tourists heading for the security gate. Two police officers stood near the metalwork, puffing warmth into their bare hands.

Steve wondered how much the officers' attire was to impress tourists. After all, Whitehall wasn't exactly a den of thieves with drug dealers doing house calls. Their uniform was a far cry from the traditional UK bobby on the beat, and conspicuously included a stab vest stuffed with restraints, cuffs, stun gun and more, judging by the bulges. They were also carrying Heckler & Koch MP5 semi-automatic carbines. It was just like being back home. Steve had his fingers crossed Dale wasn't about to say they were police officers and needed to be let through. *Aw shit, he's opened his big mouth …*

"Good morning, Officers," Dale said, extending his hand. "My name is Lieutenant Dale Franklin and this is – " he gestured at Steve, " – my partner, Sergeant Steve Abrams, and we'd like to gain access to Number 10 Downing Street."

Steve had to admit, Dale knew how to look cool under pressure, although the frigid air must've helped. Dale's outstretched hand remained frozen in motion between the two officers. Their mouths gaped like a pair of fishes out of water. Seconds passed like minutes. A blackbird on a neighbouring portico stopped by to watch the scene. A languorous, head-to-toe sizing up completed the officers' initial evaluation. It was like being scanned through a Walmart checkout by a member of the walking dead. One of the officers flipped open his pocket book.

"A lieutenant, you say," the shorter, rotund policeman said.

Dale withdrew his hand. "Detective Lieutenant, actually." But he'd pronounced 'actually' with an accent that sounded way too English. Steve could see the officer's hackles rising. "From the Kansas City Police Department," Dale clarified helpfully. Steve definitely wouldn't have added the second part. Mention Kansas City in the wrong company and you'll have a plague of Dorothy lookalikes and Wizards of Oz on your hands.

Unfortunately, the officers started laughing. It was clearly a little more than humorous to them. Their chuckles and thigh slaps sent the blackbird off into the crisply blue yonder. That was the red rag to a bull. Dale didn't exactly start snorting and pounding his feet, but a storm cloud was definitely crossing his face. The unjolly green giant could be just around the corner.

"Er, babycakes, don't you think we should leave now?" Steve said limply, reaching for an arm. That endearment proved to be another mistake. The taller officer mimed an un-pc, faggoty wrist. Dale bent until he was almost crouching, his fingers apparently about to tie undone shoelaces. *That's strange,* Steve thought. *He's not wearing lace-ups.* Dale suddenly shot up, as if pneumatically powered, until his face was just inches away from the policeman.

"I need to speak with the Prime Minister now," Dale rasped, grimacing as he forced out the words.

The rotund police officer tut-tutted, with a smirk on his face. "Aren't we forgetting our manners … *babycakes*?"

Dale turned around slowly and seized the security

gates with both hands. "I'm gonna ask you nicely, Officer. Goddamn let me through," he growled, his eyes fixed on the entrance to Number 10. As if on cue, the front door opened and various dark-suited dignitaries emerged.

"And why should we do that ... sir?" the taller policeman said, already fingering his gun.

Dale sank to the ground, his hands still clasping the vertical bars of the gate. He looked defeated – and in agony, judging by his drawn face and gritted teeth. *Thank Christ,* Steve thought. *Perhaps we can go get our coffees now.*

The taller officer dropped onto his haunches. "Are you all right, sir?" he asked, suddenly coming over all concerned. "Perhaps you should see a doctor?"

Dale turned his head to look at the police officer. "Yeah, sure. I've already seen three of them in the last 24 hours. It's not exactly curable," he said grimly. He glanced back to the view of Number 10. "But I still need to get in there." The suits had just got into a limousine.

"So you said, sir," the officer said, shaking his head in sympathy. "Perhaps you could explain why?"

"Because there's gonna be an attempt on your Prime Minister's life," Dale said calmly, continuing his steadfast gaze. The limousine was already heading towards the gate.

For a brief moment, you could have heard a pin drop. Then all hell broke loose. The officer who'd been speaking with Dale yelled at the oncoming vehicle, frantically waving his arms as the gate opened to allow the car's passage out of the protected enclave: "Stop! Turn back!" The other officer had Dale spread-eagled on the ground within seconds. Steve stood back, feeling about as useful as a chocolate teapot. He sure wasn't about to assist with the arrest of his boyfriend. Steve crouched next to Dale's head. He wasn't going to tempt fate by touching him.

"Christ, Dale, why'd ya have to do that?" Steve said into the ear that wasn't pressed against the ground.

"I am what I am. And what I am – "

Steve sighed. "Yeah, yeah, I get it. But still …"

Just then, half-a-dozen police officers in tactical gear jumped out of a vehicle that had slammed to a halt only yards away. Their faces were set hard, with the look of grim determination the British did so well in war movies. And they weren't chewing gum, either. Steve stood up and held out his hands placatingly. *Why the fuck did I tell Dale we wouldn't need our IDs?* he thought despondently.

"So, you're the joker's boyfriend, are you?" the nearest officer sneered through a slash of a mouth. He had close-set eyes, too. His badge kept personal information to the minimum; 'SMITH' was a name that got lost in the crowd.

Steve nodded. "Sorry, Officer. He's not been himself today." He glanced back at Dale. The officer restraining his arms with his knee in Dale's back was beckoning the squad to assist getting him to his feet.

"Is he mental, then?" The officer almost spat out the word.

Steve was shocked. They'd never get away with that in the US. "Jeez, no!" he replied indignantly. "Dale's got this condition. It's called 'Testiculus cognoscitiva'." Steve was good at thinking on his feet. But it had been a bitch to pronounce. He had his fingers crossed that Officer Smith had skipped Latin class in school.

Judging by the officer's blank expression, he obviously had, but he still got the testicular part. He winced. "Sounds painful. But it doesn't exactly give him a reason to go around saying provocative things, now does it?"

Steve checked the officer's feet. They were bigger than his. It was good to know where you stood in a one-to-one situation, particularly when words were his only ammunition. He shrugged in the face of inevitable defeat. "Sure, it's unorthodox, but, the fact is, he knows."

Puzzlement crossed the officer's pinkly porcine features. "He knows what?"

"He knows things. Like that, for instance – " Steve gestured in the direction of Number 10 and the deserted limousine, its doors left wide open like some *Marie Celeste* lost on the political sea, " – and this." He made bunny ears with his first and second fingers.

Puzzlement became confusion. The officer scratched a whiskery chin.

"Except he's better at knowing simple things. More complicated stuff gets jumbled up, so he's never quite sure when things'll happen. But he hasn't been wrong yet. It's all due to entangled particles travelling back in time." The technique was obfuscation. Befuddle the enemy with the bewildering and they'll lie on their backs and wave their hairy little legs in the air. Well, it worked for the low life of Kansas City …

"I don't care whether you're a policeman or a dustman, sunshine," the officer said with a particularly unfriendly glint in his eye. "I'm taking your mate in for questioning. If you want to come along for the ride, that's your choice."

Steve groaned. *Oh fuck, not again,* he thought. He could have made a stand, but macho cops weren't like psychology professors. And he didn't have an audience on his side, either.

Five minutes later, Steve found himself in the front seat of a paddy wagon, with Dale handcuffed opposite two armed officers in the back. Darting red spots danced the pas de deux from the Sugar Plum Fairy on Dale's chest. Road bumps heralded an imminent Nutcracker suite. It was overkill, but the UK's Security Service wasn't exactly renowned for its subtlety where terrorist suspects were concerned. Steve wasn't surprised Dale kept quiet. He'd been vaguely aware of his partner being read his rights, but they'd seemed conveniently abbreviated. The driver, named 'BROWN', was blue lighting to God knows where and evidently relishing every moment of his 15 minutes of fame.

"Are we allowed to know where you're taking us?" Steve asked, not expecting a reply.

Officer Brown grunted in response and gunned the gas pedal through the next two sets of lights, brutally waking up a generous handful of London's blissfully somnambulant commuters.

Steve suddenly remembered the card that Dale had slipped into his pocket on the way out of the hotel. *The sonofabitch,* Steve thought. *He'd known all along something might happen.*

"Er, Officer, you might wanna take a look at this," Steve said, holding the card out between his thumb and index finger. He didn't want to obscure the crest and MI5's motto beneath it.

Steve watched the officer's eyes flick over the card once, twice and then, lingeringly, a third time. "Shit," he said beneath his breath. "Where the fuck did you get that?"

"The Manor," Steve replied.

Just then there was an abbreviated yell as the van clipped someone on a pedestrian crossing. Steve checked the window behind him. An umbrella lay in the middle of the road. The victim had probably been happily anticipating a date with his secretary.

"The Manor?" Officer Brown asked hesitantly, his voice quivering with fear. His colleagues behind whispered the words like a ghostly echo. "You mean you were there and they let you go?" the officer said.

"Yeah, yesterday. It was Ms Jenkins who gave us the card. She told us to use it if we ran into difficulties."

Stunned silence descended on the van's icy interior. The divine Deborah's reputation clearly extended beyond the countryside. Officer Brown reached for the radio. "Delta Whiskey, this is Tango Charlie. Cancel Paddington Green. We're taking the sus … er, *officers*, to Thames House … Yeah, Thames House, Millbank. I'll explain later. Tango Charlie out."

There'd been no mention of the hit-and-run incident, of course.

As the van pulled up outside MI5's Thames-side headquarters, Dale realised that his mind had been swimming through molasses since he'd been forced to the ground. He remembered making a quip to Steve, but that was about it. Perhaps it was an adaptive mechanism to avoid data smog. He should have gone ape shit, but he didn't. Fact is, he'd been bombarded by so much crap masquerading as knowledge during the brief journey from Downing Street that he'd needed to preserve his sanity. The officers staring at him had holes in their morals that were dug deeper than Hades, and their trigger fingers could have literally blown his lid at the slightest provocation. It had been like some ancient arcade game where it was words that were being batted. Ping: he's screwing his next-door neighbour; pong: he's defrauding the departmental account. And they were both about to be found out: court martial for one of them and grievous bodily harm (viz. attempted penile amputation) for the other.

Jeez, it's all so goddamn irrelevant! Why me, for Chrissakes! Dale cursed the whole fucking world beneath his breath.

Important stuff like when or how the Prime Minister might be assassinated was inconveniently hidden away inside Ma Bell's filing cabinet, and Dale didn't have the remotest idea where he was gonna find a key. Going ballistic might help, but he was never quite sure of the direction his anger might take. There was always the risk he'd plunge a steak knife into something other than dead meat. He wondered whether the locks would have eventually tumbled open during interrogation at Paddington Green police station. Rumour had it that the secure custody suite had air-conditioning and access to movies, so they probably went in for the kill after some softening up. Hell, they might even have had a Westinghouse washer waiting for him, with its door gaping open, its womb-like interior so inviting for someone desperate to crawl back to where they started ...

And who should be waiting for them at MI5's visitors' entrance but Deborah Jenkins herself. She looked glowingly self-satisfied despite the cold air. Dale guessed last night's assignation had gone according to plan. She shook her glossy head as he was helped out of the van, his hands cuffed behind his back. Images of Darth Vader still wouldn't let up. Steve had mentioned something about phallic symbolism. Dale's weakness was silver and metallic rather than big and black. The doors of his DeLorean opened like wings, so perhaps he had a thing for angels. And Steve was pretty angelic, all things considered. Thank God his angel had remembered the business card.

"What's Lieutenant Franklin doing in cuffs?" Ms Jenkins demanded, glaring like a latter-day Medusa at the officers either side of him. Their weapons drooped under her withering gaze, their machismo sucked dry in an instant. A few indignant mutterings later, Dale had been freed from the restraints.

"Follow me," Ms Jenkins said over her shoulder, already heading for the entrance. There was a portcullis above that looked primed to descend in an instant to decapitate offenders.

Dale glanced back at his former captors. At least he didn't have the consequences of their indiscretions to look forward to. He fleetingly thought of warning them, but that would take a whole lot more explanation.

Fate's curved arrow would strike sooner or later anyway. He wished them a happy onward journey. That was the least he could do under the dismal circumstances of his godforsaken ability. He held no real grudges for being treated like a second-class citizen. But next time he'd bring his ID.

"No dawdling, please, gentlemen," Ms Jenkins said. "You're required inside. Immediately." She made that sound like a threat.

Dale glanced around anxiously as they entered the building. The gawpers outside were already being cleared from the scene. The security equipment in the reception area was surprisingly, and reassuringly, low-tech. MI5 didn't go in for 3D body scanners that trapped the unwary. He wondered how spies entered the building. The entrance seemed too public. MI5's agents probably dropped in on harnesses via the rooftop or through camouflaged subterranean entrances, stripping off their wetsuits as they ordered a martini, shaken but not stirred. He'd never been a cloak-and-dagger sort of cop; up front and out in the open was more his kind of thing. But he could see Steve was lapping it up and busily conversing with Ms Jenkins.

"I don't wanna tell tales, Ms Jenkins, but there was a hit-and-run on the way here," Dale heard Steve say as they were waiting for the elevator.

"Indeed," Ms Jenkins said, with a casual toss of her

hair. She continued staring straight ahead at the closed door. "Collateral damage happens, Sergeant. Coming from Kansas, Missouri with its history of tornadoes, you must be aware of that." Her hollow chuckle sent shivers down Dale's spine. This was her home territory and she was making sure they knew it.

As with every other public space they'd encountered in London, there were signs dotted around banning cell phones. Dale wondered whether the internet had actually been some sort of leveller for human excesses and greed. The world seemed wide open to corruption in high places now that infelicities could be kept hidden from public scrutiny. The WikiLeaks dude had tried to prove that, but look where that got him: holed up in the spare room of some backwater embassy and costing the Metropolitan Police $20 million for three years of surveillance. Some things just weren't right and the same applied to some people. But, hey, all that maudlin talk wasn't for now. It wasn't every day that KCPD cops were offered lavish hospitality at the expense of MI5 – plus a close-up view of Ms Jenkins as she examined her complexion in the elevator's mirrored walls.

"About those police officers …" Dale said.

Ms Jenkins put a finger to her lips. Dale noticed her glance up at a strategically placed camera. The elevator continued its slow ascent to the top floor. Dale had expected a smoothly efficient whoosh, but the mechanism was probably Grade II listed as well. By the time the door opened, the pint of freshly-squeezed orange juice he'd consumed at breakfast had completed its inexorable passage into his bladder.

"I'm sorry, Ms Jenkins, I need to go to the restroom," Dale said as they stepped onto the parquet flooring. It was like being back in first grade all over again.

"Hmph," she vocalised suspiciously. "This way, please, gentlemen."

Dale looked at Steve for support, but he was already in hot pursuit of her bow-like posterior as she sashayed across the polished floor towards a nearby corridor. Dale shrugged and considered the sphincter visualisation technique that KCPD advocated to prevent embarrassment at stakeouts. That had been Steve's bright idea and it had earned him a commendation.

The room they entered seemed to be an amalgam of all the worst British spy clichés. Dark wooden panelling was interrupted by floor-to-ceiling bookshelves. The tar-coloured ceiling hinted at a lifelong nicotine addiction. A mahogany desk and matching chairs without an ounce of padding gave the impression of an occupant that enjoyed the ambience of a gentlemen's club, but without any of the comfort. A birch branch for self-flagellation had to be hidden somewhere.

"Please sit while I fetch a colleague," Ms Jenkins said, going out the door they'd just entered.

"Well, I don't know about you, but I'm gonna find the restroom," Dale said, even before they'd sat down. "You coming, sweets?"

"Sure, why not," Steve said. "You could do with someone keeping an eye on you," he added with a smirk.

The restroom was just around the corner. It couldn't have been more different from the office they'd just vacated. It was starkly white, and looked like a place for cleansing the soul as well as the body. Condom dispensers were conspicuously absent. High-power hand dryers seemed destined to strip flesh from the bone in an instant. There was no communal urinal and the cubicles had walls that went from floor to ceiling.

Peeing behind closed doors made sense when you were an uptight spook with a neurosis about having your cover blown. Colonic irrigation was probably available as an optional extra. Dale noticed that MI5 even provided miniatures of mineral water so that spies wouldn't have to sully their over-cleansed guts with London tap water. Steve had just poured some into a plastic cup. He still hadn't had his breakfast coffee, of course. He must be real thirsty.

The helpful folks at Ma Bell took that opportunity to slam home a missive. It wasn't good news. And they still had a plane to catch. *Oh fuck!* Dale thought. *This can't be happening to me!*

"Steve, don't move an inch," Dale said. "And for

Chrissakes, don't inhale." The cup was just inches from Steve's mouth, the contents glistening and sloshing gently under the bright ceiling lights.

Steve turned his head in bewilderment. Dale knew the look. 'What the fuck?' was one way of putting it. Steve still held the cup. A fraction of a millimetre of the cheapest polypropylene separated his skin from the liquid. Dale reached out with both hands and grasped the cup above and below Steve's fingers. "That's it, let me have it," Dale said, carefully taking hold of the container as if it contained something precious. Frankincense and myrrh came weirdly to mind, although the contents were better suited to making an exit rather than an entrance, and at the opposite end of one's existence.

"That's hydrofluoric acid," Dale said matter-of-factly, once he'd placed the cup safely on a flat surface. A teacher in chemistry class had once demonstrated its properties. Even glass hadn't stood a chance. It was the sort of experiment that stayed with you for life. Hydrofluoric acid wasn't as good for dissolving bodies as portrayed in *Breaking Bad*, but it was definitely lethal. An alien with acid blood was a walk in the park in comparison. "We ought to step back. Inhaling the vapour is dangerous," Dale cautioned him helpfully.

Steve was on the other side of the restroom before Dale knew it, cowering against the wall. "Jeez, dude, are you sure?" he spluttered, frantically rubbing his nostrils and lips.

That question required some quick thinking. *Would I stand up in a court of law, swear on the bible, consider the balance of probabilities and state that it was beyond reasonable doubt?* "Yeah, I'm sure," Dale said, shrugging helplessly.

Steve slumped to the floor. "Oh fuck! Now I'll have to go to an ER and we'll miss the flight. And I'm meant to be inducting new recruits tomorrow … Chief Scanlon will never believe it. Oh shit!"

Dale knelt and wrapped his arms around his partner. "Sorry, sweets. I'll make it up to you, I promise."

Suddenly, there was an insistent knock on the door. "Lieutenant Franklin! Are you and Sergeant Abrams in there?" It was Ms Jenkins's voice and she definitely wasn't in the best of moods. "You'd better not be getting up to any hanky-panky," she added sternly.

Dale and Steve looked at each other ruefully. "As if," Dale murmured, scrambling to his feet to get to the door before she forced entry into their male domain.

Ms Jenkins had her hands on her hips and she looked all set to deliver another rebuke. A man in a shiny dark suit stood next to her, his hair severely buzz cut, military style. He smiled thinly, seemingly relishing Dale's discomfort. His ID tag read: 'Major Damian Carruthers'. He was glancing at Dale's hands, as if searching for something to incriminate him with. Dale's mom had made damn sure he washed his hands after going to the toilet. The major's glassy stare was like being discovered emerging from behind the baseball pavilion, fastening one's pants with the star jock sneaking off in the opposite direction.

"Well, Lieutenant? We are waiting," Major Carruthers said, his upper lip curled at the corner. His voice was reedy and high-pitched. It had to be hard pulling off that attitude with everyone falling about laughing.

Dale glanced back into the restroom. The bottles of acid looked so innocent. Had they been intended for him? "Major, you have a situation," Dale said, looking him straight in the eye.

The major cocked an eyebrow. Ms Jenkins frowned. "We know that, Lieutenant," she said. "That's why you were diverted here. And we need to know more about the threat. So, if you'll just return with us to – "

Dale shook his head. "That's not what I mean. The situation is in there." He pointed into the restroom.

"Oh, you mean the toilets," Ms Jenkins said. "They're always getting blocked. It must be the food in the canteen." She laughed. Major Carruthers didn't bat an eye. He looked like the type who'd prefer having his nutrients fed intravenously.

"No, I mean over there." Dale pointed at the bottles and disposable cups in front of the mirror. "They're not what they appear to be."

The major looked affronted. Perhaps he also chaired the restroom committee and had been responsible for procuring the water.

"The bottles contain acid," Dale said. "Hydrofluoric acid, to be precise. It's highly toxic. And Steve may have inhaled the vapour."

Ms Jenkins and the major peered nervously into the restroom. Steve still crouched in the corner. He raised a hand feebly in acknowledgement. He looked as white as one of Dale's 800 thread Egyptian sheets.

"Oh Christ," the major said, "that's all we need!" Ms Jenkins glared at him. "Okay, okay," he sighed. "I'll call for back-up and an ambulance. And I'll get the tech lab to confirm what's in the containers. We'll need to cordon off this area for the time being."

The major sprinted off along the corridor, leaving Ms Jenkins to minister to Steve. Her designer trouser suit strained at the seams as she squatted close to him.

"Oh, poor boy," she cooed. "Does it hurt anywhere?"

Steve gave a wan smile. "I don't think so. I didn't drink any of the liquid and Dale told me not to breathe, so …" He started shivering. Ms Jenkins took off her jacket and put it over his shoulders. Dale couldn't help noticing a tattoo on the back of her neck that had been hidden by her shirt collar. He couldn't identify the image, but it looked like a pair of upside-down wings. She stood up and helped Steve to his feet. Dale would have offered to take over, but Ms Jenkins's nature was too mercurial to be trusted: all cookies and candy at one moment, and then a karate kid at the next. Her fluid movements reminded him of a well-oiled machine. All she needed was a black helmet and a light sabre. His testosterone level had to be peaking again. There was definitely more to her than met the eye. In fact, according to Ma Bell, a newly created zygote had just started its descent along the fallopian tube. Her boyfriend's situation hadn't been disclosed. What was it that female black widow spiders did to their mates? Dale hoped that it'd been a swiftly delivered bite for her boyfriend's sake.

CHAPTER NINE

Back in the top-floor office, Deborah Jenkins watched Steve like a hawk. He'd recovered most of his colour and her jacket was back where it had started the day. Dale hadn't managed another peek at the tattoo, but bats and graveyards had sprung to mind.

"Now, you're sure none of it splashed on you, Sergeant?" Ms Jenkins asked with motherly concern.

Steve nodded.

"And not a drop between your lips?"

He moved his head from side to side again.

Ms Jenkins had already examined Steve's mouth and fingers for the tell-tale whitening associated with exposure to the acid – *rather too closely*, Dale thought. He had to admit to feeling jealous of the attention she'd been giving Steve. And he was still trying to decide whether she was a femme fatale or a woman with death on her mind.

"Apparently, it can cause heart attacks if swallowed," Ms Jenkins added, confirming his morbid suspicion. "It's something to do with depleting the body of calcium."

That had to be what Steve called a double bind: behave all cosy and nice, and then slam home a fucking whammy. Whatever she was up to, it was a powerful ploy. The sucker punch had to be coming up next.

"Oh, by the way, Lieutenant, how did you know about the acid?" Ms Jenkins asked, turning to give him the benefit of her penetrating look, her deep dark eyes melting him like his mom's home-churned butter on a hot summer's day.

It wasn't quite the move Dale thought it'd be. She was still gathering information like any good spook. He touched a finger to his head. The right temporal lobe, in fact. Steve had given him a crash course in brain anatomy. Ma Bell was being strangely quiet, too. *Typical when you're being interrogated,* he thought.

"Aha ... And you're sure you didn't have a portable mass spectrometer hidden on you?"

This was getting into cat and mouse territory. *The goddamn bitch is playing with me,* Dale thought. He'd never understand the British habit of belittling intelligence with sarcasm. And he hadn't even gotten around to pointing at his testicles yet.

"Sorry," Ms Jenkins said, looking flustered. "I don't know what's got into me. After all, I wasn't questioning your ability yesterday. It must have been – "

"The chocolate nemesis?" Dale suggested. "I'm told it's extremely high in serotonin."

Ms Jenkins blushed. "Yes, well ..."

The door burst open. Major Carruthers verged on animated. His forehead bore a sheen of sweat and his hair stood on end. "Well, that's certainly got the tech chaps excited," he said, his voice squeaking. "In fact, I haven't seen them that interested since the polonium scare back in – " he floundered, " – well, whenever it was. Of course, they're disappointed it isn't the real thing. Personally, I'm just relieved we won't have to evacuate the entire building."

"Aren't you forgetting something, Major?" Ms Jenkins said, looking pointedly in Steve's direction.

The major looked momentarily puzzled, but then he seemed to make a connection. "Of course, how remiss of me." He crossed to Steve and patted him on the shoulder. "You're fortunate, Sergeant. It was only a dilute solution." He paused to extract a slip of paper out of his jacket pocket. "Hmm … a mere one per cent, in fact. But it's puzzling that it turned up here in the toilet. I believe that it's commonly employed as a rust remover. Perhaps there was a slip-up at the suppliers. It isn't good enough." He tutted his displeasure.

Dale gave Steve a thumbs-up. He'd have preferred to hug him, but MI5 wasn't KCPD and the major wouldn't have approved. Steve smiled wanly and allowed himself a deep breath. The air might be tainted with conspiracy theories and military suppression, but at least it was clean. Then Steve frowned, as if something had just crossed his mind. He raised a hand. "Er, Major, I was just wondering whether there've been any unexplained deaths among employees ... like people dying in their sleep, I mean."

The major bristled. "I'm not sure what you mean, Sergeant. As far as MI5 is concerned, all deaths are explainable."

Ms Jenkins raised both eyebrows, but she seemed to be keeping her own council on the subject. Chief Scanlon would have loudly guffawed and said, "Jeez, if only!" Dale agreed with him; sometimes deaths just happen and there was shit-all to be done about them. There'd even been the occasional case of spontaneous combustion.

Steve shrank back into the seat. "Well, I was just thinking that if the acid is in all the restrooms and perhaps the cafeteria as well, and people have been drinking it for days ... you know, a cumulative effect ... and their calcium level is getting lower and lower ... well, people could die in their sleep." He looked at the floor. That hadn't been his most authoritative explanation ever, but it did it for Dale.

Ms Jenkins broke a brief moment of silent contemplation. "Oh my God! You're absolutely right! Thank goodness I've been bringing in my own water."

The major collapsed onto the nearest chair. "Oh Christ! You'd better take over, Deborah. I believe I have need of the ambulance." He undid his necktie and reached for the phone on the desk. "We'll need to check every fucking bottle of water," he groaned.

"Follow me, gentlemen," Ms Jenkins said. She shot the major a critical glance and walked towards a bookcase stuffed with valuable looking titles. She pressed the spine of an edition of *Macbeth* and a section of the wall swung out. The room they entered couldn't have been more different to the unremitting maleness of the previous office – and it was double the size. Large windows gave a commanding view of the Thames and buildings on the far bank; Dale wondered how MI5 dealt with the threat of snipers equipped with scopes and high power rifles. A sleek flat screen monitor on the desk displayed an image of the UK similar to the one they'd seen in the Brain Lab. Next to it was an ancient black telephone, with a brown braided cord, that looked straight out of an old black-and-white movie. And then Dale noticed their luggage from the hotel. The building seemed to have a surprise lurking around every corner.

"Impressive view, Ms Jenkins," Dale said. "Bullet-proof glazing?"

"Guaranteed to resist a Hellfire II, apparently," Ms Jenkins said, looking smugly proprietorial. "And there's stealth technology, too."

"The more you look, the less you see?"

"Exactly," she said. "An electro-optical seeker would be totally fooled. Of course, it's never been tried out apart from in simulations."

"Nice phone, too. State of the art, by the look of it."

Ms Jenkins chuckled. "Oh, it's only a reproduction. Left by the previous incumbent, I'm told."

"And our luggage?" Dale said, glancing at their bags.

"Well, we rather thought you'd outstayed your welcome at the hotel," Ms Jenkins said. She gestured Dale and Steve to sit down on the white leather chairs. "It was the quantum computer that gave us the alert."

"Oh?" Dale said, raising an eyebrow.

"Well, there was the CCTV feed from the hotel dining room plus the call you made about Dai." She leaned forward to pat him on the knee. "That was spot on, by the way. We'd never have thought of looking in the middle of Green Park. Thankfully, he seems to be unaffected." Ms Jenkins got up to perch on the edge of the glass desk. "Of course, then there was your rapid exit from your hotel this morning and yet more CCTV from outside Downing Street. It was all a bit obvious. Also, I believe you encountered one of our officers in the breakfast room."

Dale and Steve shared a light bulb moment. "Mr Cute," Steve mouthed.

"Indeed," Ms Jenkins said. "He was asked to be discreet and just observe, but he got carried away – " she winked at Steve, " – as did his wallet, regrettably."

"And the check?" Dale said, glancing back at their bags.

Ms Jenkins looked momentarily puzzled. "Oh, you mean the hotel bill. It's all taken care of. 'On the house', as you say back home."

Dale nodded appreciatively. "Thanks, Ms Jenkins. We're much indebted."

Ms Jenkins inclined her head. "And us to you, Lieutenant. Dai might have suffered from hypothermia if we hadn't found him in time."

"What about the major?" Steve asked.

"Oh, Carruthers is a hypochondriac," Ms Jenkins said. "He's always going off sick with something psychosomatic."

Steve looked thoughtful. His summa cum laude brain was whirring. "But you can't be sure, Ms Jenkins. We've had mass poisonings in the US. Take Amerithrax, for instance."

"That was just one disgruntled employee of the *New York Post*, Sergeant," Ms Jenkins said.

"Not exactly, ma'am. The real perp turned out to be a microbiologist working for the FBI. An inside job, in other words. And he'd managed to rope in other conspiracy theorists."

Ms Jenkins sighed. "You're right, of course. It's rarely a lone wolf these days. And it could be messy sorting it out." She turned to Dale. "I don't suppose you've received any more intelligence about the bottles?"

Dale shook his head. "Sorry, not a peep. Just the red

flag that something was wrong. So, is there anyone who has it in for MI5?"

Ms Jenkins laughed throatily. "That's a good one, Lieutenant. There are plenty of past employees who'd like to bring us down. And a 101 terrorism suspects, of course."

"Can I ask you something, Ms Jenkins?" Steve said.

"Of course, Sergeant, as long as it's not covered by the Official Secrets Act."

Steve glanced around the office. "You're not just a PA, then?" he asked with a grin.

Ms Jenkins shot him a smile. "I'm many things, Sergeant. PA one day, general dogsbody another day … to be frank, titles get in the way. And with government cutbacks, we're all essentially generic. Also, it's easier just to be what I am."

That was Steve's sentiment to a tee. "You mean, 'M'?"

Ms Jenkins raised both eyebrows. "Actually it's 'C' and he's the head of MI6, not MI5."

Steve shrugged. He didn't appreciate being put in his place. "So, what's the difference?"

"Oh, we gave up licenses to kill ages ago."

"That sounds like an invitation to lawlessness," Steve said.

"There are higher laws, you know." Ms Jenkins crossed her legs, abruptly ending that line of questioning. "Now, about the PM," she said, fixing Dale in her sights. She swept her hair back behind her right ear. Dale noticed a tiny lens glinting in the light that he guessed was part of an ear cam. "You told the police officer there'd be an attempt on the PM's life. That's pretty specific. I'm not surprised they put you in cuffs."

Dale rubbed his wrists. "Yeah, I sorta gathered that," he muttered.

"He's so good at opening his big mouth when butch men are around," Steve said with a mischievous grin.

"So, what did you expect me to do? Lie flat on my back and converse with the stars? Thanks for the support, dude," Dale said.

"You know what I mean …" Steve said. He crossed his arms.

"Okay, okay, gentlemen," Ms Jenkins sighed, settling herself on the chair opposite. "It's been difficult for both of you, but we still need to get to the bottom of the matter. When were you first aware that a situation was imminent, Lieutenant?"

Dale checked his fingernails. He'd meant to cut them. They were getting on Steve's nerves. "Before breakfast," he said. "In the shower. There was a radio on and someone said the word 'ten'. I knew I had to go to Downing Street."

"How?" Ms Jenkins bent forward, but she kept her hands to herself this time.

"Ma Bell informed me." It felt darn good announcing the name out aloud.

"*Ma Bell?*" Ms Jenkins said. Her dark eyes widened, as if to ensnare his words.

"It was Steve's idea. He said to give it a name so that it'd feel less alien." He heard Steve groan. "That's how I receive my 'knowing'."

"Oka … y," she said.

"Yeah," Dale said. "That's what I call the information I get from the exchange inside my head. There was this preacher in bible class who used to answer every disbeliever by tapping their head with a tobacco-stained finger and saying, 'That's what the knowing is all about, boy, and don't you forget it.' Well, this is *my* knowing and there ain't anything religious about it. That's the God's honest truth, ma'am."

Dale noticed Steve making a 'stop – enough' gesture with his right hand. *Cute, but this is my fucking soapbox. Hot-diggity-damn, it felt good to be talking about it! But Steve was right. This wasn't the Brain Lab. And I shouldn't have said the word 'alien' …*

"Of course, it's all metaphorical," Dale said.

"And then?" Ms Jenkins seemed to have relaxed a bit.

Dale scrunched up his face as he relived the experience. "I got slammed at the security gate."

Concern crossed Ms Jenkins's face. "You mean you were assaulted?"

"Jeez, no ma'am," Dale spluttered. "I meant I got slammed – "

"Metaphorically?"

"Yeah, just the usual pain in the nuts." He looked down reflexively. It was getting to be a habit.

"And that's when you knew about the attempt on the PM?"

Dale made a thumbs-up. "But that's all I got, Ms Jenkins. No where or how, just the fact." He paused as he remembered what went through his mind at the time. "Come to think of it, it was like receiving a single frame of a news bulletin but without any sound."

Ms Jenkins inclined her head. Dale noticed the ear cam lens glinting again. He wondered who else was watching his interrogation. "You mean a TV station?"

Dale nodded.

"And it was in English?"

Dale couldn't be sure. If there'd been no sound, how would he have known about an attempt? Perhaps there'd been a rolling headline in English underneath. He shrugged. "I guess so, ma'am."

"My God! So, the news report could go out at any minute and there'd be nothing we could do to stop it!"

"Yea ..." Suddenly a fragment of an image popped into Dale's head. He was certain he'd seen it before. It was blurry, as if the cameraman had been caught on the hop. *Oh fuck, it's happening all over again.* Dale grasped his nuts with both hands, his cheeks turning beet red. "Sorry, sorry …" he heard himself muttering. Steve stared at him wide-eyed, his mouth shucked open. And then the shot abruptly turned crystal clear: a photo of a car's interior, the doors left wide open, objects discarded in haste on the floor.

Dale pulled himself to his feet, grimacing as he went to the window. He rested his fingers on the glass. He detected a tingle, like touching a laptop plugged in to charge. The water in the Thames looked cold but strangely inviting. His dad had tried to foster an interest in fishing, but he'd never seen any point in torturing fish with barbed hooks. The Thames used to be too polluted for fish to survive, but now it was said to be good enough to drink. Vanishing beneath the surface would be difficult without weights tied around the ankles, but at least it'd taste clean.

"Perhaps it's a sign that we need to stop taking things for granted," Dale said. He was still watching the river. A paddle boat carrying tourists passed by. He would have waved, but they wouldn't have seen the window through the stealth screening.

"Excuse me?" Ms Jenkins said. She stood up and moved to his side.

"I mean the water. We pollute the water and fishes die, then we clean it up and fishes live. Perhaps someone is trying to tell us that the water should have a say in the matter."

Ms Jenkins shook her head. "I'm sorry, Lieutenant, I'm still not getting it. You're talking in riddles."

Dale turned to look directly at Ms Jenkins. "You need to get your people to check what was left behind in the limousine. The bottles of water, in particular. They'll need full protective gear."

Ms Jenkins's face dropped to the tips of her stiletto heels. "Christ, no!"

Dale nodded gravely. "I'm afraid so, Ms Jenkins. He might want His share of divine retribution, too."

"Shit, Dale, that sure was a bolt out of the blue," Steve said as they waited in MI5's lobby with their bags by their feet. There was ten times more activity than when they'd entered. Bottles of water accumulated near the scanner, awaiting testing and disposal. "What I don't get is why your source has become so obliging. Perhaps it was the sight of her legs that did it. Mind you, if you'd said anything more, she'd have slapped a 'cease and desist' order on you. What was it she added at the end? 'Ignorance is bliss, Lieutenant.' That's an awesome comment coming from MI5. And to think, you were the one who told them where to find Dai. Jeez, there's no satisfying some people."

Dale had only half listened to Steve jabbering on. He'd been wondering whether the UK government would jerk into law an outright ban on bottled water. Still, how would they tackle the bottles already out on London's streets? And why just one per cent acid? It didn't make sense. Perhaps the idea had been to instil fear rather than annihilate the population.

He'd also been contemplating what might come after the flood of acid-tainted water; a plague of anthrax-infected insects sounded about right. Whichever way you looked at it, it sure wasn't God that was behind it, even if He'd been the inspiration.

"Actually, dude, it wasn't Ma Bell that time. It was intuition," Dale said.

"Really?" Steve said. He looked impressed, but he'd been distracted by someone who'd just entered the lobby. The individual was a good-looking dude in his 20s and he was wearing a suit. His hair, still damp, was slicked back. Perhaps he'd been for an early-morning swim in the Thames. His face seemed strangely familiar.

"Hey, guys, I hoped I'd find you before you left," the stranger said. He extended a hand.

Dale's face recognition definitely wasn't up to scratch. The operators on duty at Ma Bell remained on an extended coffee break. A smile hovered on Steve's lips. The three of them shook hands politely as if they were meeting for the first time at some crime-fighters' convention. And then the man's voice struck a chord. It definitely didn't sound Irish this time. In fact, the sing-song accent seemed more pronounced than Dale had remembered from before.

"Jeez, Steve, it's Dai Williams!" Dale said, wagging Dai's hand like an old-fashioned gas pump handle.

"Yeah, good to see you, too," Dai said. He didn't look convinced.

Steve rolled his eyes. "Sorry. It's been a difficult few days. Dale's letting off steam. And he forgot your title." He bowed dramatically. "Sir David, will you do us the honour of conversing with us mere mortals?"

Dai grinned. "Apology accepted." He placed a hand on Dale's shoulder. "Look, thanks for letting them know where to find me. That's quite a talent you have. What's the secret?"

Dale felt uncertain about explaining it to Dai. Hell, he might even try to use the hocus focus on him. "Stuff just arrives," he said.

Dai crooked an eyebrow. "Stuff?"

"As in stuff and nonsense," Steve interrupted. "Sometimes it makes sense, but often it doesn't. The theory is, it's information about future events, collected by entangled particles, sent back to the present. I guess it sorta makes sense, but ..." His shrug gave away what he really thought.

"Is that what Petros told you?" Dai asked.

"Yeah, more or less," Dale said, glancing at Steve. *If Dr Kyriakides's explanation had been a load of hooey, what the hell was left?* he wondered. *Weirdsville, Arizona, here I come …*

"You know, we'd make a great duo," Dai said with a grin. "Do you fancy setting up shop?"

"What about me?" Steve huffed. "Dale promised I'd be Robin."

Dai puffed out his chest in true superhero fashion. He eyed Steve's physique. "So, what exactly would you bring to the role, er, young pretender to the throne?"

"Well, I've got the hair, the looks and I can do a mean exclamation."

"Such as?" Dale asked, intrigued by his boyfriend's revelation.

"Holy Priceless Collection of Etruscan Snoods!" Steve said in an imitation of Burt Ward's voice. "And I can do the other 361, as listed on Wikipedia."

Dale started laughing and couldn't stop. He was vaguely aware of the looks he got from people in the lobby, but he couldn't give a shit. "Christ, I needed that," Dale said finally, tears still running down his face.

"Well, now we've got a Holy Water Shortage thanks to your detective work," Dai said, glancing at the bottles. "Not to mention a nasty case of attempted mass poisoning."

Dale examined Dai's face. It looked so friendly and open. He can't have been carrying around a lifetime of emotional baggage. It must have taken guts to walk around in public with his home-made protection against EM radiation covering his face. Dale recalled Steve saying that Dai's suit was 'way too shiny'. Okay, the cloth did seem covered in a sheen of oil, but at least he looked like a professional spook.

"I heard that Petros put you in the scanner," Dai continued. "He knows better than to try that with me. It's become something of a ritual for people visiting The Manor."

Dale felt his heart rate quickening. "Yeah ..." *Nope, I'm not gonna revisit that horror*, he decided. "So, what do you recall of your abduction?" he asked, rapidly changing the subject.

Dai sneezed loudly. "Sorry, I woke up with grass in my face." He reached into his jacket pocket to retrieve a tissue. "Trouble is, it's all so hazy. To be honest, I think it might have been a dream. I'd also had a bit too much to drink. I blame her for that." He pointed at a portrait of the Queen hanging above the security scanner. She looked disapproving at being relegated to such an inauspicious position. Given that it was her government who'd consigned EM communication to the scrapheap, it seemed appropriate that ancient X-rays were left defending her realm.

"You had drinks with Her Majesty the Queen?" Steve asked, all wide-eyed with admiration.

"Yeah," Dai said. "The dogs were there, too. She thought they had bugs in their ears." He shook his head.

"If you can't remember anything, it could have been an alien abduction. Have you checked your teeth?" Steve said. He had a glint in his eye. Dale had seen the student paper Steve wrote on the Area 51 phenomenon, and he'd done a hatchet job on the evidence. His conclusion of 'wishful thinking' hadn't gone down well with the UFO cognoscenti. And his psychology professor just happened to be an avid sky watcher.

Dai looked uneasy. "Yeah, well, UFOs aren't exactly flavour of the month around here. Medically, I'm fine, though. No holes in the teeth or that sort of thing." He leaned closer. "To be honest, they're more interested in other things flying through the sky, if you know what I mean." Dai glanced anxiously around the lobby as if he expected to see ears on walls.

"So, have you noticed any after effects – apart from the runny nose?" Steve asked.

Dai tilted his head inquiringly. "It's funny you should ask, but people have been saying I sound more Welsh. I've even been changing the way I speak. You know, muddling my words I am. See, I've just done it!"

"Yup, that's documented," Steve said. "It's the Yoda transformation. Also said to be associated with living at the top of an ivory tower with a MacBook for company."

"Do you wanna swipe him first?" Dale said, turning

to Dai. But his mind must have moved on to other things. He was checking his watch.

"Look you, I must be going," Dai said. "I'll send an invitation to the wedding. Sandra is 34 weeks now, so it has to be soon. We're waiting for her – " he glanced up at the portrait, " – to come back with some dates."

"The Queen?" Steve mouthed.

Dai put a finger to his lips. "But you mustn't say anything. She wants it kept a secret. There'll be drinks afterwards. But definitely no Dubonnet and gin."

It was no limousine this time for Dale's and Steve's journey to London Heathrow: just a standard black cab with a dome-headed driver making up for his follicular loss with small talk. He had an unnerving habit of turning to look at the back seat when he should have been keeping an eye on the road. Dale was relieved to be sitting on a seat that was actually comfortable. He'd lost weight on the vacation and his ass needed the extra padding.

"Terminal Three is it? Don't you worry, I'll get you there just as soon as. The traffic's been somethin' awful this morning. Don't know why. Must be somethin' in the water."

Dale hadn't realised that London cab drivers were imbued with a sense of irony. The driver reached for a plastic bottle and took a generous swallow. Dale saw Steve lean forward as if he was about to say something, so he shook his head to stop any interruption. Having come this far, he was damned if their journey out of the UK was gonna be cut short by a few millilitres of one per cent hydrofluoric acid.

"So, 'ow was it, then?" the driver asked with over-familiarity. He wiped a hand across his mouth and belched. On balance, Dale thought that was a good sign, although his stomach could already be going up in smoke.

"Our vacation, you mean?" Steve said. He was great at easing an imminent breakdown in communication.

"Yeah. Go sight-seeing, did you?" the driver asked.

"It was okay," Steve said, but with a giveaway droop to the tone of his voice.

"It wasn't awesome, then? Don't you Americans always say things are awesome?" the driver said.

Dale and Steve exchanged a glance. "No," they said simultaneously.

"Suit yourself," the driver said. "'ow was Tussauds?" Steve shook his head.

"And 'arrods? You must have gone to 'arrods. They used to sell elephants, you know. Don't know 'ow they got them in the lift. Then that foreign geezer went and ruined it."

Dale was ready to flip his lid all over again, but the cab's radio intervened in the nick of time. It was a news bulletin that declaimed in a serious voice: "We interrupt this programme ... attempt on the Prime Minister's life earlier today ... Londoners are warned not to drink bottled water."

Fortunately, the cab driver was able to execute an emergency stop without incurring any casualties.

CHAPTER TEN

The dark-clothed figure returned to the table and tentatively touched the outside of the cauldron. As usual, it was a few degrees warmer than the room itself, which meant it was ready for action.

Although cauldrons weren't remotely alive, they absorbed energy from their surroundings. And being matt black, they were near-perfect black bodies. In a warm environment, the furnace black surface could become too hot to touch. In fact, cauldrons had been known to hop of their own accord as a result of the metal expanding. Any imperfections in the construction could also cause a cauldron to make a screeching noise similar to nails scraping on a blackboard. There'd been productions of *Macbeth* where a cauldron left under bright lights had upstaged the actors with its antics.

The other hazard with employing a real cauldron in the play was due to issues with Shakespeare's text. It was reputed that Christopher Marlowe had left the witches' chant on his desk so that the self-styled 'Bard of Avon' would gleefully espy it, hide it in his doublet and hose and then appropriate it as his work. Although Will couldn't have known it at the time, the line 'Double, double toil and trouble' initiated the summoning of a befuddling hex. The naughty Christopher's intention had been to terminally confuse his thespian rival so that he'd be rendered incapable of scribing any more plays.

What Mr Marlowe couldn't have anticipated was the subsequent popularity of the work, which meant that countless audiences had been subjected to the heinous crime of attempted witchery. All that came to a head when Queen Victoria and Prince Albert attended a performance in Drury Lane, London. Neither of the Royals were amused by what they witnessed and the Prince Consort died shortly thereafter. *The Times* reported the cause of death as "the direst affliction of typhoid fever". The Queen considered that "a nonsense and a whitewash" and stuck to her view that witchery wasn't to be trusted and represented a threat to her commonwealth. She was right, of course; a misdirected befuddling hex could cause horrendous stomach cramps and would never have been picked up at any 19th century post mortem.

As Prince Albert discovered rather too late for his good health, an actress unaware of her witchery abilities and an authentic cauldron made a lethal combination. If the opening line was misquoted as well – substituting 'hubble' for the first 'double' – all hell could break loose. The British Shakespeare Society rightly preferred that ceiling plaster and chandeliers didn't fall onto unsuspecting audiences, so their advice was to stick with replica cauldrons and screen out actresses with long noses, pointed chins or disfiguring excrescences.

Dress was another issue. While a trio of hags helped the verisimilitude of the witches' scene, productive incantations were due to the innate skill of the witch. Pointed hats and musty rags for dresses only leadened the lily. The other consideration was the number of witches. No one could understand why Christopher Marlowe had decided on a trio, but that had stuck in the public consciousness like a boil that refused to burst. In fact, in the case of the divination hex, anything more than a single witch was overkill. The fact that a certain Ceri Edwards from Pontypridd, South Wales, had attempted the divination hex had spread like wildfire through the community. The cheek of it! Still, she'd get her comeuppance soon enough.

But back to the present. The cauldron on the table still hadn't moved a millimetre or screeched the slightest squawk. In fact, apart from a few dry runs it had lain pretty much dormant since 1872. That explained the shards of glass on the floor and the pockmarked tabletop. Simulating multiple energy streams was never straightforward. It had only been a tiny orb, but the slight wobble in the alignment had sent it careering around the room like a mad thing. But there was one picture that had remained unscathed and his gaze seemed more intense than ever. "Soon," the figure said to the room.

The sound of someone screeching at the top of her voice brought her back to the here and now.

"Coming, Mother." Christ, the cow could be such a witch! She giggled at the thought of it and said three Hail Marys.

•••

"Lieutenant, are you telling me you've got nowhere with the case?" Chief Scanlon said, his feet up on the desk. The odour of dog excrement emanated from his right sole. Dale couldn't identify the breed, but it enjoyed a rich diet. He'd brought in a mixed selection of oxynuts, but air freshener would have been more apt. In any event, the box remained unopened. The chief seemed to have embarked on a 'get healthy, get dirty, get hard' campaign and Dale wasn't in the mood to reciprocate. His nuts might have been niggling, but he wasn't getting a message about the case in question, or, in fact, any fucking case. Impotent would be another way of putting it: The Mighty Thor without his goddamn hammer.

The good Greek doctor had been dead right about EM radiation being different back home. Perhaps he should pay a visit to a friendly nuclear facility for a quick top-up of the waves that kept his 'knowing' in business. On second thought, that'd definitely agitate his nuts. He'd also been niggled by Steve's insistence on paying Joseph junior in Two Rivers another visit. Steve's excuse was that the kid wanted to show him something, but Dale suspected an ulterior motive. Relationships sucked – or cops were habitually paranoid. Both, probably.

"Sorry," Dale said, wishing to hell he could tear his acutely aware senses away from the chief's feet. "I guess it's just one of those things: sometimes it works, sometimes it doesn't. A bit like your urological problem, in fact." Dale honestly had no idea where that insight came from. It had just said 'howdy' to his frontal lobes without so much as a by-your-leave. Somehow Ma Bell had been bypassed and he'd received the information pre-filtered. *Was that the knowing finally waking up?* he wondered. One thing was certain, though. 'Hard' was missing from the chief's campaign and Dale could see that hurt.

"What?" Chief Scanlon spluttered. "I mean, who the fuck told you?"

Dale guessed he thought his wife had been telling tales. If he said she hadn't, the chief would probably head downtown to shoot his specialist. If he said she had, although she hadn't, their marriage would be over and the entire precinct would pay for it. So, he decided to let the chief stew. "Dunno," he said. "It just came to me."

Chief Scanlon put his feet where they ought to be. He paced round his office for a circuit or two. His shoes squeaked. Dale felt sorry for the carpet. The neighbourhood roaches were probably already packing their rucksacks for an overnight stay, meal included. The chief eventually settled his butt on the edge of the desk. A view of his expansive belly was almost an improvement on his feet. The chief sighed and put his hands out, palms up, ready to equivocate.

"Okay, you got me, Lieutenant." The chief looked defeated. "The fact is our sex life has been on the rocks for years." He ran both hands through what remained of his hair. "Jeez, I know I'm big, but you oughta see the size of her!"

Dale could well imagine Donna Scanlon's ample proportions. "I'm sorry to hear that, Chief," he said, doing his best to look sincere. Unfortunately, the chief's wife's body had morphed into a blubbery beached whale in his imagination, and he'd had to stifle a giggle – which Chief Scanlon had just noticed.

"Anyhow, that's my problem." He crossed his arms and looked Dale straight in the eye. "Look, Lieutenant, I'm just not getting the minor affliction that you've brought back to our fine city. Couldn't you have chosen a stick of Blackpool rock, for Chrissakes?"

Dale disagreed on both counts: it was an ability rather than an affliction – albeit unreliable and frequently irrelevant, even when it was working – and he'd never thought of Kansas City as being particularly 'fine'. Give him the beautiful, rolling Northern Plains and he'd agree with that description. But KC was way too functional in the worst possible way. And the chief's geographical knowledge had to be even worse than his if he thought Blackpool was anywhere near London.

"You're right, Chief. You've hit the nail on the head. You'd better finish what they started in the UK. You can put the cuffs on and take me to the cells. I'm a danger to everyone."

"Don't be a smartass with me, Lieutenant," the chief said, the veins on his forehead standing out like worms. "I'm trying to understand, for Chrissakes!" He cracked his knuckles and emitted a long, audible breath with way too much garlic. "Okay, Dale, take me through what happened in the UK, but try sticking to the important stuff."

Dale also sighed, but he couldn't say whether it was with relief or resignation. "The big stuff? You mean, predicting the end of the world and that sort of thing?"

The chief glared and raised his right index finger in fair warning. Dale's wind-up routine took some getting used to.

"Okay, okay. I'll give you the honest-to-God truth," Dale said. "It started as soon we got off the airplane. I had this excruciating pain in the nuts and – "

"*Nuts?*" Chief Scanlon asked. "You mean …" He pointed at his amply upholstered nether regions.

"Yeah," Dale replied bitterly. "But I was also getting these weird jumbled up ideas, kinda like Twitter on steroids, if you know what I mean."

The chief harrumphed; his pet hates were social media and baseball players abusing drugs, so Dale knew he'd be sympathetic. He nodded for Dale to continue.

"I got checked out in an ER to make sure it wasn't something physical. Would you believe it was all free and they didn't even charge me for a scan? Jeez, I don't know how they make a profit." The chief cracked the knuckles on his other hand. "Anyhow, the next day we visited Trafalgar Square. You oughta pay it a visit. Impressive statues. Awesome stone lions. Great architecture. Too many fucking pigeons, though." Chief Scanlon had extracted his cell from his pants' pocket and was checking for texts. It was a sign to cut to the chase. Dale felt sweat beading on his upper lip. It was like returning to ground zero. Perhaps Steve had been right about post-traumatic stress. He grasped the edges of the seat. "That's when I saw them," he croaked.

"Them?" the chief asked, his fingers caught mid jab above the cell phone's screen.

"The kiddies," Dale said, the Marshall's kitchen nightmare returning like the umpteenth sequel of *Nightmare on Elm Street*.

The chief's porcine fingers remained frozen.

"The triplets in the Marshall case, their mouths open,

trapped in the stroller, trying to scream ... oh fuck," Dale blurted.

Chief Scanlon put his cell on the desk. "Go on," he said. "I'm listening."

Dale shook his head, trying to erase the image. "I don't know how, but I saw them as clear as day. Then this family appeared out of the blue with the same kiddies in a stroller. They started hollering their heads off. It felt as if they were screaming at me for not saving them. And then there was the siren and the squad car and I was running ... and running ... and too goddamn late to prevent them from being carved up by the fucking SUV ... and there was just so much blood ... and their shattered bodies on the sidewalk ... oh shit ..." Dale put his hand over his mouth and rushed out of the chief's office.

At least the restroom had been vacant. He'd thrown up yellow bile. Schoolyard taunts of 'scaredy-cat' resulted in similarly vivid vomiting. Why the hell couldn't he stand up to whatever his fucking ability was doing to him? For all the patient explanation the doctor had offered, it'd had as much impact as pissing in a gale-force wind. He splashed water on his face and watched it trickle down the drain. He found the gurgle strangely comforting. It reminded him that he'd skipped breakfast. His mom had been insistent on brushing his teeth herself. She knew how to scrub. He tongued his gums for any sore spots.

Dale glanced up and saw his face shining unhealthily in the overhead lights. His cheeks looked sunken and he had bags under his eyes. What the hell did Steve see in him? The more he stared, the less he recognised his features. His hair had gone dark and was receding fast. Something was going on with his mouth: it had turned mean and pinched, like the worst sociopath you could imagine. His eyes had become small and close set. They blinked at him, slowly and menacingly. *Oh fuck! I know the face!*

Dale dashed out of the restroom, narrowly missing the chief. He was carrying the box of oxynuts. "Are you – " the chief spluttered.

"I know who it is!" Dale yelled, as he entered the Violent Crimes office. "I saw the fucker in the mirror! He's gonna kill again!"

Faces that he knew well regarded him uncomprehendingly, their voices cut short mid-sentence. Dale slammed himself onto the chair in front of the nearest workstation. He was dimly aware of Chief Scanlon drawing up a chair alongside. "That's okay, Dale, take your time." He didn't find that reassuring, as time led to the inevitable where serial killers were concerned. And this one tortured. For a brief moment of amnesic madness, Dale couldn't remember his password. Thankfully, there was a limit to the number of permutations on Steve's birthday. Jeez, his birthday was next week and he hadn't bought him a present!

Problem was, Dale couldn't place the man's name. He'd seen the face somewhere, but that was all. He'd start with a Google search. People littered the internet with their identity clueless about what they were doing. Someone else would be checking for a criminal record. He jabbed at the keyboard, trying to stop his shaking fingers from hitting the wrong keys. 'THOMAS BIGNEW' was how the name had sounded to him when he heard it inside his head.

"I'll check to see whether he's got a Triple-I," the chief said. He entered the name to search the FBI's National Crime Information Center database, then surrendered to the temptation of the oxynuts. His and other hands dived in. They watched the progress on the screen while they chewed the pastries.

Dale scrolled through the images associated with the name until his eyes glazed over. Fuck-all matched. Shit. Where the hell had he come across the man's face before? Chief Scanlon still had his eyes glued to the screen and drummed his fingers on the desk. He sure knew how to irritate. Dale sighed and reached across for his all-time favourite oxynut. As taste sensations went, Genovese pesto still rated the best. He opened his mouth ready for the rush of basil and pine nuts.

"That name could be Polish," someone said

from behind. "Try spelling it 'T-O-M-A-S-Z Z-B-I-G-N-I-E-W'".

"Yay! Give the man a p☐ czki!" a female voice said.

Dale and the chief exchanged a look. "Let's try it," Chief Scanlon said. He stabbed at the keyboard with fingers stained by beetroot pesto.

"Christ! That's him!" Dale said as he scrolled the first page of images from the search. He felt multiple sources of hot breath on his neck as people crowded around to view the screen. The air-con compensated by wafting a cool breeze across his thinning crown. It was awesome to be reminded of one's failings at moments like this. The photo was small and in low resolution, but it was definitely the individual he'd seen blinking at him in the restroom mirror. The image showed him smiling, evil and calculating, like an undertaker from hell sizing up a body. An icy coldness shivered its way up Dale's spine.

"Sexy," the female voice said.

"Yeah, you'd be right up his dark alley," a male voice said.

"Dickwad," the female voice said beneath her breath.

Dale clicked on the image. No, that can't be! He'd been redirected to the website for the City Prosecutor's Office just a block down the street. The page heading read: 'Assistant Prosecuting Attorneys'.

"You're kidding me," the chief said.

"If only. That's him," Dale said with a certainty to his voice that bore no similarity to how he felt inside. A dash to the restroom loomed again. He wondered what colour it'd be this time.

"You're absolutely sure?" the chief asked, drumming his fingers even louder.

"As fall follows summer," Dale said. But, as he registered how fucking annoying the tapping was, something bizarre was happening inside his head. It was as if someone was using a cell phone to spy inside a closet and he was the camera. He saw latex-covered hands pull away a partition and extract a pair of shoes. Were they his hands? A sudden splash of light revealed trainers spoiled by multiple dark dots. It didn't require much imagination to determine the origin of the stains. His dad would have beat him soundly if he'd messed up his shoes like that. *For Chrissakes, dude, show me your hands! I need to know!*

"Well, Lieutenant?" the chief seemed to be saying from a distance. His voice sounded different, as if it was being speeded up and then slowed down. Somewhere between Darth Vader and Looney Tunes. Darn unpleasant, whichever way you heard it. At least the tapping had finally stopped.

"He's got killing shoes," Dale said, returning with a jolt to the present. "It's a bit like Dexter and his glass slides, but a whole lot messier. They're covered with blood spatters and he hides them at the back of his closet ready for his next slaughter."

Blood had drained from Chief Scanlon's usually ruddy face. Their colleagues' fruity expletives bounced around the office like buzzards scouting for carrion.

"How the fuck do you know that?" the chief said. He'd spoke it so deliberately it seemed he'd have preferred not to ask. The chief was the sort of man who'd still use 'd'you' officiating in a marriage ceremony.

Dale shrugged. "I'm there ... or, at least, I think I'll be there."

"You what?" the chief spluttered.

"It's what my 'knowing' is all about, Chief. Meaning that events in the future are fed back to me in the present." Dale held up his hands to pacify his colleagues. They'd probably already started speed-dialling for the men in white coats and a straitjacket. "Yeah, yeah, I know it sounds screwy, but that's God's honest truth." He'd made the sign of the cross without knowing why. *Shit! Is that to protect me from myself?*

The chief scratched his head. "Christ, Dale, I don't wanna say that's a load of baloney, but ..." He looked around for support, but all he received were shrugs. "Okay, okay, so how do I explain all this to the judge when I ask for the search warrant?"

Tomasz Zbigniew didn't have a criminal record, but he did drive a 1967 V8 Chevy Impala renowned for its generous-sized trunk. They'd discovered that snippet of information from an overly talkative clerk at the Kansas Division of Vehicles whose troublesome ex also drove a Chevy, although of a lesser vintage. A rather more functional Social Security check revealed that he'd bought a condo just a few blocks from Dale's apartment. Downtown KC was clearly on the up *and* the down.

Presiding Municipal Judge O'Connor had raised a bushy eyebrow when the search warrant was requested, but he was no stranger to dealing with misconduct in public office. To his eyes, incriminating material was incriminating material, no matter the source of the intelligence. The notion of the Law being bamboozled by a suspected felon with a law degree merely added grist to his mill. A warrant for the arrest of the assistant prosecuting attorney had been the icing on the cake, and he'd have willingly gone along for the ride. But a four-course lunch, with a bottle of fine Burgundy, beckoned instead.

Dale had been given the task of identifying the location of Tomasz Zbigniew that crisp fall morning. His colleagues were far from unanimous on the appeal of marching into the City Prosecutor's Office with warrants and handcuffs. On the side of positive thinking, it was hoped the attorney would fulfil his civic duty, come quietly, and say, "It's a good collar, you've got me dead to rights, Officer." On the negative side, an egg/face scenario would be deeply embarrassing for the department.

Dale discovered with some relief that Mr Zbigniew, J.D. was on compassionate leave from the City Prosecutor's Office following two unexpected deaths in the family. That was when Dale realised how he knew the man's name and face: he'd featured in KCTV5's account of two Holocaust survivors who'd been found brutally murdered with their fingernails removed ante-mortem. Mr Zbigniew had given a touching eulogy at his relatives' funeral, although there'd been something distinctly creepy about holding the service in a crematorium. *Christ, what a sick bastard!* Dale thought bitterly. Matching DNA on the trainers would be a pain in the butt if the CSI team hadn't kept any specimens. So, it would be guns cocked and loaded and a lunchtime raid on his condo. Dale had arranged a takeout from Joe's Diner for when they got back and the chief had even offered to pick up the tab. Things were looking up.

"So, where's the Chevy?" Chief Scanlon asked as they checked the immediate surroundings of the brownstone building.

"Dunno," Dale said. "Perhaps he keeps it in a lock-up. It's a collector's item, after all."

The chief nodded without comment. His home was

a shrine to baseball memorabilia and collecting was in his blood.

A janitor was on hand with the passkeys. Dale and the rest of the posse stood back with guns raised. Chief Scanlon knocked on the door. The noise echoed along the length of the corridor, reverberating in the still, musty air. No one responded from inside the condo. The chief rapped again, louder. They heard the sound of door bolts being pulled back. "Brace yourselves," the chief said. "If he's armed, take him down. I don't want no casualties."

A head full of curlers emerged tentatively from the apartment to the left. The woman stared wide-eyed and a gasp escaped her mouth as half-a-dozen, state-of-the-art firearms swivelled smoothly in her direction. She raised shaking hands above her head. "Please don't shoot me," she whimpered.

The chief raised a mollifying palm. "It's all right, lady. You'd best be going back inside."

The neighbour lowered her hands and patted her rollers. "He's in there, you know. I heard him close the door about – " she looked at the watch on her scrawny wrist, " – an hour ago. He must be making lunch. He's got something cooking on the stove. Smells good, too." She reached into her robe and put on over-sized spectacles. "My, there are a lot of you. Has he been a bad boy, then?"

"Something like that," Chief Scanlon grumbled. He pointed an index finger at the neighbour. "Inside. Now. If you don't mind, ma'am."

"Well," she said. "I was only trying to help."

As the door closed behind the woman, the chief motioned the janitor to step forward with the passkeys. All eyes were on the door as he turned the keys in the lock. "One … two …" Chief Scanlon flicked his eyes over his troops for a fraction of a beat, "three …"

Half-a-dozen police officers lurched into the apartment like the creature from the black lagoon. Massed eyes out on stalks scanned for anything approximating to the human form. The owner had furnished the living room straight out of a cheap catalogue. There was a galley kitchen to one side and something was definitely roasting, but the cook wasn't to be seen. The Maillard reaction was developing nicely. The aroma was so rich and meaty that a cow would have turned carnivorous. Dale reached for his radio.

"Any movement down there, Mike?" he asked the officer stationed at the bottom of the fire escape.

"Nothing human," came the tinny reply, "although the south-westerly wind is gusting up to 30 miles an hour. The pressure is falling, too, so there could be a storm brewing." The officer had aspirations to be a weather anchor and he'd recently purchased a wind meter app for his iPhone.

Chief Scanlon raised an eyebrow. "Dale, you and Franco take the bedroom. We'll check the rest. There's something not right about this."

That was the understatement of the year. Chefs didn't usually leave their steaks sizzling. Dale's testicles had started aching, too, so there had to be something in the air apart from the meaty smell. And Officer Franco was smirking, which was just as bad a sign.

"Fancy a quick romp?" Franco asked, his eyebrows arched.

"Dumbass," Dale said, checking the rounds in his Glock.

"Is that a pistol in your pocket or – "

"Christ! Give me strength!" Dale muttered. He'd have a word with him later about his unprofessional behaviour.

"Right, I'll go in first. You cover me," Dale said as they approached a door on the left. He snapped on latex gloves.

"How do you know it's the bedroom?" Franco asked. His lascivious grin had morphed into puzzlement.

"I know. Trust me." As usual, Dale's cojones had had a say in the matter.

Franco shrugged and adopted a firing position as Dale put his hand around the doorknob. Their entry was executed as smooth as silk. It was too easy. The bedroom was a whole lot tidier than Dale's. He sniffed.

There was a remnant of some fragrance in the air. It was sweet and clashed with the roasting aroma that had spread throughout the apartment.

Dale and Franco swung open the doors to the closet with a co-ordinated yank. Clothes had been arranged in separate sections with neat gradations in colour. Luggage was stored on shelves at the top. If anyone had left the premises, it couldn't have been with much more than an overnighter. Dale parted the white shirts and found a barely noticeable crack in the back panel. He pressed the wood and a rectangular section swung back, revealing a cavity cut into the wall behind the closet. Dale reached in and gingerly withdrew a pair of Nike trainers.

Franco stared disbelievingly at the well-hidden evidence. "Jesus! How the fuck did you know where to look?"

Dale tapped the side of his nose. "Intuition, my friend. You ought to try it sometime."

Franco shook his head. "You're weird, man. I just don't – " He was interrupted by a dull thud from somewhere else in the apartment. "I'd better go see what's happening." He left the room with his firearm raised for action.

Dale inspected the trainers. They were exactly as he'd seen inside his head back in the department. The soles looked unworn, but the grey uppers had been liberally sprayed with dark dots. The shoes had a musty, metallic odour that was due to more than just sweaty feet. Dale checked the inside. Something had been pushed into the end of one of the shoes. The paper had been folded, origami-like, to resemble a bird. Dale almost dropped the trainers when he saw his name written on one of the wings. His heart thumping, he carefully unfolded the paper. The handwriting was small and neat: 'IT TAKES ONE TO KNOW ONE', he read. *Christ! What the fuck is going on?* He quickly pocketed the slip.

"Chief Scanlon needs you," Franco said, putting his head around the door. His swarthy, Mediterranean complexion had turned unwholesomely ashen.

Dale deposited the trainers on the bed and followed his colleague along the short corridor. Another officer pushed past. "I'll direct the paramedics," he yelled. Everyone else had gathered in the bathroom. The door had been forced open and the jamb was splintered. Chief Scanlon bent over a man lying prone on the vinyl floor. The checkerboard pattern contrasted neatly with the dark suit and white shirt on the body. Mr Zbigniew had put on a black tie for the occasion. Some unusual accessorising with black leather gloves suggested he'd chosen his funeral attire. The chief perspired heavily from his exertion.

"For fuck's sake, Dale, where've you been?" he gasped. "You take over. At least you've done basic life support." He glared at the other officers who shuffled uncomfortably.

Dale and the chief exchanged places. Dale looked down at the body. The chief hadn't opened the man's shirt and had been crushing his abdominal organs. Dale tried to avoid looking at the face as he felt for a pulse in the neck. Mr Zbigniew's complexion was deathly white, as if covered by a layer of chalk. "So, what happened?" Dale asked, as he commenced compressions.

Chief Scanlon stood half bent over, his meaty hands on his thighs, huffing and puffing like the Big Bad Wolf in a very bad mood. "Fuck," he panted. "Someone get me some fucking water."

One of the other officers filled in the story while the chief's liquid refreshment was located. "We had to break the door 'coz the janitor didn't have a key. Looks like the perp hanged himself with a belt – " he pointed at a fixture that had come away from the wall, " – so we cut him down. There was blood in the tub, but we – "

The raucous sound of what could only have been the stove's buzzer interrupted the officer's account. Dale realised he was salivating. His mom had a habit of banging on the pan when she was about to serve the Sunday pot roast. Still, he had to admit, the contents of the oven smelled pretty darn good. A bit of moderately strenuous CPR sure gave one an appetite.

"Go check what the fuck that is, Officer!" Chief

Scanlon said, after swallowing the contents of a glass in a single gulp.

"Excuse me, gentlemen," the officer said in his best English butler's voice. "I do believe luncheon is almost ready." He went off to attend to the noise.

"Jeez," the chief said with a snarl. "What have I done to deserve this crap?"

The tension in the air was thick enough to cut and serve in a sub. Dale didn't appreciate Chief Scanlon's intense scrutiny when he was just doing his job.

"Shouldn't you be giving him some air?" the chief asked pointedly, waggling a sausage-sized finger at Mr Zbigniew's mouth.

"Mouth … to … mouth … is dead," Dale said, trying to keep up the rhythm of 100 compressions a minute.

"Who said?"

"The … American … Heart … Association … in 2010."

"Oh."

Three police officers rushed through the door, bringing a halt to all further discussion about the latest CPR guidelines. They clutched their stomachs. "Shit! Fuck! Christ!" they gasped as they hurled themselves at the toilet.

The officer with pretensions to servitude made his entrance a moment later. He held an ominously smoking tray. "Ta-da!" he announced. "Luncheon is served."

Dale immediately knew why the man had put on gloves before hanging himself – and the source of the blood in the tub. "I'd … say … he's … giving …us … the … finger."

Chief Scanlon looked blank … and then looked at the tray. He put his hand to his mouth. "Jesus Christ! What a sick motherfucker!"

Like yawning, vomiting could be just as contagious given the right conditions – all of which had been met in the condo's checkerboard bathroom. As Dale puked his guts out for the second time that morning, it occurred to him that he'd forgotten to take his gloves off when he discovered the trainers. Perhaps that had never been on the cards, though. If he'd removed his gloves when he hadn't been meant to, a paradox might have rippled its way through time and obliterated God knows what. There again, if he'd taken no notice of what he saw inside his head, and had left the trainers where they were, perhaps fate would have got its own back and allowed Donald Trump to win the race to the White House. It was like being a plaything for some Mr Big who got his kicks out of waggling monumental carrots. But at least he could do CPR – not that that had made any difference to Mr Big … *Zbigniew … Christ, my head hurts!*

CHAPTER ELEVEN

Five minutes in, and Steve Abrams's second visit to the Two Rivers psych facility was already going a whole lot better than the first. The woman on intercom duty seemed imbued with the milk of human kindness, although the increasingly husky tone in her voice hinted at something more down to earth. She'd even requested his cell phone number, in case of 'administrative issues'. Steve then noticed that the sticky tape over the camera lens had been uncovered, so she could see him, although not vice versa. He'd smiled winsomely and the woman buzzed him in with a demurring sigh that probably still lingered on the line.

Inside, the unit seemed quieter than before. Steve guessed the zombie teens must have been in medicated lockdown. A patient even offered to direct him to the nursing office. It was fortuitous he'd felt the back pocket of his pants before the door closed. 'Where there's a will there's a pickpocket,' was the saying back home, but he wouldn't be pressing charges.

"To be honest, Officer Abrams, we didn't expect you back," Nurse Elliott said, after soundly scolding the miscreant. "Most who come to visit don't do repeats unless they're attorneys or relatives. I think you made quite an impression on young Joseph."

"Yeah?" Steve had heard that before and it tended not to mean undying admiration. 'Foot-in-mouth disease' was the way his mom put it. And he had size 14 feet. His psychology professor would have sewn his mouth up if he could.

The nurse nodded. "As I said on the phone, he has something to show you."

"Yeah, that's got me intrigued," Steve said. He wondered whether the kid had progressed to pecans and walnuts. "So, how's he doing?"

The nurse nodded encouragingly. "He's doing okay. The meds have made a difference. Joseph isn't out of the woods, but he's getting there. We're switching him to a day care program next week."

"You mean, basket weaving for boys and how to bake a perfect Victoria sponge," Steve said with a twinkle.

"I'll have you know, Officer, their sponge has won awards at the county fair," Nurse Elliott said. "Not to mention basket weaving being excellent for attention and concentration." He grinned. "To be honest, I wish they did do that kinda thing. It's all group this and group that. In my experience, teenagers just don't wanna talk unless someone's paying them to do it."

Steve was the exception to that rule. He'd even started a debating team in high school. "Actually, I'm thinking of going to psychology grad school and Joseph is a case

I'd like to write up. You know, brain lesions and art."

The nurse cocked an eyebrow. "Well, you'll find even more to write up now. He's taken over the art room."

As soon as Steve entered the art room, he could see Nurse Elliott hadn't been kidding. The room was awash with light, and row after row of canvases had been stacked against the walls. Joseph currently stood halfway up a ladder, recreating a scene straight out of Dante's *Inferno*. He'd located purgatory in the bottom left and paradise in the top right. Steve could imagine it as a road map for someone's righteous path. It also bore uncanny similarities to Dai Williams's description of the inside of Lady Leanne's brain. The only thing missing was Bugs Bunny sprawled on a chaise longue, chewing a carrot and saying, "Eh, what's up, Doc?"

"Whaddya think, then? It sure beats drawing peanuts," Joseph said, swivelling around on the ladder rung to check out his visitor.

Steve walked up to the painting and pointed at what appeared to be golden sex toys hovering over the lava-strewn landscape. "I bet they didn't have those in the 14th century."

"Oh, you mean the winged phalluses?" He grinned. "Wouldn't it be cool to pluck a BJ straight out of thin air?"

There was a park near Dale's apartment where getting frisky alfresco happened most evenings, but

Steve wasn't about to give the impressionable Joseph the heads-up on that. He hemmed and hawed, and examined the painting some more. It definitely wasn't portraying thin air. In fact, the fiery sky was so thick with activity that even air traffic control wouldn't have coped. Naked angels were engaged in lewd behaviour that would have made every one of the Promised Land's 72 virgins blush. Joseph still had sex on the brain, which wasn't an encouraging sign. Still, there was something to be said for getting one's fantasies out into the open, and his artwork would be good for some healthy discussion in the day care group.

"What's the painting called, then?" Steve asked. "*The Nine Circles of Hell?*"

"Oh, no." Joseph looked puzzled. "It's *Coming Out the Other Side.*"

Well, that's an original way of doing it, Steve thought. "Nurse Elliott mentioned you had something to show me. Was this it?"

Joseph jumped to the floor. "Er, not exactly, Officer," he said. He inspected Steve's face close up. "Yup, I thought so." The teenager reached into a stack of canvases and withdrew one measuring about 18 inches square. "I hope you like it." His hands were shaking as he handed it over.

Steve reversed the canvas and rotated it through 90 degrees. He'd had plenty of photos taken of him over the years, but Joseph's pen and ink drawing was a first. Somehow the boy had recalled how he'd been sitting on his first visit, and had caught his thoughtful posture and half-amused look as he'd watched Joseph draw the 3D peanut with its Dali-esque ears. He'd even added a couple of realistic-looking moles.

"See, I remembered that," Joseph said. "So, whaddya think?"

Steve realised he'd been touching the mole beneath his right eye. Dale used to kid that it made him look like Enrique Iglesias. Steve glanced at the teenager. His bright-eyed keenness reminded him of how easily his enthusiasm had been dashed by some teacher's smartass put-down. But the drawing was unnerving in its precision. Creepy, in fact.

"It's awesome, Joseph," Steve said. "But I don't get how were you able to draw that having only met me the once. Surely you must've taken a photo on a cell without my knowing?"

The teen looked shocked. "I'm not stupid enough to risk that again, Officer. And, anyway, they've all been confiscated."

Big feet in mouth strike again, Steve thought. He slapped himself playfully across the cheek. "I'm such an idiot, Joseph. Will you ever forgive me?" He dropped to one knee with his hands held up in mock piety.

Joseph giggled. "Yeah, but only if you let me show

you something else, although you'll have to promise not to tell anyone." He bounded over to a larger stack of paintings and extracted a canvas that was double the size of the previous drawing.

For once in his life, Steve was lost for words. Rather than a black and white drawing, the canvas was a photo-realistic painting, and Joseph had somehow been able to visualise him without any clothes on. It was also uncannily accurate – with the exception of the six-pack abdomen the teenager had given him. "Jeez, Joseph," he said, sweeping his hair back from his forehead.

Joseph looked deflated. "You don't like it, then," he grumbled, staring at the floor.

Steve put his hands on the boy's shoulders and looked him in the eyes. "Joseph, it's quite probably the best painting I've ever seen in my life, but – "

"Okay, okay, I know I exaggerated parts of you," Joseph said blushing.

"Er, no, not exactly – " Steve felt blood incriminating its way towards his face, " – it's just a bit weird drawing someone unclothed without seeing them naked." X-ray vision had to be a first for the art world, with the exception of the guy who dreamed up Superman for DC Comics.

"It's a painting," Joseph corrected.

"Okay, it's weird *painting* someone naked," Steve said. He sighed. "And it takes way too much explanation. I mean, I can't exactly show that to my partner."

"Well, I wasn't gonna give it you, anyway," he said with a toss of his head. "But it might go in my first exhibition," he added with a grin.

"You dare!" Steve said.

Steve caught up with the nurse as he was leaving. "I see he's given you the drawing," Nurse Elliott said.

"Yeah," Steve said. He wished he didn't blush so easily. "It's amazing. How the hell does he do it?"

"The brain damage seems to have liberated an artistic ability. That sometimes happens with people who've had strokes. He's also developed a photographic memory. Some of that might be due to the meds, but we're not sure."

"Has this happened with any of the other patients?" Steve said, already thinking of expanding his write-up.

The nurse nodded. "Yeah, we've seen something similar in other kids, although not to the extent of Joseph. One girl is writing symphonies. She was tone deaf before. Another is writing poems. The guys that developed the medication are crowdfunding the drug as a cognitive enhancer. They've named their company 'Cogniz'."

"Cool name. So, what do Joseph's folk think about his talent?"

Nurse Elliott sighed. "Well, they're not exactly over the moon. He was all set to go to Harvard Law School and follow in his dad's footsteps. But they've come round to it. Shit, they should be relieved he's pulled through! Anyhow, he's taking a year out studying art in Italy. So plenty of life classes, I guess."

"They won't know what hit them."

The nurse chuckled. "Yeah, he's certainly got a knack with his brushes."

•••

Dilys was all ears when Ceri told her about the chat she'd had with her mum. She said her parents had always suspected there was something strange about the Queen. People didn't reach the age of 88 without their fair share of gammy legs, cancer of one sort or another, going doolally and a bedside table covered with pills. Dilys thought that if it wasn't witchery, then it had to be a pact with Satan, which was almost more exciting. It had also been her idea to use her mum's kitchen for their second attempt with Granny Betty's cauldron. Dilys thought moving the cauldron to somewhere without so many memories might make it behave itself. *She's a bright spark that one,* Ceri thought.

"Are you sure your mam won't be back until later?" Ceri asked, looking out of the window at the bicycle-strewn front path. She'd almost dropped the cauldron on her right foot dodging the spare wheels and other cycling detritus.

"Of course, silly. It's her bridge club afternoon and she never leaves until she's had tea and scones," Dilys said with a sniff. She'd just tried lifting the cauldron and couldn't budge it from the floor. That had made her sweat like a pig, which didn't do much for her complexion. In fact, she'd been blushing an awful lot ever since she saw that poster in the library.

Ceri took over and hoisted the cauldron onto the solid oak breakfast bar as if it was an empty saucepan.

"I don't understand," Dilys said, shaking her head, her arms crossed sternly over her chest. "I mean, I'm just as strong as you, Ceri bach."

Ceri looked at her friend. As long as she wasn't toppled by her ample bosom, that was probably true, but the cauldron clearly had different ideas. "That's the variable mass I told you about. Don't know how it works, though," Ceri said with a shrug.

Dilys switched on the halogen spots and the two of them peered into the brightly illuminated interior of the pot. Ceri had expected it to reflect something back, but it remained a dull black that got darker the more she looked. She touched a finger tentatively just below the rim and immediately withdrew it, uttering a yelp.

"Jiw, jiw! It's boiling, Dilys bach."

"No way," Dilys said, extending an inquisitive digit towards the mysteriously self-heating vessel. "Gosh, you're right! It's scorching!" She frowned. "I don't get it. How can it be so hot? It's only a lump of mangy old iron and it's not even on the stove."

They heard a sound like metal grating against metal. It was brief but insistent and came from the cauldron. It could even have been someone rattling their chains before they had their head chopped off. Ceri enjoyed a bit of horror when she'd finished her homework.

"You hear that?" Ceri said, peering cautiously into the pot. "It sounds like it's groaning." She could feel warmth on her face. There was a curious smell, too. It reminded her of the spices her mother put in a curry, but there was something sharper as well. She coughed to clear her throat.

"That's odd, that is," Dilys said, shielding her eyes and squinting in concentration. "Perhaps it's the light. Mam's always going on about the halogens giving her a headache." She took a sniff and her face suddenly lit up. "Wow, that's like chicken tikka masala!" Her stomach rumbled loudly. "So, are we going to try the hex or not?" she said. "I'm getting hungry."

"Look, I don't need the pressure. Let me think, Dilys bach." It was only a day until Dai's wedding and Ceri wanted to find out more about the Palace's involvement. According to her mother, the Queen had arranged it herself at a nearby church, which seemed unusual. She must have had more important things to do on a Saturday afternoon. The Queen was definitely meddling.

Ceri had been surprised to be included on the invitation list. Dai had said something about bygones and burying the hatchet – or maybe that had been her mother's interpretation. Her mother had said she could go if she promised to be on her best behaviour. Well, really! She *was* 15, after all.

And she also had to practise her witchery on something. So, she'd come to the conclusion that one more attempt couldn't do any harm. She wouldn't do the whole divination hex this time. It would just be a gentle peek into what went on in the Palace. She reached into her school satchel and extracted a photo. She'd obtained it from the *Pontypridd Observer* offices. It wasn't the most flattering picture and showed her mother talking with the Queen at the opening of the new medical unit. The photographer had caught her with her mouth hanging open.

"Where are the scissors?" Ceri asked, looking around.

Dilys was busy stuffing a packet of chocolate digestives into her mouth. In between handfuls, she passed Ceri some scissors from a drawer next to the stove. Ceri trimmed the photo to remove her mother from the picture. The cropped image looked as if the Queen was talking to a vacant space. Ceri peered closer and noticed that there was something green hanging from

Her Majesty's lower lip. "Look at this, Dilys," she said, pointing at the photo. "The Queen's got a blooming garden growing in her mouth!"

The two of them cracked up laughing. Ceri wondered what counted as treason these days. "Shush," Dilys said, her voice collapsing back into giggles. "The cauldron might tell tales on us. She might feed us to her corgis." Dilys spluttered bits of biscuit all over the breakfast bar.

"C'mon, let's get on with this, Dilys bach," Ceri said, brushing away tears of laughter. "I'll put the photo in the cauldron and give it a stir. What've you got to put in it, then?"

Dilys reached into a cupboard and took out something that looked like a small doll. Ceri took one look at the miniature version of the Queen and tears streamed again. Dilys wound the key at the back of the figure and its gloved right arm waved jerkily up and down.

"Oh, that's wicked, that is," Ceri said. "Where did you get it?"

"Dad brought it back from one of his business trips. It's like one of those waving cats in Japan. He said it's meant to bring good luck so long as you keep it wound up. Of course I'm always forgetting. That's why I've put it in the cupboard with the biscuits."

Ceri added the doll to the cauldron with its arm still wagging. She tossed in some freeze-dried eye of newt and toe of frog for good measure. She consulted a slip of paper she'd taken out of a pocket. "Here's the incantation. It's just two lines, so I reckon it'll do the divination without causing any damage."

Dilys raised an eyebrow. "It'd better, Ceri bach, or my mam will never forgive me."

Ceri glanced around the pristine kitchen. "Better fill a saucepan with water just in case. That's how my mother got rid of the orb on All Hallows' Eve. She said it just fizzled to nothing."

The two of them started reciting the incantation while Ceri stirred the cauldron with an ancient wooden spoon:

She is the one who led Dai astray
She is the one whose home we open up

According to Ceri's great grandmother's book, the sound of the words did the trick by making the cauldron resonate. Female voices were said to be more effective than male voices, which explained why good male witches were rare. Inhaling helium was one way of getting around that, but chipmunk voices made cauldrons get up to way too much mischief. Another option was castration, but that had gone out of fashion apart from in the transgender witchery community.

At first, nothing seemed to be happening in the cauldron, but then they saw something like fog creeping over the bottom of the vessel. The temperature had dropped, too. As the vapour climbed up the sides, they could make out the doll's hand moving. *But was it waving hello, goodbye or saying, 'Help, I'm drowning!'?* Ceri wondered. The vapour formed into a peak in the centre, then became a ball that rose until it was just above the cauldron. It started spinning with a whooshing sound and turned translucent. Ceri and Dilys chanted louder, willing it to turn into a window looking in on the Palace. *Perhaps it'll open up inside the Queen's bedroom,* Ceri thought. It was definitely becoming clearer. Then they saw an eye whizzing around inside the ball. Or it could have been many eyes; it was hard to tell. It felt as if they were being watched. The eye blinked once and disappeared. The ball regained its vaporous quality and sank back into the cauldron. Then the mist vanished altogether.

"What the fuck was that?" said Dilys, all wide-eyed.

"Dunno," said Ceri, equally dumbstruck. "The hex definitely wasn't bloody meant to do that. Let's look in the cauldron and see what's been left behind."

They leaned over the cauldron until their heads were almost touching. The two objects they'd put in the pot were still there. Ceri cautiously plucked out the photo with some tongs and put it onto the counter. At first glance it didn't look any different, but then the sharp-eyed Dilys noticed something.

"Look, Ceri bach, she's signed it!"

Ceri looked at where Dilys's finger was pointing. It was the Queen's signature. "Gosh, you're right! But how … Let me check the doll …"

Ceri extracted the doll with the tongs. It had stopped waving its arm, but otherwise it looked like it did before they'd put it in the cauldron. Dilys turned the key to wind it up. The arm didn't wave, but the head rotated through 360 degrees and then stopped. It could have been a trick of the light, of course. As Dilys's mother had said, those halogen bulbs were far too bright. Ceri wondered what sort of lights the Queen had in Buckingham Palace. Perhaps she'd find out tomorrow. An icy draft had entered the kitchen and was lapping around their feet.

•••

"You're kidding!" Steve said, yanking at the recalcitrant zipper on his bag.

Dale paused his packing and stood with his hands on his hips. It was meant to look butch, but it failed abysmally. He had the same problem when he attempted line dancing. "Dude, do you think I'd kid about oven-roasted digits served up to Chief Scanlon with authentic Kansas City barbecue sauce?"

Steve considered that carefully. "Possibly, but it'd depend on whether I'd been restricting your diet recently."

Dale rolled his eyes. "Okay, but you gotta admit it's a pretty mean trick to play on the department."

"You think it was all planned, then?" Steve said, still tugging away at the bag.

Dale nodded. "You might say that I knew it."

"What ..." Steve couldn't quite get the words out, but at least the zipper had finally come unstuck.

"In fact, he'd left the trainers in a hidden compartment in the closet and Ma Bell let me see my finding them."

"Shit, you're kidding me!"

Dale shook his head. "There's more. He'd left a note saying, 'It takes one to know one.'"

"Jeez! So he knew that you'd go looking for them before you knew you would yourself."

Steve could see that Dale was pondering the logic. "That kinda sums it up," he said.

"Fuck! But how?"

Dale shrugged. "I was thinking of phoning the doctor to find out, but you know what he'd say."

"Yeah. Yet more entangled particles or something." Steve rubbed his eyes. "Jeez, that's just so weird. Still, the chief must be pleased you nailed the creep. Shame he's dead, though."

Dale cleared his throat. "Er, he may not be."

"What ...?" Steve's jaw had hit the floor.

"The body went missing somewhere between his

condo and the ER."

"Jesus!"

Dale chuckled. "Yeah, it's a tad too like Lazarus for comfort. Anyway, the chief isn't blaming me for the fiasco. In fact, …" Dale dug into his jacket and extracted a sheet of folded paper, which he unfolded and handed to Steve.

Steve couldn't believe his eyes. "Wow, business class seats!" The surprise sank with a thud. "Fuck – you haven't sold the car, have you?"

"Let's say the chief and I reached an amicable agreement," Dale said with a wink. "Actually, I promised to do overtime through Christmas. I also mentioned we'd be meeting the Queen. He almost prostrated himself at my feet."

At least Dale hadn't offered to do extra shifts over Thanksgiving. Meeting his folks was still the next big step in their relationship. "So, what d'you think she'll be like?"

"Hmm, a bit like Rose in *Golden Girls*. But with pearls and a tiara. And not so ditzy."

"So, we'd better be on good behaviour. No kissing coppers T-shirts this time."

"And we're taking our IDs. I guarantee there'll be no detours to custody suites on the way to the church."

Dale continued with his packing while Steve watched. He was surprised how methodically Dale approached the task. "Hey, did you hear about Staley High and Virginia Ironside?" Steve said.

"Nope, should I have? Has she been arrested for abusing minors?"

Steve laughed. "No, better. She got the axe along with Principal Davies after he was videoed at Missie B's with his hands in some guy's pants. She seems to have vanished off the face of the Earth."

"I always thought she was an alien. Jeez, those horn-rimmed glasses!"

Steve actually thought that Virginia Ironside's glasses were a positive feature. But Dale's quip about her abusing minors wasn't far off. She seemed to take a sadistic delight in belittling students who'd been summoned to Principal Davies's office. Still, it couldn't have been easy for the school dealing with the aftermath of the Marshall case.

"Chief Scanlon said the bottled water shortage in London is over," Steve continued, trying to sound tactful.

The Thames House incident hadn't been Dale's finest hour, all things considered. MI5 had concluded that the acid in the water was an inside job. The restroom they'd used catered for both sexes, so anyone on the top floor could have been the target. From what Steve had been reading about the British Secret Service, backstabbing went with the territory.

Dale went red-faced. "Yeah, but it's not easy distinguishing one bottle from another."

"So, the Prime Minister was never in any real danger?"

"Nope. Someone had been trying to save money by refilling them with tap water, so the seals were broken. I guess that's what Ma Bell picked up on. So I don't think I'll be getting a knighthood anytime soon." Dale stood up, his packing completed. "Okay, I'm done."

"Any premonitions I should know about before we head for the airport? No saving the world from nuclear Armageddon on anything like that?"

Dale looked thoughtful.

"Please, dude, don't tell me you're gonna have a *Final Destination* moment in the airport lounge!"

Dale scrunched up his eyes. "No, all clear at the moment," he said. The doorbell rang. He grabbed his travel bag and suit carrier. "Last one downstairs picks up the tab."

Steve took his time, checking they had everything they needed for the flight. They wouldn't be taking any shortcuts on this occasion. Perhaps he'd even get a photo of them with the Queen. That should convince his folks he'd done something meaningful with his life.

•••

Elizabeth Alexandra Mary Windsor pulled herself up to her full height of five feet four inches, give or take an inch. She'd developed a slight stoop over the years. 'Curvature of the spine' was how one of her personal physicians had put it. At least that sounded kinder than 'dowager's hump'. A touch of osteoporosis was probably the cause, so she had to be careful where she put her feet. Plenty of milk was advised, too. Staircases were a particular hazard, especially when they were attached to aircraft and buffeted by crosswinds.

She'd decided a long time ago that she wouldn't use a stick. Her sister had done that and it hadn't suited her at all. Mind you, Margaret's unsteadiness was more because of her predilection for G&Ts. She'd never been the same following scalding her feet when making tea. Brewing a nice pot of Earl Grey was still one of life's simple pleasures, but it was best avoided when one was tipsy.

Looking at herself in a full-length mirror was so different to seeing a photograph. She wasn't vain, but imperfections seemed more obvious when the image moved. Bits of oneself did tend to bulge. In the early days, she'd kept a scrapbook of all the photographs taken of her and Philip, but then some Palace official had interfered by appointing a press secretary. Still, the internet had brought some of the old excitement back; all she'd had to do was enter her name in a search engine and, within a blink of an eye, she could view thousands of photos taken over her reign. Some of the pictures were even of people dressed up to look like her. Helen Mirren was terribly good. There were even some women who made a living by impersonating her. Such cheek!

What she found most difficult was not to look like how people expected. Everything she wore officially was basically the same shape: not too fitted and with a pleasing fall to the fabric to help her appear taller and slimmer. Her hats followed the pattern, too, and she had an awful lot of them. She did have more informal clothes, but the standard combination of a gilet and headscarf had become just as much a uniform – and instantly recognisable. Many years ago, when Margaret wasn't wooing some young man, they used to go out on the town for cocktails and didn't bother about a disguise. Nowadays, with those unpleasant paparazzi people around, it was almost impossible to slip out incognito. Of course, the rot had set in with Diana who only had herself to blame for attracting the wrong sort.

On this occasion, it was imperative that she disappeared into the background. She didn't want to upstage the two young people getting married. Her name would be on the guest list, but she'd be listed as 'Mrs Lilibet Sinword'. Her disguise would be subtle but effective. A soft, low-brimmed hat of the sort worn by Greta Garbo would take care of her candyfloss hair and she'd foregone any make-up. The long charcoal grey skirt and high-buttoned jacket had been a couturier's experiment that she'd kept for a rainy day. The complementing shawl, draped loosely over her shoulders, was another break from tradition. There definitely wouldn't be anything tartan in sight. She'd left her customary white gloves in the drawer. It would be rather pleasant going out without an oversized handbag draped over her left arm. A silver clutch bag would be much more convenient. She'd fastened a small, silver broach to her right shoulder, but it would be hidden by the shawl. Softly tinted sunglasses had completed the transformation.

The Queen checked her watch: there was three-quarters of an hour to go and it would take her 15 minutes to walk to St James's Church in Piccadilly. She'd had a word in the right ear so that the wedding fees were waived. The Privy Purse had paid for the flowers, too.

St James's was a large church and she wondered how many guests would be in the congregation. At least it would be easy for her to slip in and out unnoticed. She'd never attended a wedding where the bride couldn't speak. She would like to have attended the reception, but that would have been too complicated. She'd invite the couple to tea instead. But definitely not for Dubonnet and gins! David had been in enough scrapes already this year.

The Queen pulled down her hat, smiled at the mirror and reached for a catch hidden in the frame's ornate decoration. The mirror swung opened smoothly with barely a squeak. She touched the initials that she and Margaret had scratched into the woodwork when they were teenagers. She reached for the rope to switch on the light. Her sister's sign, which read 'Pull me at your peril', was still there after all these years. She doubted that the dusty light bulb had been replaced since her coronation. She walked cautiously down the wooden stairs, keeping a lookout for rotten steps. A few of the bulbs had failed and she made a mental note to have them changed. On second thought, she'd exchange them herself; it would be tiresome having to disclose her secret after so many years.

The bottom of the stairs opened onto a Clapham Junction of choices. She'd used the leftmost corridor only recently, but Charles was none too happy when she'd arrived unannounced in Clarence House via the servants' toilet in the basement. She'd been fortunate it wasn't occupied at the time. "Mother, that is simply not acceptable," he'd said. She thought it entirely reasonable for mothers to want to drop in on their children every now and again. They were close neighbours, after all. Anyway, he should have been keeping an eye on her after the stroke. The doctors at the Royal Infirmary had informed her that she'd have died without David's intervention. She hadn't let on what he had done, or, indeed, what she'd been attempting to do, sitting on the bench. That would have to remain a secret like the Palace's tunnels.

The best part was emerging from the exit in St James's Park. It was one of the few original telephone kiosks left in London and had a touch of stealth technology so that it merged into the background. It also helped that the telephone was permanently out of order. Climbing out of the tunnel felt like her escape from Colditz. She could have taken a more direct route along The Mall, but she'd have had to contend with coachloads of tourists taking selfies, with her home as an ostentatious backdrop for postings on social media. She stood for a moment to watch the ducks bobbing for fish in the lake. She heard rustlings from her right as someone fumbled with what sounded like a bag of breadcrumbs.

"It's so peaceful here, isn't it?" the stranger said.

The Queen huffed to herself, but turned to examine the unwelcome intruder on her privacy nonetheless. The woman looked about ten years younger and her appearance was a little shabby. Her grey hair hung lankly around a pale face and she had dark rings around her eyes. She was the kind of person who hung around the back of crowds searching for someone to share memories with. The Queen warmed to her, although she wasn't certain why. "Yes, it is. Have you come to feed the ducks?"

The woman nodded. "It gets me out of the house."

She sighed deeply. "It's been difficult since my Jack died."
She stared across the lake and then turned back, misty-
eyed. "What about you, then? Do you live nearby?"

"Yes, we – " the Queen caught herself, " – *I* do. Quite
near, in fact."

The woman paused, staring open-mouthed. "Oh,
I'm sorry, love, have you lost someone, too?"

"Not exactly," the Queen said. "My husband doesn't
get out much these days. It's the flu, you know."

"Oh, I know, love," the woman said. "My GP is
always trying to get me to have the jab, but … well,
I can't see the point, really …" Her voice trailed off
and she resumed her watery gazing. "Sometimes I think
there's no point in …"

The Queen looked at her watch. "Goodness, I must
go. We are due at a wedding."

"Oh," the woman said. She seemed taken aback.
Going to a wedding must have seemed an unlikely
excuse considering where they were in London.

"Maybe we will bump into each other again," the
Queen said, holding out her hand.

The woman smiled sadly, but eagerly accepted the
Queen's gesture. "That would be nice. I'm here this
time most days." She froze, staring at the Queen's hand.
"Goodness! That looks valuable!"

The Queen reddened. The one thing she couldn't
disguise was Philip's wedding gift bracelet. She should

have taken it off, of course, but she'd become such a creature of habit. "Thank you, my dear. They're synthetic, of course. The original is kept with the Crown Jewels. One can't be too careful these days."

The woman laughed. "That's a good one. I suppose you're going to tell me you live in that place next." She pointed at the Palace, but forgot that she was holding the bag of breadcrumbs, which promptly emptied onto the ground at the Queen's feet. "Oops, silly me. Jack always said I was a clumsy so-and-so. Anyhow, love, what's your name?"

"El … er, Lilibet," the Queen said. She should have practised it some more.

"Lilibet?" the woman said. "That's unusual. A nice, old-fashioned name. Not like the silly names people use nowadays. I'm Emily, by the way."

CHAPTER TWELVE

Dai was already waiting in St James's Church, chewing his nails, wondering whether he'd got his tie right and generally trying to avoid thinking about everything that could go wrong. At least Sandra didn't need to be concerned about her voice drying up.

"Are you nervous?" went Dai's thought, delicately placed inside Sandra's head, assuming he'd got the layout of the church right.

"Not really," she responded in kind. Dai wondered how many feet of stone their communication had to pass through. Sandra had been rehearsing the vows and responses with the sign language interpreter. Telepathy would have been so much easier.

"Well, I am," Dai sent back. *"Going to church always reminds me of funerals."*

"Me too," she replied. Dai thought he detected a change in tone to Sandra's thoughts. Perhaps she hadn't been permitted to attend her parents' funeral. *"I wasn't,"* she added. Dai did his best to groan inwardly. He was still rubbish at using thought boxes.

"What are you doing at the moment?" Dai asked, hoping that he'd be on safer ground.

"Practising signing," Sandra responded. *"It isn't easy."*

"Any sign of the Queen?"

"Not yet. Dr Jones is keeping a look out for her. Will she be in an official car?"

"Dunno. Perhaps she'll walk here. It's not far from the Palace. Oh ... the music's started."

"I can hear it."

"Walk carefully, darling. Don't trip on the train."

Dai heard something like a giggle inside his head. Petros nudged him. "Was that the bride?"

Dai jumped. "How did you know?"

"Oh, you go all spaced out when you're on the receiving end of telepathy. It's just like me and chocolate."

•••

The Queen walked the rest of the way with a spring in her step. She couldn't recall when she last spoke with someone just as one person talking to another. Even Balmoral didn't afford her that anonymity. Perhaps she would pay St James's Park a further visit in the hope of having a longer chat.

The streets were busier than she had expected, so she was relieved to see the church spire ahead of her as she turned off St James's Square. She wasn't pleased to be sworn at by an unpleasant young man in a white van as she crossed at the junction. He had St George's Cross flags sticking out of the windows, too. Apart from that, no one had paid her much attention, which is exactly how she had wanted it, although she appreciated why widowers like Emily complained of feeling abandoned.

She was surprised to see a street market underway in the church courtyard. A young woman called out something to her. She smiled back and wondered whether she should buy something that was old and blue to give to the bride. Then she remembered she didn't carry any money. She laughed to herself. Superstitions such as the Evil Eye would be irrelevant with David around to protect his bride.

"Good afternoon, madam. Bride or groom?" the usher asked abruptly as she entered the church discreetly through a side entrance. He handed her the order of service.

The Queen hesitated briefly. "Groom," she said, although she regretted that when she noticed how empty the left side of the church was. Both of Sandra's parents had died under, what MI5 euphemistically termed, 'unfortunate circumstances'. She chose a pew halfway down the nave and sat next to a square wooden column supporting the 'upper circle'. She couldn't remember when she last visited a cinema. The days of wholesome epics like *Doctor Zhivago* seemed such a long time ago. She examined the vaulted ceiling; Sir Christopher Wren must have been on first name terms with the Almighty to build something quite so magnificent. A polite cough brought her back to the present.

"I'm sorry to bother you, madam. Are you sure you wouldn't like to move nearer the front?" the usher whispered. "As you can see, there aren't many guests."

The Queen took in all the empty spaces. "We are fine, thank you. We might need to – " she pointed at the open door at the back, " – you know …"

"Oh, of course. My nan has the same problem," the young man said. "Oops, sorry. That didn't come out quite right." He blushed and fidgeted. "Anyhow, I'd better go and rustle up a few more guests, if you don't mind. Sorry again." He backed off sideways, crab-like, waving apologetically. Most of her subjects tripped over their feet when they attempted that manoeuvre.

The Queen couldn't help smiling as the young man retreated to the safety of the front entrance. That wasn't a conversation she'd ever imagined having: a normal person talking about normal things with cack-handed informality. She looked across to the rows on the left. She hoped the pews would fill up. St Mary Magdalene Church in Sandringham could be just as quiet on a chilly winter's day. Just then, she noticed a woman sitting at about the same level as her. Or at least, she assumed the individual was a woman, as she wore black and had a covering over her head. Of course, it could be someone finishing their prayers. St James's had an open door policy that she approved of, even if it meant never being certain of one's neighbour. And it didn't comply with her government's enhanced security measures, either.

•••

"Impressive place," Steve said, staring up at the vaulted ceiling of the church. "Sir Christopher Wren built it."

"All on his own?" Dale quipped, shifting his weight on the unyielding bench. After the business class seats on the flight over, the wooden pews were like stepping back in time. He wished they'd get on with the goddamn service.

Steve gave him a playful dig in the ribs.

"Ouch!" Dale said.

"Sorry, sweets," Steve said. "I didn't mean that to hurt."

"No, no, it's not you." Dale grimaced. The pain was peaking. "It's just that – "

"Your nuts?"

"Yeah, they've started up again. Great timing." He smiled wanly and then a thought hit him like a Missouri tornado. "Jeez!" He flicked a frantic look around the church.

"What is it, Dale?"

"Something's about to happen."

"Of course, dude. They're getting married."

"Oh Christ, Steve! It's bad!" So, too, was the tsunami-like wave of panic that was threatening to engulf him. Avoiding barfing on his shiny new shoes was the number one priority. There had to be a restroom somewhere. Dai and Dr Kyriakides were looking at him strangely. The doctor came over and placed a hand on his shoulder. It should have been reassuring, but it wasn't.

"Are you all right, Lieutenant? You're looking very pale."

Dale grasped his testicles and tried to catch his breath. He wished he'd brought his cell phone for protection. He looked helplessly at Dr Kyriakides.

"Oh my God! You're having a premonition!" the doctor said, turning a lighter shade of tan, his beard bristling to attention.

"Yeah," Dale spluttered. "And it's a big one."

"What are you getting?" Dr Kyriakides asked. Dale saw him waving at Deborah Jenkins to attract her over. He mouthed something Dale couldn't make out.

Dale grasped his head. "It's weird. It's like blackness turning into a blinding light." He tried shaking his head to sort his thoughts. "It keeps repeating in a loop. No structures, no words, just … Christ, perhaps it's an explosion!"

Deborah had reached his side. She gaped at him. "You must be kidding, Lieutenant!"

Dale shrugged. "I wish …"

"Great timing," she muttered. "So, where and when?"

Dale concentrated. The image was cycling more frequently. "Dunno, but it's definitely somewhere dark."

He wished he could give her more, but Ma Bell wasn't exactly in a churchgoing mood.

Deborah motioned Dai over. "Sorry, Dai, it's urgent. Can you try pinging the lieutenant? He believes an explosion is about to happen. We need more information." She extracted a radio from a pocket and thumbed a button. "Code nine. I repeat, code nine."

Dale noticed shadowy figures in the church gallery scurrying purposefully. He guessed that MI5 agents outnumbered the congregation. Dai looked uncertain. Dale sympathised. Life couldn't get any weirder or more inconvenient. "It's okay, dude, go ahead," Dale said. "But be gentle."

Dai looked at Dr Kyriakides. "Where should I look?"

"Try the dorsolateral prefrontal cortex," the doctor said.

"Left or right?"

"Perhaps the left would be – "

"No, go for the right," Steve said. "It's more involved with waking thought and reality testing."

"Okay," the doctor shrugged. "He's the better psychologist."

Dai moved to stand in front of Dale. "This won't hurt a bit."

Dale remembered him examining the burn patient in West Hollywood. It'd been a massive leap of faith to accept what he'd done back then. And now? Perhaps they were cut from the same cloth, after all. He watched Dai's face as he engaged the hocus focus. His pupils constricted and then dilated as if he'd suddenly gone into the dark. The image inside his head continued to repeat, but the focus seemed to have shifted. The light had become golden and it was very bright. Then he heard voices: "Scaredy-cat, scaredy-cat." They sounded like the kids that used to torment him when he was little. Dale felt heat on his face despite the coolness of the church. He was getting hotter by the second. He needed to escape …

Dale looked down both sides of the church. "Oh shit," he said. "It's here."

Deborah shouted into her radio: "Code ten, code ten! This isn't a drill! We need to evacuate!" But the music had already changed and drowned out her words.

Then the door at the entrance to the nave opened …

•••

Near the front, on the bride's side, the Queen glimpsed the dark features of Deborah Jenkins. She reminded her a bit of her sister, Margaret. Her glossy hair was topped with one of those frivolous fashion items called a 'fascinator' that her granddaughters were forever wasting money on. She was talking loudly and gesticulating wildly to a young man next to her, which seemed rather rude inside a church. She would need to have a word with her. Glancing ahead, she noticed the hirsute attributes of Dr Kyriakides who was standing next to David. She didn't recognise the two men standing adjacent to them. They wore identical suits, but their haircuts were different. One of them had been bending over and seemed to be in some discomfort. Perhaps he had problems with a shoelace.

Suddenly the music changed. The Queen recognised Mendelssohn's 'Wedding March' immediately, although it had been played at the end of her ceremony rather than as she walked down the aisle. How times change. She turned to watch Sandra make her entrance. The sunlight silhouetted her dark hair, which had been arranged in ringlets cascading onto her shoulders. She looked so radiant … and extremely pregnant. And then she saw who was giving the bride away. How appropriate that it should be Emma Jones. She'd been such a help to Sandra in discovering her gift and then liberating her from the unfortunate clutches of that scoundrel Major Chisholm. To think that he'd had the nerve to place one of his spies in the Palace.

"Please watch out, Ma'am!" Goodness! That had to be David. Now, what did he mean by that?

The stained glass windows cast colourful patterns onto the motes of dust that drifted lazily in the reverberant sound of the organ. The Queen sensed a vague movement to her left accompanied by a barely detectable current of air. The woman in black had pushed back the covering over her head. The Queen was certain she'd seen the face somewhere before. The woman stood up with difficulty and opened her mouth. Time seemed to freeze as a stream of energy emerged from her mouth and coalesced with similar effusions from David and his troublesome niece. The Queen had heard of a triple-headed obliteration hex, but she'd never witnessed one before. It was one of the reasons why Mr Brown used to burn an effigy of Siandi Da'aan every Halloween at Balmoral Castle; "kill the witch's fire with fire," was the way he'd bluntly put it.

The Queen quickly checked around the church and saw that she was the only one still able to move. Deborah and some of the other guests close by her had their hands inside their jackets as if they were about to pull out firearms. The organist's hands remained above the keys, but somehow the sound lingered in the air. David seemed to be in the process of moving in front of Sandra to protect her, but he was immobilised like the rest of the guests. In the meantime, the streams of energy had assembled into a golden orb that hovered in mid-air above the pews. And it had started rotating. The Queen covered her ears against the shrieking noise it made.

"I'm sorry, Ma'am, I've let you down," the Queen heard distantly inside her head. She'd been looking at David, but his lips hadn't moved. His curious disappearance

and reappearance in Green Park, seemingly unscathed, made sense to her now. How cunning. But David's kidnapper couldn't have known about his telepathic ability.

"What should I do?" she communicated to him. The orb was spinning faster and tendrils of energy were snaking out into the church. She touched the broach on her right shoulder. It was hot under her fingers and she could feel the warmth seeping into her body. David wasn't responding. *"Are you there, David?"* she attempted again. The only thoughts in her head remained her own. After so many years of having things done for her, it felt strange to be so out of her depth. She walked over to David. His mouth remained wide open as if he was trying to scream a warning. She looked into his eyes, hoping that somehow he'd tell her what she should do. Instead, she saw the reflection of an old woman wearing a funny hat and even more ridiculous sunglasses. She sighed and placed her disguise on the floor.

As she stood up, she was sure she detected something burning. She turned and noticed the rector's richly embroidered white and gold vestments smouldering. Someone had left a bottle of water near the end of a pew. She bent down and threw the contents at the vicar's clothing. There was a brief fizzle. The priest still had his arms outstretched to welcome the happy couple. Water dripped from his face, which remained creased in a rictus of a smile. She shuddered. She'd always been suspicious of religion's trappings of power despite being the head of the Church of England. What hypocrisy. But who was she to talk. And she had her subjects to save.

The Queen walked into the body of the church, unpinned the broach and held it out under the spinning orb. One by one, the lightning streams pulled back from the far reaches of the church and formed into a huge glowing ball around the orb. The object pulsed with sinuous currents, as if thousands of serpents were ready to spit their fiery venom and reduce her to a pile of ashes. If someone had wanted to frighten her with an image of hell, they were doing an exceptionally good job of it.

She wondered what her dear sister would say if she could see her battling with this fearsome foe. They'd been brought up on Agatha Christie and Enid Blyton, and she was sure the Famous Five never had to deal with anything like this. She could imagine George's eyes dancing with excitement at the sight of it while Timmy yelped his way out of the church with his tail between his legs. Her corgis would have barked the thing back to where it came from.

But this wasn't the time to reminisce. What should she do next? If she let go of the broach, the swirling monster above her might do its worst and reduce

Piccadilly to a barren wasteland. Imagine London without Buckingham Palace – or afternoon tea at The Ritz. She tried to recall David's instructions. She closed her eyes and imagined the two of them back on the bench on the hill above Balmoral Castle. It was all a bit muddled. Her memory hadn't been so good since the stroke.

"Oh, Margaret dear, what should we do?" the Queen asked the church.

She held her breath and listened. The orb continued to wail like a banshee, but it had also developed an ominous hiss. She recalled witnessing a screeching singer shatter glass at some tawdry Royal Variety Performance. The tightrope-walking dog had been much more amusing. She glanced anxiously at the stained glass windows. She was sure she'd heard her sunglasses crack on the flag-stones. They'd been a gift from a distant king in an even more remote outpost of the commonwealth.

"Lilibet dearest, use the way," she heard whispered inside her head.

Of course! Even if David couldn't send her a message, she might be able to find out what he'd been thinking. She'd used 'the way' on him before, even if he didn't know it. She turned around to look at the stationary figures, frozen like statues. If she'd been a child, she'd have gone up and said, "Boo!" Except she wasn't a child and she had their lives and the continuing existence of countless others in her hands. Could this be what she'd been waiting for all these years?

"Sorry, David," she relayed gently before peeking inside his head. Usually she encountered embarrassed resistance and had to tease under the surface. Mr Blair always had plenty of legal obfuscations up his sleeve. This time, it was just too easy. And for someone so keen on popular culture, she was surprised to see how empty David's thoughts were. It was as if his past life had been sucked out of him. Then she saw it, carefully placed for her to find: an inverted funnel, sculpted out of something like pewter. Of course, it had to be Welsh slate!

She repositioned herself under the orb and its hellish surround. The pulsations were becoming more insistent and bulbous protrusions periodically broke the surface. She could make out faces and they seemed to be laughing at her.

"Who are you kidding, old woman?" one of them jested.

"You're too old to rule a dog's home," another sneered.

That was it. She'd had enough. How dare they mock her! She held the broach under her chin and stood with the sphere a couple of feet from her head. She felt static electricity lift her hair and a tingling sensation against her face. She closed her eyes, took a deep breath and imagined herself back at Balmoral, sitting on the same, much loved roughly-hewn bench, opening her mind to connect to the sky … funnelling everything that was evil into the vastness of space …

•••

"So, who was that old woman?" the organic preserves stallholder asked as she completed clearing up for the day. She disengaged her Beats by Dre earbuds from her tortured ear canals. Leaking hi-hats added their sizzling crispness to the air. "I noticed her smiling at you."

"Yeah? So what?" the next-door purveyor of the finest bric-a-brac said. "She looked the sort who'd recognise quality."

"Quality? Huh," her neighbour said, sniffing snootily at the sight of the randomly arranged tat on her rival's trestle table.

"Actually, she reminded me of someone … you know, that ancient actress … whatshername … yeah, that's it … Greta Garbo."

The jam seller frowned from the lack of familiarity and then cocked her head to one side. "What's that?"

"What's what?"

"There's a strange wailing noise. It's like a cross between Kate Bush and Björk."

The trestle table owner shuddered. "It's your tinnitus. I've told you before you'll go deaf from the stuff you listen to."

The stallholder shot her a glare. "Anyway, I think it's coming from the church."

"It's probably just the organ that's got stuck – or bats in the belfry objecting to the bloody wedding. I mean, why can't people be satisfied with a registry office?"

"Well, I'm going to investigate. It doesn't sound right."

Bric-a-brac followed organic preserves up the front steps of the church, listening out for something that wasn't quite ringing true. "You're right," the former said. "The noise is coming from inside."

The two of them grabbed hold of the brass rings to open the double doors, but let go immediately, their fingers sticking to the metal. "Christ, that's freezing!" organic preserves said. They tried a second time with their jacket sleeves as protection. There was some resistance and the whiny noise got much louder as they opened the doors a crack.

"Oh my God, did you see that!" bric-a-brac said. "There's something glowing!"

"Wow! It's like a fireball from Warlords of Draenor!" preserves said, her jelly-like body going all of a quiver.

The doors slammed shut of their own accord. The two stallholders looked at each other, finally in full agreement. They ran in the direction of the nearest shop to call for the fire brigade.

•••

… time must have passed, but the Queen couldn't be sure for how long. She felt strangely light-headed. She'd been thinking about her sister and her concentration had been wandering. She was still clasping the broach as if her life depended on it. In fact, it was getting hotter by the second and she'd have to drop it soon. She should have worn gloves, of course. But somehow the pain didn't seem to matter. She slowly opened her eyes and was surprised to find that she was looking into the body of the church from a vantage point high up in the roof.

Well, what a sight! There she was, an old woman with her hair standing on end – her long-suffering hairdresser would never forgive her for that – with a glowing ball hovering overhead and rivulets of energy shimmering their way up into the roof's apex. Logically, that had to mean she was dead, or else she wouldn't be having an out-of-body experience. But she was also still standing up and dead people didn't do that. And then there were the people standing around, motionless. Why weren't they bowing, curtseying and applauding her – or rushing to their monarch's assistance if she was already dead? But, goodness, it was so wonderful to be free and unencumbered. Perhaps, if she relaxed a little more, she'd float even higher. She craned her disembodied neck upwards.

"Oh, good Lord! We can see the light!" the Queen uttered silently to the infinitely welcoming cosmos.

•••

Dai's jaw ached like he'd had his mouth open for hours of root canal treatment. He checked his left hand: there was no ring. He looked over at Sandra. She stood 20 feet away next to Dr Jones. Her veil was still down and she was glancing around, clearly just as puzzled as he was.

"What happened?" she asked, her telepathy uncharacteristically hesitant. *"Are we married?"*

"Dunno," Dai replied truthfully. *"One minute I was here, the next I'm still here and my jaw aches like I've been at the dentist."*

"Well, I'm aching all over." She peered down. *"And my flowers have wilted."*

Dai inspected the single carnation in his buttonhole. It, too, was drooping. Then he noticed the body on the floor. The figure looked as crumpled as their wedding bouquets and its white hair stood on end, like a Dr Frankenstein scared shitless by his abominable creation. Its hands were held pressed together, as if the figure had been struck while engaged in prayer.

"Oh Christ, that's Her Majesty!" Dai shouted. A chord of dissonant pedal notes from the organist's abruptly relaxing feet added the frisson of a film soundtrack to the urgency of his proclamation.

Those guests who were still recovering lurched into full consciousness with hands planted over their ears.

Dr Jones staggered over to the recumbent body. "Someone call 999," she yelled over the bone-shaking racket. "And kill the bloody organ while you're about it!"

Hands dived reflexively into jacket pockets and extracted nothing but thin air. "Perhaps there's a phone in the vestry," someone said. Dai heard several pairs of feet running in search of the elusive landline. He felt he was reliving his moment of helplessness in the Scottish Highlands. There didn't seem much chance of telepathy saving the Queen's life this time. He vaguely recalled something emerging from his mouth before everything ground to a halt – and Her Majesty ending up unconscious on the floor. *Oh shit, is it my fault this time, too?*

"Of course it isn't, silly boy," the Queen communicated in a clipped tone that was still as cut glass as Granny Betty's best vase.

"You're alive, then?" Dai responded, immediately regretting that he hadn't stopped to think before he thought.

"Well, we haven't joined the spirit world quite yet," she replied with a chuckle that felt more like a tickle. *"It takes more than a triple-headed obliteration hex to dethrone us. Mind you, we do believe that our hands are rather burnt."*

Dai went over to Dr Jones who was checking the Queen's pulse. "She's okay, I think, although some of what she's saying doesn't make much sense," he said, whispering in her ear. "She was going on about an 'obliteration hex'. Perhaps her brain was starved of oxygen."

Dr Jones looked at him piercingly. Dai was sure her eyes were up to something sneaky. Mixing green and blue always spelled trouble. She turned back to the Queen and continued her examination. "You may be right, David. Something hit her for six, although I don't believe she's had another stroke. Her face is symmetrical, as you can see."

Dai looked at the Queen's face. He wished his grandmother had looked so serene on her deathbed. He was starting to appreciate the true nature of Granny Betty's demons and he had a sneaking suspicion that the Queen knew a whole lot more than she'd let on back in the Palace.

"Wise words, David," the Queen said inside his head. She opened her eyes and blinked. "Well, that was a nice rest," she announced to the church. "A cup of tea would be most pleasant. Although ..." She looked at her hands which held something silver between them. "Perhaps we were a little foolish, but at least they no longer hurt. We imagine the nerves have been damaged by the heat. It reminds us of that time when our favourite horses were caught in a fire at the stables ..." She tailed off, misty-eyed.

"I should be wearing gloves," said Dr Jones, gently taking hold of the Queen's hands.

"So should we," Her Majesty said. She shuddered and looked away.

The Queen winced as Dr Jones commenced separating her hands, starting with the base of the thumbs. Dai held his breath, his senses ready to be assaulted by the sight and smell of burnt flesh. He, too, shared memories of burnt and blackened bodies.

"Good heavens!" Dr Jones said, her jaw dropping in amazement.

The exposed palms revealed the extent of the damage. The silver surround of the broach had melted, but the stone remained attached to a pentacle design in the centre of the jewellery. Dr Jones lifted the broach cautiously from the Queen's fragile skin. Her right palm bore the shape of the broach, but otherwise looked entirely healthy. In fact, neither hand seemed burnt. The red stone, on the other hand, lacked the usual lustre of a gem and the edges of the facets were blunted and chipped. It looked as if it had been to hell and back, and not by the scenic route.

The Queen ran a finger over the stone. "The Dulled Ruby of Hallowed Life," she said reverently.

Dai and Dr Jones looked at each other, as if to say, "Eh?"

"Of course we were not sure it would still work after all these years," the Queen said. "But we still had to try."

"You knew something would happen?" Dai asked, shaking his head.

The Queen allowed herself a wry smile. "Unlike your American friend, we wouldn't say we *knew*, but we did think it might prove too good an opportunity to pass up. Sadly, we have become something of a target for extremists."

Dai guessed she was referring to the spy placed in Buckingham Palace by MI5's double-dealing Major Chisholm. His former boss was rumoured to be tending his roses under house arrest while the government decided what to do with him.

"So, Ma'am, what exactly is the 'Dulled Ruby of Hallowed Life'?" Dr Jones asked.

The Queen smiled. "It's what some people describe as an amulet. The pentacle is said to be particularly powerful against, er, *fiery* hexes. And the ruby – "

"Works like a laser in reverse?"

The Queen nodded sagely. "That is the theory, Dr Jones. But one still has to expel the transmuted energy somehow." She looked at Dai. "And that's when we recalled our little experiment at Balmoral." Her eyes twinkled in a grandmotherly way. "Although we have to admit we got a little confused between tunnels and funnels. One of those 'senior moments', we suppose."

"Wow!" Dai said, staring at the Queen. "So, you imagined a funnel to get rid of the energy?"

"Of course, David," said the Queen. "And how clever of you to think of it in Welsh slate. Impervious to flame, it would seem."

"If you don't mind me saying, Ma'am, you really are a wily old bird!" Dr Jones said.

The Queen looked surprised. "Well, thank you, Dr Jones. We do believe that is the nicest thing anyone has said to us for a very long time."

•••

"I don't suppose you've got CCTV here, have you?" MI5's Deborah Jenkins asked rather optimistically given the distinctly lo-tech environment of the vestry.

The rector fingered his damp vestments with the disdain of the precious touching the leprous. "CCTV? Oh, you mean video. Yes, of course. We've got Wi-Fi, too." He caught himself. "Sorry, my mistake. We *had* Wi-Fi."

The three of them watched the monitor as the video played back. The screen was small, but the image was crisp and in colour.

"Good Lord!" the rector said as they observed the orb forming from the streams of energy.

"Jesus!" Deborah said. She checked nervously behind her on hearing the door creak open. Dr Jones and Dai were escorting the bedraggled figure of the Queen into the vestry. "So, what the hell was that?" she said, turning back to the video monitor.

"A triple-headed obliteration hex," the Queen

said, as she was lowered gently onto a chair. "Highly dangerous and last used in 1872, if my memory serves me correctly."

Deborah and the rector looked at each other. "A hex? You mean, as in witchcraft?" he asked, incredulity spreading all over his face. "*Ma'am,*" he added, lowering his head, his ruddy complexion deepening.

"Ms Jenkins, would you get us some water, please?" the Queen said, before turning to her questioner. "We believe the term these days is 'witchery', Rector. Witches regard their ability as a calling rather than a craft. Rather like a surgeon practicing surgery, we would imagine. And they have no need to dress up to practise what they preach."

Deborah heard a harrumph from the priest as she filled a plastic cup with water from a cracked sink in the corner. If he hadn't been wearing gold, he probably wouldn't have been struck by the energy from the orb. She sniffed. There was a smell of something scorched with an undertone of damp animal. Perhaps he wore a hair shirt for penance.

"Apologies, Ma'am. It was the only thing I could find," Deborah said. The Queen viewed the water suspiciously but drank from the polystyrene cup of life nonetheless.

"Now what about the wedding?" the Queen, her eyes glinting in amusement. "Should we let a bit of foolish witchery ruin their day or continue what we started?"

CHAPTER THIRTEEN

Who would have believed that she'd be having tea at Buckingham Palace? It certainly beat afternoon tea at The Ritz, not that Sandra Williams *née* Evans had ever been to that fine establishment. It was the Queen's idea to have their wedding reception at the Palace. Her Majesty had said it was the least she could offer after the near conflagration of the congregation in the church. MI5 hadn't been too pleased on the Queen's insistence that the wedding should continue, but they'd capitulated when the rector offered to perform an abbreviated version of the service in the vestry.

Sandra glanced around the room. Staff outnumbered guests by two to one and they were seated at a table that seemed intended for state banquets, judging by its football-pitch length. Sandra felt as if she'd tumbled into a rabbit hole and happened across the Mad Hatter's tea party in full swing. She half-expected Alice to come running through the door, with Tweedledum and Tweedledee wobbling behind, in pursuit of high calorie sustenance. They wouldn't have been at all impressed by the glassy tiers of dainty sandwiches and bite-size gateaux.

Still, the tea flowed freely and there was a champagne

toast to look forward to. She wished she wasn't pregnant, as she wouldn't mind getting a little drunk. Perhaps she would anyway. 'Rat-arsed' is how her father would have put it. She recalled drinking cola and pretending it was champagne when Dai came to her room in The Manor for the first time. A smile crossed her lips. She noticed the Queen looking at her quizzically. What had she just given away? This could be a Diana moment. She had the sneaking feeling that the Queen might jump up from the table at any moment and screech, "Off with her head!" or push her down the stairs.

"You have been very quiet, my dear," the Queen said a little too searchingly. There was that unmistakeable glint in her eye that Dai had warned her about. The Queen had loosened her tongue on a previous occasion, but there was fat chance of her doing the same thing this time. Too many people were looking at her. She had a choice between smiling sweetly, grunting non-committedly or sending an apt riposte. So, she opted to do all three, which was no small feat for someone trained by MI5 to shout inside someone's head with a complete lack of empathy.

'I was thinking in private,' Sandra conveyed telepathically, accompanied by a grunt and a grin.

"Aha," the Queen said, communicating in kind, although without the additions. *That is something of a luxury these days, Ms Evans –* " she tittered into her hand,

realising her error, *"– er, Lady Williams."*

Sandra bobbed her head. *"I use thought boxes, Ma'am."*

"We know, my dear."

"I know you know, Ma'am."

"Of course you do, Sandra. David told me."

That came as a fist in the guts although she didn't show it. Her baby had felt it, too, and was kicking to get out. Sandra had to know more about the witches. Why did they want to attack herself and Dai? She would have to leave questionable allegiances until later. She shouldn't have been surprised that skull digging and skulduggery were quite so enmeshed where the Royal Household was concerned. But Dai, too? She noticed the Queen and her new husband share a look. *'I'm sorry, darling. I had no choice,"* she heard inside her head. Dai was doing his best to appear suitably contrite. She smiled to keep them all happy, but inwardly she was seething. What else had he shared?

"We should talk," the Queen said. She moved her handbag to the right side of the table. Sandra saw one of the footmen take his cue and scoot the dogs out of the room. The rest of the waiting staff extracted earplugs from their liveried jackets and inserted them in their ears. They stood to attention to await further instructions.

The Queen cleared her throat and looked across the table. "My great great grandmother ... Queen Victoria

– " she smiled as if enjoying some memory, " – was unusually interested in magick. So much so that she kept a journal in which she recorded what she believed were instances of witchery. Her husband, Prince Albert, bought Balmoral Castle principally for her to observe what our Scottish friends were getting up to. Unfortunately, he died after they attended a performance of *Macbeth*. She believed that was because of a Welsh actress dabbling in the dark arts. His death spurred her on to use Ynyshir Hall in Wales in a similar fashion to Balmoral, and it subsequently became the Wooden Torch Institute."

Sandra noticed that one of the American detectives looked puzzled. He'd been introduced as Steve Abrams. He was far too handsome to be a police officer. "Sorry, Ma'am, but don't you mean Torchwood?" he asked.

"Oh no, young man," the Queen said. "The Wooden Torch Institute is far more real than Torchwood ever was." Her expression softened. "Actually, we suggested the title for the television series. We thought it might be useful to help light the way." She smiled at her play on words.

"And then the Wooden Torch Institute moved to a Jacobean manor house in Oxfordshire," Dai said, "with stone lions called Patience and Fortitude guarding the entrance."

"Indeed," the Queen said. "Princess Margaret and

I discovered Queen Victoria's journal in the drawer of a locked bureau. We found it to be most interesting reading. Queen Victoria was greatly concerned by the enmity between the various factions of witches and she feared it might tear the Empire apart. Her monitoring stations allowed her to keep a check on their activities. Unfortunately, her ghillie John Brown was in alliance with Scottish witches and very nearly eradicated their Welsh counterparts."

"By burning the effigy of Siandi Da'aan every year at Balmoral, you mean?" Dai said.

"Exactly," the Queen said. "It was crude, but it proved to be an effective form of population control. Fire has long been a way of eliminating witches and burning the effigy destroyed the foetus in the witch's womb."

Sandra had been feeling increasingly uneasy and all the talk about killing babies only made her feel worse. There was something about what the Queen had said that struck home, but she didn't yet know why. *"And so where do I fit into all of this?"* She chided herself for omitting the 'Ma'am' again. She knew she was acting like a spoilt child.

The Queen smiled gently. "Sandra has just asked me how this might concern her. Would anyone care to hazard a guess?"

Sandra observed blank faces. Even her husband was

keeping strangely quiet.

The Queen extended her hand to touch Sandra's fingers. Sandra felt a tingle course its way up her arm. She tried to move her hand away, but her brain was refusing to connect with her extremities. "You must have been most upset by your mother's death, my dear," the Queen said. "We seem to recall that it was a car accident."

Sandra nodded glumly. She didn't understand why the Queen was raking over the same old ground. She'd been through it countless times with Major Chisholm. The bastard had never let her forget it.

"And we gather you blamed yourself." the Queen said.

Sandra inclined her head. Tears still welled up far too easily. She felt hideously exposed in the over-decorated ballroom with its stuffed antique chairs and even stuffier footmen. Her legs shook under the table. Some wedding reception this was turning out to be. Why the hell had Dai agreed to it? They could have been off on their honeymoon weekend by now.

"You were not to blame, you know," the Queen said softly, but still far too audibly in the huge, and far from private, space.

This is getting ridiculous, Sandra thought to herself, *I'm walking out of here.* She pushed her chair back and made to get up. Dai was looking daggers at her. She didn't want to hear what he'd say when they got home. She was angry with him, she was furious with herself and she was hopping-mad with the Queen. How could the bitch say such a thing?

"We understand," the Queen said, patting her hand. "In fact, it was your father. He made you believe you tampered with the brakes. Unfortunately, the silly man misdirected the hex and got into the affected car with your mother." She tut-tutted. "Such a dreadful undoing for all concerned."

Sandra couldn't believe what she was hearing. The stuff about witches and hexes was pure mumbo-jumbo. The guests around the table were as open-mouthed as she was. They didn't believe the Queen, either. Of course she was to blame. She remembered cutting the brake cable as clearly as yesterday – not to mention the look on her mother's face as she stared out of the car window at her murderous daughter. So, why the fuck was her husband telling her, *"Yes, it's all true."*?

Sandra rocked in her seat, her eyes shut to the stares of hate she knew she was getting. She felt warm, protective hands around her – hands that she didn't deserve. She was a monster. She'd killed her parents. She deserved to be locked up for good and her baby taken away from her. "No, you're wrong," she said softly but clearly. Her voice seemed to echo around the room, the words taunting her with the flat denial. Dai held her tighter. She only half-registered that she'd got her voice back.

"Your father was a witch who then became a warlock," the Queen said. "He meddled in the darker side of magick. Unfortunately, young girls were involved. Your mother found out and threatened to expose him." She raised her shoulders in a delicate shrug. "It was as simple as that."

Something seemed to have changed in the ballroom. It was almost imperceptible, but the motes of dust seemed more at ease and the sunlight streaming through the endlessly tall windows was a little warmer.

"And me?" Sandra said, looking first into Dai's eyes and then back at the Queen.

"You are not a witch, my dear," the Queen said. Sandra thought she detected relief in her voice. "You are someone with a paranormal ability, which makes you far more of a threat to witches. They are helpless without their potions, cauldrons and wooden torches. You can do it all with your mind."

Sandra nodded. She'd probably known it all along. Perhaps it was something ingrained in the walls of The Manor that had encouraged its reluctant visitors to accept the truth about themselves. Discovering her voice was unexpected, but it had happened once before in the Queen's presence when she and Dai went to Balmoral Castle. Apart from that, she'd been silent for years. She was relieved, but it wasn't enough to prevent her from shivering.

"And then, of course, there is your husband, who must be of huge concern for witches with limited abilities," the Queen said. "So, when it came to your wedding, it was an ideal opportunity for someone to settle a score or two."

It was a lot to take in. Sandra was still reeling at her father's duplicity. Rediscovering her voice seemed almost an irrelevance.

"But there is more, my dear," the Queen said. The glint in her eyes had returned. "Although David isn't a witch – " Sandra saw him silently mouth, 'Phew!', " – his great grandmother, Elizabeth Williams, was probably the greatest witch ever. So, given that your father had the calling, it is highly likely that your child will inherit from both."

Sandra realised that it was she who was open-mouthed now. "My baby, a witch?" she asked.

"With paranormal powers," Dai said. "A super-superbaby, in other words. She might even be able to ping." He'd have had to tell Sandra sooner or later.

Sandra nodded. She was dumbstruck, but in a good way. It was finally all making sense. Even what her father did to her seemed to be fading into the past. She looked around the room at the other guests, trying to imagine what they'd made of the story. Dale and Steve had seemed totally engrossed. Did they have witches and warlocks in Kansas City? Perhaps there was a grain of truth in the story of the Wicked Witch of the West, after all.

•••

"So, Your Majesty, what actually happened in the church yesterday?" Dale said, eager to break the silence. He could see that Sandra was still struggling with the Queen's revelations. Jeez, they all were! "I mean, I've seen fires, but that was sure unlike any fire-setting I've ever witnessed before."

"Put simply, Lieutenant," the Queen said, "David was used as a Trojan horse. During his period of incarceration, a witch we believe to be Elspeth Brown – a descendant of Mr Brown – found his Achilles heel and introduced a fire-setting hex into his body. The hex obliterates organic matter but leaves inorganic material untouched. So, when the fire brigade arrived, they would have found piles of clothes, but no bodies."

"Clever, Ma'am," Dale said. "But Deborah Jenkins mentioned seeing three streams of energy on the church's video. I guess that means there were three Trojan horses in all."

The Queen sighed deeply. "That is a highly pertinent comment, Lieutenant. We believe that Elspeth Brown included David's niece and also herself as vessels for the attack, thereby completing the triple-headed obliteration hex. Of course, self-sacrifice amongst witches has a special significance and may actually enhance their powers."

Dale whistled through his teeth. "Hot diggity, Ma'am! That's some MO. And to think all I brought to the party was knowing there'd be a fire."

Steve nudged him with an elbow. "Remember it's Her Majesty the Queen you're talking to!" he whispered tartly.

The Queen looked at Dale sternly. It was like being back at Sunday school all over again. "Young man, your compatriot Mark Twain once said: 'Truth is stranger than fiction, but it is because fiction is obliged to stick to possibilities that truth isn't.'" The Queen smiled coyly. "You must excuse an old woman for using obscure quotations. We find they are a bit like doing crossword puzzles. They are so good for the brain. *The Times* is still the best, of course."

Dale saluted. "Gotcha, Ma'am." He had an aunt like that, although her puzzles were on the back of cereal packets. He leaned across the table. "But one thing that's still bugging me is how you put out the fire. I mean, you didn't exactly have a hose with you."

The Queen glanced at what Dale took to be a bone china cup. "You see the steam coming off from this tea, Lieutenant?"

Dale nodded. Perhaps the Queen was going to say

that she huffed and puffed and blew the fire out.

The Queen continued with her explanation: "We see our world like a cup of tea: somewhere between cold and hot, typically murky, and with whispers of unrest emerging from the calm surface."

"That's deeply metaphorical," Steve said in his partner's ear. Dale wasn't convinced. Plain loony is how he'd have put it under usual circumstances.

"So, when we realised what was about to occur," the Queen said, "we imagined hoovering the carpets at Balmoral and sucking up the destructive force of the hex – "

"Into the vacuum of space, Ma'am?" Steve said.

"Exactly!" the Queen said. "We are not nearly as adept as David in these endeavours, but it did the trick. Did you know that the hoover was invented in the United State of America? By a Mr Hoover, we believe. Not J Edgar Hoover, of course." She chuckled. "Sadly, one doesn't hoover often, but we do find the pastime most therapeutic – a bit like ironing, really." She looked wistfully at the carpet.

"So, Ma'am, how did you manage to stop before it went too far?" Dai asked eagerly. "You know, like at Balmoral when …" Dale could see he was getting into dangerous territory. Details of her space-time incursion was kept under wraps, on a need-to-know basis.

"Oh, that was easy, David. We thought about putting

our feet up and having a Dubonnet and gin. It was really rather exciting." The Queen sighed. "It is amazing how one can teach old dogs new tricks. Who would have thought …" She was becoming pensive again.

"What I don't understand, Ma'am, is how the whole witchery thing remained hidden," Steve said. "Surely we'd have known about it, what with all those movies and books?"

"A good point, Sergeant … Abrams, is it?" Steve nodded, beaming at the Queen's acknowledgement. "The Institute realised they had to do something," she continued. "There were too many reports of people going to hospital with strange injuries. Burns from wooden torches and misfired hexes were particularly common. The cover story was spontaneous lightning strikes, but the BBC's health correspondents were becoming suspicious. So, we had a word in a certain publisher's ear …"

"You're saying that was a goddamn smokescreen all along?" Dale said. "Jeez! Who would have thought it?"

"Precisely," the Queen said. "So, if someone went to hospital complaining of being afflicted with a crucifix hex or a nasty case of hobgoblin poisoning, no one batted an eyelid. It was brilliant, even if we say so ourselves."

"And then the government blew it out of the water," Dai said.

The Queen sighed. "Unfortunately, yes. Without radio waves to dampen the witches' excessive activity, it suddenly became open season, with the Scots against the Welsh, the Welsh fighting with the English ... I mean, really." She tut-tutted her exasperation. "I'm afraid MI5 have rather had their work cut out dealing with indiscriminate hexes."

"And now, Ma'am?" Steve asked keenly. "If you've sent something that was meant to destroy us into outer space, is that the end of it?"

The Queen looked up at the ceiling. Dale could guess what she was about to say.

"There's a certain rule that dictates what happens to undelivered hexes," the Queen said, turning to Dai, "Your aunt and a certain young lady named Ceri should know all about *that*."

"They come back to haunt one, Ma'am?" Dai said.

The Queen nodded sagely. "Exactly, although it is a little difficult to predict when. Suffice to say, one should be keeping an eye on the sky for many hundreds of glowing balls."

Hearing that, Dai was relieved they'd moved from the top of a tower block to a first floor flat. He took a quick look at his bride. She was happily talking to Steve. Amazing. Who would have believed that she could recover her voice just like that? At last the truth was finally out in the open. But what would happen now that the Queen had exposed herself as an adversary of witches? He wasn't exactly out of the woods, either. His kidnapping ordeal remained as blank as ever. At least his speech was back to normal. Perhaps the attack of Welshness was a sign of his body attempting to deal with the hex. Granny Betty would have expected nothing less.

So, how was the hex put into him? Christ, perhaps it was in the Pringles! No, he'd vomited them over his shoes. Aha, he'd remembered that. He also vaguely recalled a white van, although there was a lot of them around. Rumour had it that the police used 'Mobile Interrogation Units' to deal with the pressure on Paddington Green. *Hmm, a witch in a white van with an obliteration hex kept under her pointed hat? No, Dai, that's getting crazy.*

"So, what will you be doing next, Ma'am? A trip in Sir Richard Branson's Virgin Galactic, perhaps?" Dai asked.

The Queen smiled the wisdom of nearly fourscore years and ten. She inclined her head. *"Actually, we believe there is more work to be done here and we are counting on you assisting us."*

What could he say to that? *"Of course, Ma'am, I remain your humble servant."*

The Queen moved her handbag to the opposite side of the table. "More tea, anyone?" she said, returning to her guests. "Darjeeling or Earl Grey? Both are excellent, although we prefer Earl Grey in the afternoon. We find it so refreshing. Of course, Philip hates it and calls it 'slanty-eyed tea'."

Dai watched as footmen leaped back into action, freed from their Borg-like hibernation. The guests had laughed politely at her much-practised joke. The Queen seemed surprisingly back on form despite the bizarre events in the church. And he *was* her humble servant. A quote from *Star Trek* came to mind: "I have been ... and always shall be ... your friend." It always brought tears to his eyes, but, for once, what bubbled up was based in reality. He reckoned there'd be exciting times ahead on this insignificant little planet called Earth.

The footmen had just discreetly poured glasses of champagne. Dai felt hot breath around his ankles. A corgi or dorgi – he was still useless at telling them apart – was panting for attention. He bent down and inspected one of its ears. The little black mites were still at home. One jumped species onto his finger. Close up, it moved rather jerkily and had a tiny silvery protrusion, which he was certain nature had never intended. The Queen had been right all along: it was a nanobug and probably of Chinese origin. With the mobile phone industry on the decline, their factories were occupied making even smaller things to get on people's nerves. No wonder she'd sent the dogs out.

"You see what we mean?" the Queen said inside his head, pointing at the offending technology. *"The little blighters are all over the place. But we won't let that spoil our annus mirabilis."* She stood up, holding a flute of champagne.

"Please be upstanding for Her Majesty the Queen," one of the footmen intoned solemnly.

"Please raise your glasses," the Queen said, smiling broadly. "To Sir David Williams, soothsayer to ourselves the Queen of England, Scotland, Northern Ireland and – " she winked at Dai, "– most definitely Wales, and his charming bride, Lady Sandra."

As they tipped their glasses, Dai became aware of a tinkling sound that didn't seem related to the bubbly drink. Sandra had gone ashen and she had her hands on the arms of the chair, as if in the process of lifting herself up. Her waters had broken … onto the priceless Chippendale chair … and the heirloom Axminster carpet … and just a few feet away from the Queen.

"Can someone call for an ambulance?" she said shakily.

CHAPTER FOURTEEN

The Queen had been most understanding about the mess on the carpet. Her Majesty had slipped into the maternal mode in the blink of an eye and had ordered a limousine and outriders to take Sandra to hospital. She'd even offered for Sandra to go to the Lindo Wing at St Mary's, Paddington, the private maternity unit used by the Royal Family. That had been a tough call, but Granny Betty would have rolled over in her grave and cursed the lot of them if Dai had taken the soft option.

"Well, that was certainly a dramatic end to a wedding reception!" Dr Jones said as they arrived in the maternity unit. "And I hadn't even finished my champagne."

Dai shuffled his feet. "I feel really bad about the carpet. I can't exactly offer to replace it on the salary MI5 pay me."

"Well, at least Sandra finding her voice should make the midwife's job a whole lot easier," Dr Jones said. "Let's go and see how she's doing."

A couple of hours later, they were starting to regret the wisdom of Dr Jones's remark. Sandra's vocal cords might have been unused for years, but there was no doubting her ability to swear like a trooper.

Dai also discovered that telepathy was an effective

way to do the visualisation exercises Sandra had been taught to manage pain – when she wasn't screaming at everyone, of course. It took him back to the days when they first met in The Manor and exchanged imaginary bouquets of flowers and drank virtual champagne. There'd been fireworks and symphony orchestras, too, but he'd save those until after the baby was born. He'd been warned they could be in for a long wait.

"Jesus Christ! Why won't the fucking thing come out!" Sandra yelled after pulling heavily on the Entonox before the next contraction peaked.

"Because it's a baby, dear, and babies do what babies want," the generously proportioned midwife said, smiling grimly. Dai noticed that she wore a large, wooden cross around her neck. He wondered whether she endured the swearing as penance for all her overeating.

Eventually, the baby did pop out with a wholly unimpressive plop. By then, everyone was so exhausted that the delivery came as an anti-climax. Dai had long since forgotten the *son et lumière* celebrations. The most impressive feature of the new-born child was her hair, which was unusually abundant and raven black. She had strikingly dark eyes, which bore into you as you gazed on her sweet face. The midwife completed her night's duty by placing the baby in a cot by the side of Sandra's bed. Dai settled himself in the chair alongside. The three of them had definitely earned a restful night.

•••

The phone rang by the bedside. It didn't have the usual sound Steve remembered from back in Dale's apartment. It definitely seemed more strident and insistent. He grumbled to himself and reached for the handset.

"Yeah …" Steve said sleepily. The caller's accent was strange but somehow familiar. It wasn't American. The voice mentioned a baby. Steve jolted into alertness within seconds. "Oh fuck! Yeah, sure, we'll be there. Don't do anything."

Steve nudged the recumbent form next to him. Dale was snoring and the noise sounded like his DeLorean backfiring. Steve planted a kiss on his lips. It was a pretty mean way of getting his attention, but it wasn't every day that a knight called for their help. Dale grunted and extended his arms from under the bed clothes like a sleepwalker fumbling in the dark.

"That was Dai," Steve said, watching for a reaction. "The baby has gone missing."

"You must be fucking joking!" Dale said, jerking bolt upright. His eyes seemed to stare right through him.

Steve shrugged. "Sorry, sweets. That's the honest-to-God truth. The baby was taken at – " he checked his watch, " – zero three forty. The graveyard slot, in other words." He grimaced. "I didn't mean that, of course."

Dale was out of the bed in an instant, pacing the room and grasping his head with both hands. "Fuck! I should have seen that coming."

Steve stood by observing his boyfriend. He'd come to appreciate that Dale's manic moments should be watched rather than interfered with. Dale went to the window and drew back the curtains. It was still dark outside. His body looked so slim and muscular from behind. Dale started tapping his fingers on the window like some weird version of Morse code.

The doorbell rang, rudely interrupting Dale's communication with the outside world. Steve grabbed a bath towel and dashed to the door, hoping it was news about the baby. He opened the door a crack. It was someone they'd seen on their side of the church, although they hadn't been introduced. What with all the business with the hex, he probably wouldn't have remembered anyway. The woman wore a night robe, so she must've been staying in the hotel. She looked worried.

"Have you heard about …?" Oops, she'd just made the mistake of looking over his shoulder. "Oh … g-gosh, I'm s-sorry," she stammered. "I'll come back in a few minutes."

Steve glanced back into the room. Dale was still standing naked in front of the window.

"Hey, dude, cover yourself up," Steve called out. "We've got a visitor."

Dale turned to face the two of them. Just then, the

hotel guest was joined by a girl. They both stared wide-eyed at Dale.

"Don't look," the woman said, covering the girl's eyes with her hands.

"Stop it, Mam!" the girl said, grabbing angrily at her mother's fingers.

"Christ, Dale!" Steve yelled as he ran back into the room and reached for something to cover Dale's manhood.

"I know what you've been up to, missy," Dale said, pointing a finger at the girl, still apparently oblivious to his condition.

The girl went red-faced. "Excuse me, sir," the woman said, "what the hell do you mean saying that to my daughter?"

"Out of the mouth of babes," Dale said with a throaty chuckle. "That was clever. Yessiree, darn ingenious."

The woman and her daughter shared a puzzled look. "Sorry ..." the woman said.

"Yeah, aren't we all," Dale said, reaching for some clothes. "The business in the church was just the start. The bastards are playing with us. And what's better than using a baby as a lure?" He clicked his tongue in admiration. "You've gotta hand it to them."

"Jeez, Dale! How d'you know?" Steve said.

Dale tapped the side of his head. "Trust me. I know." He turned to look at their visitors. "Now, if you ladies would excuse us. I suggest we meet in reception in ten minutes."

The woman nodded and pulled the door closed without saying a word. The girl could be heard shouting as they walked back to their rooms. Steve dressed, waiting for Dale to say something. The silence was painful.

"So, who exactly were they?" Steve asked.

"Dai's aunt and her daughter," Dale said.

"How do you know?"

"I saw the guest list at reception."

"Okay, but what was all the pointing about? You weren't exactly being Mr Congenial."

Dale shrugged. "I have my reasons."

"And why so hard on the girl? She's only a teenager for Chrissakes."

Dale put his hands on Steve's shoulders. He was shaking. His metabolism seemed to be in overdrive. "Because she needs to feel guilty." He grabbed at a jacket. "Hurry up. And don't forget your ID this time."

"What the fuck ..."

But Dale was already out of the door.

"I'm sorry, sir, I'll need to see some ID," the receptionist said through a hatch at the entrance to the maternity unit. "We have strict rules about visitors."

Dale cocked an eyebrow. "Like this morning, you mean?" He flipped his badge open.

The woman flicked her eyes over the ID. "Americans," she muttered, as if coming from the other side of the pond was something shameful. "Anyway, the local police have already been here. And they've advised us not to let anyone in."

Steve stepped up to the window. "Please make an exception, ma'am. We're friends of Sir David," he said, smiling winsomely.

For a moment, Dale thought the receptionist was about to concede defeat. Steve's eyes were particularly come-to-bed given his half-asleep condition. "No," she said, looking at him without a flicker of emotion.

Mrs Edwards bustled her way to the front. She smiled sweetly. "My dear, I'm Personal Assistant to the Chief Executive at the Royal Glamorgan Hospital and I'm about to register a complaint for the negligent care of my nephew's wife. So, if you don't mind ..." She pointed at the door to the unit.

Sandra had been allocated a side room. Dale knocked gently and eased the door open a crack. She appeared to be sleeping. Dai was sitting in a chair next to the bed, his eyes closed and head lolling to one side. He still had on the shirt and pants he'd worn to the reception and his hair was mussed up. The empty cot had been left next to the bed. A pink blanket embroidered with animals hung over the edge. Dai jerked into consciousness as the four of them entered the room and he leaned forward to check the contents of the cot. He sighed and looked over at Sandra. She hadn't registered the presence of visitors. Dai brushed away a lock of hair and kissed her on the cheek.

"Sorry, I haven't had much sleep," Dai said. He looked exhausted and hollow-eyed. He yawned and attempted a smile. "Hey, thanks for coming. I could do with some friendly faces right now."

Mrs Edwards's daughter rushed over and gave Dai a hug. "I'm so sorry, Dai bach. I shouldn't have …" Ceri burst into tears. Her mother went over to join them for an embrace. Ceri had taken the first bite of Dale's bait. If she was a goddamn witch, now would be a good time for her to prove it.

The air in the room was institutional and stuffy, and carried more than a hint of why they were there. A bodily odour was the best way of describing it. Dale detected the sickly aroma of the milking parlour. Air-con would have helped. He was sure glad they'd skipped breakfast. He cleared his throat. "Have the Met interviewed you yet?"

Dai looked at his wife and nodded. "They didn't get much. Sandra couldn't speak again and started hitting herself, so they had to sedate her." Anguish spread across his face. "I'm useless, that's what, just like Grandmother always said. Christ, I can't even protect my own daughter!"

Mrs Edwards put an arm around him and made comforting noises. Ceri seemed to be on the verge of saying something.

Dale glanced around the room for cameras. All he could see was the tell-tale sign of water ingress. The upkeep of Victorian buildings sure was a bitch. If hi-tech surveillance existed in the place, they'd certainly hidden it well. "So, what about video?" he asked.

Dai thumped his seat. "They've got CCTV, but it wasn't working. I mean, fuck ..."

Dale wasn't surprised. This was a no-frills establishment with lax security and no air-con. He pulled up a chair and looked to the room for inspiration. The baby's parents had to be the starting point. "Dai, did you see anyone behaving suspiciously?"

Dai looked across the bed at Sandra. Her head hadn't budged an inch since they entered the room. At least tranquillizers were the same the world over.

"Not really ..." Dai said. Deep lines spread across his forehead. "Hang on, there was this midwife. It wasn't so much her behaviour, but what she was wearing. She had this large wooden cross dangling from her neck."

Mrs Edwards leaned forward. "That sounds pagan to me."

"You mean, rituals and stuff like that?" Steve said.

Mrs Edwards blanched. Dale guessed what had crossed her mind. *Surely not in this day and age?* he thought.

But if the Scots hated the Welsh that much …

"Paganism is a collection of ancient religions – witchery included, although it's invariably benign," Mrs Edwards said, far from convincingly. Her statement sounded straight out of a press release; 'invariably' never meant 'without exception' in Dale's experience.

Ceri raised a hand sheepishly, just like a teenager ready to fess up to something. "Can I say something, please?"

Mrs Edwards shuffled uneasily in her chair. "Go on, cariad, but remember what your great grandmother would say."

Thanks to Chief Scanlon's tutelage, Dale was a past master at recognising a loaded message. Wales must be a tough place to grow up when it came to breaking with tradition and grandmothers wielding a wand.

"I think the baby's been taken because of me," Ceri said, breaking into sobs.

Dale hoped she'd say that.

"And all because of that fucking cauldron!" she added, smoke as good as billowing from her nostrils.

Mrs Edwards winced at her daughter's language. "What she's trying to say is that she and two of her friends were playing with – "

"We weren't playing, Mam," Ceri said. "It was a divination hex."

"Yes, I know, Ceri bach," Mrs Edwards said. She

sighed. "Unfortunately, they were using Grandmother's cauldron and it got out of hand."

Ceri reddened. "Um, that wasn't the only time."

Mrs Edwards glared at her daughter and muttered something under her breath. It didn't sound like any English that Dale knew.

"Dilys and I tried again just before the wedding," Ceri continued. "Someone sent us a message ... it wasn't exactly friendly ..." She looked at the floor.

Mrs Edwards tsk-tsked, shaking her head. "So, thanks to you, they now know that witchery is alive and well in Pontypridd. I should have got rid of that bloody cauldron ages ago."

"When you say 'they', do you mean Elspeth Brown?" Steve asked.

Mrs Edwards went ashen. "How do you know about her?" Her voice seemed to be shaking with fear.

"Her Majesty told us about her at the reception," Dai said. "Of course, you weren't there, Auntie."

Mrs Edwards reddened. "Ceri wasn't feeling well. I told you that, Dai."

"Well, if you had been, you'd have heard that the Queen believes Elspeth Brown was responsible for the events in the church," Dai said.

"Oh, dear God!" Mrs Edwards said with a gasp. "That means they must have Siandi Da'aan's cauldron."

The room went quiet.

"That brings us to the next question," Dale said. "How the hell are we going to find this witch, the cauldron and, hopefully, the baby?"

A few seconds passed.

"I've just had a thought," Steve said. "When Dr Kyriakides showed us those maps of EM radiation, there was a load of new activity. What if that's related to the witches?"

Steve had gotten their attention. "Go on," Dale said.

"Well, I was thinking that if we tracked back the activity to the business in the church, we might see where the obliteration hex originated from. Perhaps that's where the baby is."

Good thinkin', Batman, Dale thought. *Now all we need is a Batmobile to get to the depths of Oxfordshire.* And then he remembered the flat screen on the divine Deborah's desk.

Thankfully, Dai's aunt had stayed behind to be with Sandra in the maternity unit. Ceri had insisted on coming with them and Dale had surprisingly agreed to that. There had to be method to his madness. Dai just wanted to be doing something remotely useful.

They'd tumbled out of a black cab with the 86 hectares of Victoria Park straight ahead. The flat screen on Deborah's desk had displayed an orange blob of intense EM activity at the exact time they should have been getting married in St James's Church. As Deborah had pointed out, there couldn't be many Scottish witches, living near the park, dispatching dangerous hexes at 2 p.m. on a Saturday afternoon. The only problem was that the blob covered half a square mile.

"Dai, you take Ceri and head towards that church," Dale said, pointing at a steeple about a hundred yards away. "We'll go the opposite direction. See if anything stands out as unusual. Use the radio if you find something."

Dai glanced behind as he and Ceri commenced their check of the area. Dale and Steve walked purposefully towards a row of houses, as if they already knew where they should be heading.

"Sorry," Ceri said, looking glumly at the ground. "I'm always messing up."

"Who says?" Dai asked gently.

Ceri sighed. "My mam. She's so critical, you know. I can't do anything right."

Dai paused to consider that. With teenagers it was best to think before speaking your mind. But he already knew what to say: "Well, I think it's cool you're a witch. Granny Betty had always been hoping for the day when the right person discovered her cauldron." *That was a fib, but Ceri wouldn't know that.* "So, what does your mother think about you being a witch? I mean, that's not exactly usual, even in Wales."

Ceri pondered for whatever passed for a few seconds in teenage time. "I suppose so. Actually, I think she's quite proud. She even called me Caridwen."

"After the Welsh goddess, you mean?"

Ceri nodded. "The way she said it made it sound as if she thought I *was* Caridwen."

Dai whistled his approval. "Wow, that *is* cool."

"Yeah, I suppose so." Ceri almost sounded pleased.

They'd just reached the church. The building looked dark and forbidding. The board at the front proclaimed it to be a 'Presbyterian Ministry', but the letters were a decayed brown rather than burnished gold. Dai couldn't imagine wanting their daughter baptised in the church's murky font. The street sign nearby read, 'Cadogan Terrace E9'. The area had to be home from home for a Scottish witch. There was even a hint of haggis in the air. Dai reached for the radio.

"Dai here. I'm sure this is the street. Over."

The radio squawked Dale's reply: "Yeah, and we've found the house. Over."

"We're on our way. Dai out," Dai said, already starting to run. "C'mon, Ceri bach!"

As they ran, Dai heard Ceri muttering wheezily about wishing she had a broomstick.

"Are you sure this is the right place?" Steve asked. "It looks kinda dead."

•••

Steve was right. A 150 years ago, Number 1 Cadogan Terrace would have been one of the best residences around. Nowadays, similar clapboard houses in the US got turned into heritage B&Bs that earned a few extra bucks moonlighting in *American Horror Story*. This particular horror fest didn't have a square inch that hadn't been pockmarked in some way. The house seemed to have been blasted with shrapnel. Perhaps what had gone up in the church had already descended and done their work for them. And the front door was conveniently open, as if enticing them to witness the evidence of Elspeth Brown's final destruction. Dale just prayed the baby had been left somewhere safe. But there was no sound of any crying.

"What a dump," Ceri said breathlessly, as she and Dai arrived outside the house. "How d'you know it's the right place?"

"Dale's just gonna check his intelligence," Steve said. "But he'll need Dai's assistance."

"Uh?" Ceri grunted. Dale guessed she had problems finding her bearings in the puzzling world of adults.

Dale was almost certain it was where they should be, but Ma Bell seemed to be in a teasing mood. His nuts had been tingling rather than aching, and the only snippet of knowledge he'd been offered was a grainy photo of dubious vintage. Whoever was on switchboard duty enjoyed winding-up her callers. She probably gorged on virtual carryouts while she decided what next to divulge. Dale had tried informing the entangled particles that a poor little mite's life was in danger, but nothing had started grumbling down below or insinuating its way in up above.

"Okay, dude, I'm ready for the poke," Dale said.

Dai sighed. "It's ping, not poke."

Dale shrugged. "Whatever. Let's get on with it. We're running out of time."

Dai put both hands on Dale's shoulders and looked him in the eyes.

"This isn't a gay thing, is it," Ceri piped up, "'cos my friend Dilys says – "

"Shush, Ceri bach," Dai said. "I'm trying to focus out and zero in."

"Well, it still looks a bit gay to me," Ceri huffed.

Dale closed his eyes. Watching Dai perform his hocus focus trick was too damn unnerving, particularly when he was the subject. He had his fingers crossed the kids at his old school weren't on their morning break. It was all silent so far. *Shit! I spoke too soon.* Except it wasn't children taunting him this time. The sound was soft at first, like the gentle rustling of trees in the wind. Or was it rushing water? The brook wasn't exactly babbling. It was getting louder and he heard laughter, but not of the happy sort. Crackling and cackling was hardly a winning combination inside anyone's head.

And then the image hit him, like a thump in the guts: Siandi Da'aan and her familiar, the witch's eyes looking so warm and all-knowing; the black cat on her lap on the lookout for prey, ready to pounce on the poor and pathetic. Both were on fire. Even as the flames tore the flesh from their bones, their eyes continued to observe the man who'd put the tinder to the pile of wood and the watcher who'd sat back to enjoy the spectacle.

"Sorry, I'm out of practice," Dai said with a grimace. His forehead glistened with sweat. "That was tough."

"Yeah. For me, too," Dale said, massaging his temples. "Poor bitch."

"Poor cat," Dai said.

"Excuse me," Ceri said petulantly, hands on hips, not wanting to be left out.

"I saw something," Dale said. The fuller description would have to wait.

"And I saw what he saw," Dai said. "Your mother was right."

A look of horror mixed with awe crossed Ceri's face. "You don't mean Siandi Da'aan?"

"You got it, missy," Dale said, "and her cauldron is ready and waiting for us."

"Don't call me ..." Ceri started to say, but something ancient and powerful had gotten hold of her tongue.

"So, what's gonna be our approach?" Dale said. "Low and stealth-like or charging in regardless?"

"Well, they're gonna be expecting us," Steve said. "And it's not as if we're armed to the teeth."

Dai put his hand up. "I can try turning up the ping, if that helps."

"And I'm a witch," Ceri said, this time as if she meant it.

"Okay, that's agreed," Dale said. "We run in hollering our heads off, grab the baby and then get the hell out of the place. But keep a watch for any stray energy streams. And black cats with wandering eyes. This is some mean sonofabitch we're dealing with." He'd always been good at psyching up the troops.

They paused briefly on the top step, staring into the depths of the dark hallway. Dale set his jaw, engaged a stance from his ill-fated attempt at Navy SEAL training and imagined himself as Indiana Jones, complete with his hat and whip. There'd better be no snakes. "Okay … one … two … three …"

True to Dale's instruction, they ran en masse into the house, making as much noise as they could and headed for any doorway that was already open. It all seemed so easy. They reached what must have been the back room of the house. At least there were no more doors. It was so damn dark. Someone sure liked curtains. Success! There was the cauldron on the table and they could see the baby in some sort of basket. Easy-peasy, grab and run. Wham-bam-slam!

Something had stopped them from moving. Their hands should have been hitting thin air, but it didn't want to give. They were stuck like bugs in treacle.

A black-clothed figure stood with its back to them in the corner. It turned and threw something silvery into the cauldron. It said a few words, but they didn't sound like any language Dale knew. Guttural, primeval, angry. A small orb rose from the vessel and started spinning, sending out flickers of plasma-like energy. The figure threw back its head covering and grinned, although its teeth were blackened stumps.

"Jeez! That's Virginia Ironside!" Dale said.

"Principal Davies!" Steve said.

"It's Major Chisholm!" Dai said.

"No, it's Miss Donn!" Ceri said.

The four of them looked at each other and then back at the figure. Now, the figure looked like the Queen and it waggled a white-gloved finger at them.

"Christ, you're gullible. That's the oldest trick in the book, although honed to the nth degree by yours truly." The Queen's doppelganger fixed Ceri with a gimlet eye. "I bet you never discovered that in Granny Betty's potions book. And to think she called it 'Recipes'. Huh! What a joke. Oh, and by the way, I gave you a 'Fail'. Such a shame you didn't complete your project. So, do you want to see some real magick, young witch?"

The figure uttered a few words under her breath and the baby rose until she was a few inches from the ceiling. Dale looked for wires, but he couldn't see any. The baby seemed more dead than alive.

Dale shook his head. "I don't geddit, lady. Why d'you want a helpless baby if you're so goddamn powerful?"

The figure laughed. "'I don't geddit", she said, mocking his voice. "You call that English? Jesus H. Christ!" Suddenly, the voice was that of Virginia Ironside, PA to the Principal at Staley High School. "Is that better, boys?" she said, leering, in a grotesquely exaggerated Mid-West accent. She glanced at her chest. "Sorry 'bout the boobs. They're a bit flat these days. Not that that'd interest you gay boys, of course. I can rustle up a porn star if you'd like. I'm just so fucking versatile. Oops, there's a child around. Jesus, can you imagine what it's like listening to snivelling kids for all those years? The only thing that kept me going was the man you destroyed. Yes, you!" She pointed a finger angrily at Dale and Steve. "How dare you destroy our lives!" The figure abruptly switched her attention to Dai. "And don't think you're getting off the hook, matey, whippersnapper from the Valleys and lapdog to Her Majesty. Oh, we know all about your intimate titty à titty on the bench at Balmoral! I should have locked you away in the white van for good – or fed you to your pigeons. Hocus focus. What a laugh! And don't get me started on that bloody play and Christopher's witches."

The orb had begun to wobble ominously on its axis. The figure turned to the other side of the room. "Oh, mother, you might want to watch this. It should get rather interesting." The accent had switched to Scottish. She flicked another handful of something silvery into the cauldron. The orb added some ominous whining to its activity. "I said, watch this, you old hag!" the figure yelled. A high-backed chair in the far corner turned slowly by itself. There was a pile of black clothes and a hat on it. A smell of burnt fur and flesh filled the air.

Dale couldn't quite put his finger on how he decided their strategy, but it had become a now-or-never situation, and he was damned if some power-hungry bitch of a witch was going to have her way. Working in Kansas City had its advantages when it came to dealing with crazed old ladies. A few flicked looks exchanged between the four of them and the plan was set.

"That's better," the figure said. "She's rotting in hell quite nicely. Now, where was I?"

That was the last thing the witch said as any of her multiple personalities. Dale guessed that Dai's ping must have made its mark. Being confronted by flashbacks of your very worst deeds would scare the bejeebers out of the hardiest soul. He'd never forget her look of outright terror. Steve leaped forward as soon as the barrier came down and caught the falling baby. Ceri threw the cauldron at the figure. The witch didn't exactly explode. Instead, she appeared to flicker between all her 101 identities and then lost cohesion. What had been Elspeth Brown became smoke that drifted slowly upwards and through the ceiling. The smell of smouldering hair lingered in the air.

"That's my girl," Dai said, taking the baby in his arms. She woke up, stretched her tiny arms and made contented cooing noises. "I think I should get you home to your mother."

Dale and Steve looked at each other. "And I need to get you back to Chief Scanlon before you cause any more mischief," Steve said.

"Will you promise me something, sweets?" Dale said.

"Er, okay," Steve said uncertainly.

"When I get old and gnarled like that witch, will you still be there to look after me?"

Steve shrugged. "Yeah. As long as you get me the Robin outfit for Christmas."

"Eurgh, that's just so gay," Ceri said. She blew her nose loudly. "So, what about me then?"

"You can take the cauldron home with you," Dale said, glancing at the now redundant lump of metal embedded in the lath and plaster wall.

"Gosh, thanks," Ceri said. She went over to where Elspeth Brown had disappeared and effortlessly retrieved the heavy cauldron, which she dangled from her hand as if it was the latest, must-have fashion accessory. "Cool," she said, as she admired the decoration around the rim. Dale glimpsed the pattern: pairs of upside-down wings. Cute. And then he made the connection – without the assistance of Ma Bell. He'd been right all along about the divine Deborah and her dark side. MI5 had a reputation for dirty work. They'd better get the hell out of the place before her spooks arrived with the clean-up squad. Dai could deal with the debriefing. He could always zap them with the hocus focus if it got too heavy.

CHAPTER FIFTEEN

"Yeah, I know the timing sucks, but this is a chance to make a real difference for the kid," Steve said. "And anyway, I want you to see how talented he is."

"You mean, loads of lira for him to blow on dope and sex?" Dale said, as good as extending his claws.

It was two days before Thanksgiving and the car was playing up. Dale needed to get under the hood rather than go to some art gallery – particularly one with an exhibition by an exhibitionist. Steve had put his drawing on the wall above his desk. It was a darn good likeness, but ...

Dale sighed. "Okay, sweets, but only for an hour. I need to work on – "

"Your DeLorean," Steve said with a groan. "Look, you sure you don't want to marry the car instead?"

Dale closed his eyes and affected a wistful grin. "Yeah, that's quite a thought ..."

"Awesome!" Dale said, as they entered the gallery foyer. The exhibition had been titled 'Coming Out the Other Side'. He'd been vaguely aware of some guy dressed in black handing him a sheet of paper, but his mind was busy taking it all in. The exhibition space was industrially proportioned, with exposed pipes, bare brickwork and lights criss-crossing the cantilevered ceiling. The centre of the gallery was occupied by screens and video projectors. A sign on the wall nearby read, 'START'; 'END' was over on the right. Dale appreciated the straightforward intention.

"I guess we should begin there," Dale said, pointing towards the left. He recognised the first picture from what Steve had told him after his first visit to Two Rivers. The drawing had no title, just the number 1 by the side, although it was written in letters. 'ONE' could have been about the boy groping for an identity, establishing his oneness with the cosmos or identifying as a peanut – albeit with two ears attached.

Dale heard the sounds of someone struggling behind him. He whipped round and saw a video playing of the boy from the ER being manhandled by burly nurses attired in white. He guessed the artist was struggling for the sake of his sanity and art. That was juxtaposed with footage of fanboys queuing up at the altar of Apple to buy the latest cell phone. They proudly held high their silvery rectangles like Olympians holding up their well-earned medals. Little did they know that they were holding tainted technology that would spell the end of their freedom. The final shot in the sequence was a news bulletin about a Foxconn employee plunging to his death after 48 hours on an assembly line with barely any sleep.

"Whaddya think?" a young-sounding voice asked to his left.

Dale did a double-take. It couldn't have been the same guy they'd seen in the ER – could it? He had on a suit and dress shirt, and his hair looked immaculately groomed. His only concession to an artistic temperament was an iridescent green tie that matched the sparkling intelligence of his eyes.

"The look on your face says it all, Officer," Joseph Gardiner said, smiling broadly.

"Jeez! You did that?" Dale asked.

Joseph shrugged. "Sure. But that's just the beginning. Wait till you see the rest," he said, bright-eyed and brimming with enthusiasm. "Tell me, how d'you like the videos? That was Nurse Elliott's idea. I think they're just so cool." He gestured to a man nearby, dressed in nurse's whites, to come over.

"So, you're Steve's partner," Nurse Elliott said, looking him up and down. "Yup, I was right, you are a cutie."

Joseph yawned theatrically. "Sorry, he's like that with all the guys. Look, I want to show you something, although – " he leaned forward to whisper, " – Steve doesn't know I've put it up."

"Will I like it?" Dale asked.

"You'll love it, dude," Nurse Elliott said with a wink.

Dale allowed himself to be led past a huge

centrepiece painting that had already attracted a large crowd. Steve seemed to be deep in conversation with someone resembling Father Christmas. But he hadn't started patting his fat belly and saying, "Ho-ho-ho". Dale guessed he was some know-it-all critic, ready to describe the work as being "unzipped with transcendently surging symbolism". Sex certainly figured in all its liberated forms. The take-home message seemed to be about venturing onwards and upwards to the promised land, with intercourse as the driving force to get folk to their chosen destination.

"Ta-da!" Joseph said, as they reached the destination he had in mind.

Dale guessed he looked like an idiot, with his jaw on the floor and eyes all bugged-out, but seeing one's partner displayed naked, life-size, on a wall, took some getting used to. To complicate matters, the real body in question had just joined him by his side. He was almost tempted to suggest Steve stripped for a quick side-by-side comparison.

"Oh fuck!" Steve said, reddening in a flash.

"Oops, I guess I should have warned you," Joseph said sheepishly, "but it's the best thing I've done. In fact, the gallery owner liked it so much, he's bought it for himself. See, there's the 'SOLD' sticker." He pointed a finger at a large red dot at the bottom right of the painting.

"How?" Dale asked pathetically, hoping there was a less than obvious explanation than Steve posing in the buff. "And don't say it was X-ray vision," he grumbled.

"X-ray vision?" Joseph inclined his head and flicked a look at Steve. "Yeah. I dig that." He shrugged. "Actually, I just imagine what people are like without their clothes." He turned to look straight-on at Dale. It was like being back in the Walmart scanner, although a whole lot quicker. "Okay, I'll paint you next, Lieutenant, but I might shift it to the middle so you're symmetrical."

Dale's blush response was even quicker than Steve's.

"That is ... awesome," intoned a non-US voice from just behind them. Dale and Steve swivelled around and their eyes nearly popped out of their heads. The speaker had warm brown eyes, skin like polished onyx, razor-sharp cheekbones and a slender body that seemed to stretch on forever. He wore a loose-fitting black suit and a T-shirt that had a multi-coloured logo printed on it. Steve let out a low whistle and reached out to shake the man's hand.

"Jeez! You must be Jacob Ngali!" Steve said, clearly awestruck by more than the dude's reputation.

"It is I," Jacob said with a polite little bow. "And who might I have the pleasure of ..." He frowned, glanced at the painting and then back at Steve. "You are most handsome, sir," he said, apparently in all sincerity.

Dale was all set to drag Steve away from his strangely old-fashioned admirer with his schoolroom English. Jacob Ngali might be Caltech's whizzkid, but Dale was just as old-time when it came to social etiquette and someone taking an instant shine to his boyfriend.

Just then they were joined by another man wearing the same T-shirt but over jeans. It was a lot easier to make out the 'Cogniz' logo. He had a Harpo Marx halo of golden, curly hair. "Oh jeez ... sorry," he said, grinning and putting a hand on his friend's shoulder, "Jacob isn't exactly used to social situations and says the first thing that comes into his head. I'm Peter Griffin, the CEO of Cogniz."

Dale shook his hand. "Good to meet you, Peter. I'm Dale Franklin." But judging by the adulation on Jacob's face, Steve remained in the firing line of Cupid's scope-equipped bow. "Umm, your friend's object of desire just so happens to be my boyfriend, Steve Abrams. We're both with the Kansas City Police Department and we worked alongside Dr Cathy Sven – "

"I like frat parties!" Jacob piped up. He leaned forward until he was a few inches from Steve's neck and inhaled deeply. "Hmm, bergamot, verbena, nutmeg, black pepper, patchouli, vanilla, civet ..." He scrunched up his face for a moment then beamed. "That is Noir by Mr Tom Ford. He is also a very handsome man."

Peter rolled his eyes. "Sorry, guys. We saw *Perfume* in

a movie theatre last month and he's been trying to guess the ingredients of men's colognes ever since – "

"I do not guess, Peter; I know," Jacob said, evidently in all seriousness.

Peter shrugged. "Yeah, you probably do, too." He turned to Dale and Steve. "He's memorised all the chemical formulae, would you believe it? The next thing you know we'll be crowdfunding a perfume store."

Jacob's eyes lit up. "I would like that. It is good to make people smell nice." He seemed to remember something and pulled a cell phone out of a pocket. "See," he said, flipping through pictures on the screen, "these are our children, David and Jonathan. I am teaching them math. They are very good students."

Dale and Steve exchanged an 'eh?' look. Jacob's cell displayed two animals that could have been rats. They stood on their hind legs, their forepaws held out like some parody of Charles Dickens's *Oliver Twist*, with their beady black eyes focused greedily on the person behind the lens. Dale shuddered. Feeding time back home had been a similar battle of wills when his dad was worse for drink.

"They're ex-lab rats," Peter said. "I gave them to Jacob when he moved in to my place. They were among the first to be given the cognitive reparative therapy. And it's true he's teaching them math. They must be the only first graders that sniff their way to the answer. He's making them add for their supper."

"Isn't that the drug from some African plant?" Dale asked. He'd remembered some news report about start-up companies muscling in on the aftermath of 'the screaming'. "'Ashtanga' or something?" He shrugged, knowing he'd used the wrong word.

Jacob suddenly looked wise beyond his years. "It is *ashwagandha*, sir," he said. "It is very special to my people."

"Okay, yeah? ..." Dale said. He wasn't exactly up to speed with cultural stuff.

"Jacob's right," Peter said, nodding and grinning simultaneously. "An extract of the berry is biologically highly active and marginally improves memory in some subjects. A bit like ginkgo biloba, in fact. Jacob's genius with chemical structures enabled him to see that some minor alterations to the active constituent would allow it to slot into the beta amyloid molecule. Hey presto, that gave us enhanced hippocampal neuronal transmission and regulated beta amyloid turnover. A win-win for affected teens like Joseph. And a couple of super-intelligent rats, of course."

"Holy Houdini!" Steve said. "That's like finding the Holy Grail of neuroscience!"

Jacob beamed. "Thank you, sir. That is a great compliment." He turned serious again. "It is God's work, of course. We must atone for our sins."

Peter blushed. "Yeah, sure, babe." He turned to Dale. "Sorry, it's the old bible babble thing. You know, 'swirling around in a cesspit of their own creation' and all that crap."

Dale laughed painfully. "Yeah, don't I know." He looked around to check for others of Godly persuasion nearby. "So, Peter, what's your connection with – " he gestured at the generally sacrilegious exhibits around them, " – this show?"

"The gallery owner is the main investor in our company," Peter said. "And Joseph has agreed to be in our publicity campaigns."

"I said I'll be on my best behaviour," Joseph said, smiling from ear to ear. "So, no tits or dicks on display."

"I like dicks!" Jacob said way too loudly. He frowned, bent down to rub his hands on the floor and then rubbed his palms briskly against his cheeks.

"Hairshirt?" Dale asked beneath his breath.

"Yeah, something like that. I'm sorta working on it, but it's like walking on eggshells," Peter said, smiling ruefully.

Dale nodded. He'd once had a girlfriend who breathed fire and brimstone during sex. Marriage might have sorted her fornication guilt trip, but she'd have found another way of bringing God into the bedroom. Now it was Sodom and Gomorrah all the way and there was no turning back. Even the delights of the darkly devious Deborah Jenkins had been consigned to the annals of a past life.

"Is the gallery owner here?" Steve asked, looking around keenly. "I'm kinda interested to meet the guy who's bought Joseph's painting of me."

Dale was thinking along similar lines. He was weighing up the pros and cons of throwing him a sucker punch; best after the first wink at his boyfriend, he decided. He was off duty, after all, and some well-aimed performance art could be just the audience's ticket. Although perhaps that'd been the plan all along. "Holy rat in a trap!" as Steve would put it.

Peter shook his head. Ringlets rearranged themselves in a languorous way that was straight out of some cheesy shampoo commercial. Dale decided that was a good enough reason to distrust him. "That's the weird thing," Peter said. "We've only ever dealt with him through an intermediary. Still, as long as the money keeps on coming, it doesn't really matter. He wanted the drug for himself, too. I guess he could be in the early stages of Alzheimer's disease. Perhaps he's been delayed by the weather. It's fucking slippery out there."

"Well, that was interesting," Dale said as they walked to the door. "You'll be needing a secretary for your fan club soon."

"You're jealous," Steve said.

"No, I'm not."

"You are too!"

The wind had picked up when they emerged from the gallery and the street lights glistened on icy patches on the sidewalk.

"Jeez! Where did the chill come from?" Dale asked, rubbing his hands for warmth. "Fancy a glass of vino?"

"I thought you had a date with the car?" Steve said, grinning like the cat that got the cream. He'd been let off the hook and he knew it.

"Yeah? Oh, that can wait. That art's got me thinking." Dale turned back to look at the gallery. The sign read: 'THE BIG NEW GALLERY'. He liked that. Plain and simple; nothing remotely artsy-fartsy. But he still didn't like the idea of some creep hanging the picture of Steve on his living room wall. Perhaps Father Christmas had gotten lonely and needed a companion for the cold winter nights. It was the season of goodwill, after all. And he didn't really mind the attention Steve had received from Jacob, either. Weird dude, mind you.

"Dale, take two steps back," Steve ordered. "Like now!"

Dale's primitive brain kicked in without him giving a second thought. That was the whole point about chain of command. If you stopped to question it, chances are you'd get hurt. He stepped back and waited. He wouldn't have been able to say whether it was for a minute or a second. The street had been clear apart from a station wagon a 100 yards away. He'd always been good at judging distances. Perhaps the driver had been collecting a Christmas tree. The bigger, the better these days, it seemed. Throwing them out with the trash didn't do much for green credibility.

Dale caught a snatch of sound of revellers a block away. Too much festive liquor, he imagined. The noise was joined by something much closer and louder. Squealing brakes, engine noise and tires hitting concrete merged into one. The station wagon careered out of control down the sidewalk just feet in front of him. Dale thanked God he'd been well trained to follow orders. The vehicle came to a halt amid a pile of trash bags and dumpsters left out for the morning pick up.

"Fuck!" Dale said, shocked to the core. It was like being zapped by electricity and realising you'd escaped death by a whisker. "How the hell did you know?"

Steve looked puzzled. "Dunno. It just came to me."

Dale's scalp still prickled. "Let's check the driver. You call 911." He ran to the driver's side. The guy was elderly and had slumped against the wheel. Dale opened the door and reached in to turn off the engine.

"Are you all right, sir? You've had an accident."

The driver groaned and moved a hand feebly to his head. At least he was conscious and moving. And he'd still be around to enjoy Christmas.

"It's okay, sir, don't move. Help is coming."

"An ambulance is on its way," Steve said, arriving alongside. "He's got a flat on the left. He must have skidded on the ice. He's damn lucky."

Yeah, so am I, Dale thought ruefully. *But was it actually luck?*

"Er, Steve, how are your nuts?" Dale said.

"Fine, last time I looked … oh fuck! Not me as well!"

Dale shrugged. "Could be. We could set up shop. Your specialty could be predicting vehicular accidents, while I do crime. We can share dealing with threats from witches. I can see the sign: 'Franklin & Abrams, Precognitors'. Sounds cool, don't you think?"

But Steve had already gone off to say howdy to the paramedics, who'd arrived in record time for a call received during the holiday season. Dale noticed they even had a 'HAPPY THANKSGIVING' sign on the back of their vehicle. They'd probably been pigging out on turkey and pecan pie in a nearby diner.

Talking of signs … Dale glanced back at the gallery. Something about the banner was bugging him, but he couldn't quite put his finger on it. The strengthening wind was busily wrestling the banner away from its attachments, as if it had done its job and was ready to be set free. With a final gusty tug, the sign parted company with its moorings and spiralled gracefully to the ground. Just then the gallery doors slammed shut with a dull clang. The show was over … or, on second thought, perhaps it had just started. The Big New Gallery had a captive audience.

ABOUT THE AUTHOR

David Graham lives in an ostensibly carbon zero house, converted from a chicken shed, with his partner and two cats amid fields of maize, orchards of apples and poly-tunnels of strawberries. He would like to live entirely off the grid, but a 3G mobile network mast stands sneakily camouflaged as a tree in an adjacent field. When he isn't enjoying the ever-changing Kentish landscape, gale-force winds and torrential rain, his mind is drawn to strange imaginings about what lurks beneath the surface of the world around him. This is his fifth novel.

ACKNOWLEDGEMENTS

The prequel to this book, entitled 'The Screaming', is published by Urbane Publications (eBook) and Austin Macauley Publishers Ltd (paperback).

Matthew Smith kindly offered a different deal that breaks the mould of traditional publishing. I'm proud to be a member of the Urbane Publications family.

Henry Andrews, Harmony Kent and Dayna Harding-Hubbard were my beta readers. They did a great job. Thanks, guys.

Ben Way was my editor. He's a stickler for accuracy and I really appreciated that.

The characters Emma Jones, Sandra Evans and Dr Petros Kyriakides first appeared in a self-published novel entitled Looks Could Kill.

The character of Dai Williams is borrowed with permission and adjustments from Paul Nagle's excellent first novel, Bogus Focus. His music is still awesome.

The character of Betty Williams is modelled on my Great Aunt Maggie, who used to inhabit a drafty, smoky farmhouse in North Wales that had a wheezy harmonium in the corner of the kitchen. She wasn't a witch, but I'm sure she could have been in another life.

I spent the first few years of my life in a bleak and

windswept place called Borth, just outside Aberystwyth. My father was born and raised in Aber, too. And I play the harp. I hope that makes me sufficiently Welsh.

My grandfather's nanny Letitia Evans used to say 'Jiw, jiw!' at just about every opportunity. It stuck in my mind. It means 'Good God!', or words to that effect. The other thing I remember about her were her fantastic pommes frites. Oh, and accidentally hitting her on the forehead with a toy gun. Sorry, Letty bach.

Secret tunnels under Buckingham Palace were mentioned in an article in *The New Statesman* in 1980 and have been the subject of urban myths ever since. Possible destinations include Green Park, Windsor Castle, Number 10 Downing Street, the Houses of Parliament and Scotland. An underground Tube stop has also been rumoured to exist. Buckingham Palace has always declined to comment. Boo.

The Dynion Mwyn tradition was established between 1282 and 1525, by descendants of the Bards of Prince Llewellyn, the last true Prince of Wales. The pagan religion of Dynion Mwyn was revitalised in the 1950s and 60s by Taliesin einion Vawr. I'm not sure what they get up to, but I don't think spinning orbs figure.

The Association of Cymry Wiccae is an assembly of traditional Welsh covens in the US and has no connection with the Cymry Wiccae Association mentioned in this book. It's curious that the ACW doesn't exist in

Wales itself, but the Welsh have always been adept at exporting themselves, viz. Y Wladfa, the Welsh colony in Patagonia.

A Course in Welsh Witchcraft was indeed authored by Taliesin einion Vawr and Rhuddlwm Gawr. Sadly, it's out of print.

Shandy Dann was the name given to the effigy of a hideous old woman put on the bonfire every Halloween at Balmoral Castle. Queen Victoria was said to be much amused by the spectacle. A *shandrydan* is also the term given to a rickety, ramshackle vehicle like a hand-propelled cart. The name Siandi Da'aan is entirely made up.

Scottish witches seem to have been frequently hunted down and burnt at the stake, which may have led them to be jealous of their more protected Welsh rivals. Life ain't fair.

The Third Level of Reality: A Unified Theory of the Paranormal by Percy Seymour (Cosimo, Inc., 2003) is one example of surprisingly many attempting to explain abnormal phenomena in terms of particle physics. I haven't read it, but it just goes to prove we're all thinking along similar bidirectional lines.

Urbane Publications is dedicated to
developing new author voices, and publishing
fiction and non-fiction that challenges, thrills and
fascinates.
From page-turning novels to innovative
reference books, our goal is to publish what
YOU want to read.

Find out more at
urbanepublications.com